# CLAIRE DE LUNE

FOR MORE OF CLAIRE'S STORY, CHECK OUT

# NOCTURNE

# CLAIRE DE LUNE

*Christine Johnson*

SIMON PULSE

NEW YORK LONDON TORONTO SYDNEY

This book is a work of fiction. Any references to historical events, real people, or real locales are used fictitiously. Other names, characters, places, and incidents are the product of the author's imagination, and any resemblance to actual events or locales or persons, living or dead, is entirely coincidental.

SIMON PULSE

An imprint of Simon & Schuster Children's Publishing Division

1230 Avenue of the Americas, New York, NY 10020

First Simon Pulse paperback edition July 2011

Also available in a Simon Pulse hardcover edition.

For information about special discounts for bulk purchases, please contact

Simon & Schuster Special Sales at 1-866-506-1949 or business@simonandschuster.com.

The Simon & Schuster Speakers Bureau can bring authors to your live event.

For more information or to book an event contact the Simon & Schuster Speakers Bureau

at 1-866-248-3049 or visit our website at www.simonspeakers.com.

Designed by Karina Granda

The text of this book was set in Adobe Caslon Pro.

Manufactured in the United States of America

2 4 6 8 10 9 7 5 3 1

The Library of Congress has cataloged the hardcover edition as follows:

Johnson, Christine 1978—

Claire de Lune / by Christine Johnson. — 1st Simon Pulse ed.

p. cm.

Summary: On her sixteenth birthday Claire discovers strange things happening, and when her mother reveals their family secret, which explains the changes, Claire feels her world, as she has known it to be, slowly slipping away.

ISBN 978-1-4169-9182-3 (hc)

[1. Werewolves—Fiction. 2. Mothers and daughters—Fiction.] I. Title.

PZ7.J63092Cl 2010

[Fic]—dc22

2009036269

ISBN 978-1-4424-0766-4 (pbk)

ISBN 978-1-4424-0641-4 (eBook)

*For my husband, Erik,*
*whom I love beyond description*

# Prologue

SHE KILLED HIM in the darkest part of the night, before the dew had settled on the grass.

It was easy. He came to the window when she'd tapped her claws against it. It was exactly what she'd hoped he would do. Sliding up the square of glass. Sticking his head out to investigate. Like an idiot. Like prey.

One less moron in the world. She licked the blood off her mouth, the coarse whiskers sliding against her tongue.

He didn't even have time to scream. He was no different from any of the others. His eyes had gone round as coins, his cheeks turned fish-flesh white.

*It was when their mouths made that terrified* O *that she sprang.*

*It was the perfect moment. They saw her coming for them. They knew what was about to happen. But none of them ever had a chance to make a sound.*

Except when their necks snap. That makes a sound, *she mused.*

*She'd expected to feel more fear, breaking the rules like this. Instead, she'd discovered that she liked it. The power of deciding who and when. Letting her instincts take over without worrying about the consequences.*

*After all, she wasn't the one who would take the blame for killing these sad little rag-doll humans. She wouldn't get caught—she was too good. Too careful.*

*It was the other one who would pay.*

*Dizzy with success, tantalized by the so-close gleam of revenge, she disappeared back into the woods.*

# Chapter One

THE SMOOTH MIRROR of the pool's surface shattered as three boys cannonballed into it at the same time. Shrieks erupted from the cluster of girls who got splashed.

"Claire, this is the *best* party!" Emily gushed, nibbling on a potato chip.

Claire scanned the crowd in her backyard. Bikini-clad girls and soaked boys in swim trunks perched on the patio furniture, drinking soda and laughing. *Anyone'll come to your party if you have a pool,* she thought. She scratched the backs of her hands against the sharp edge of the table and wished they'd quit itching. It was like the worst poison ivy ever, only there weren't any bumps and it wasn't red.

"Yeah, I guess," she said. Claire had known most of these people since elementary school, but aside from Emily, she had never been close with any of them. It was the hottest June since 1910, and the huge pool in her backyard had made Claire instantly popular. Which still wasn't saying very much—more than a few people at the party had been surprised to find out it was Claire's birthday. *Oh, well, I guess having people come just to use the pool is better than not at all. Yep. That's me—glass always half-full.* She sighed.

"What do you mean, 'I guess'? Aren't you having fun?" Emily's mouth curved into a worried little frown.

"No—I mean, yeah, it's fun. I just don't know a lot of these people so well."

"But they're here, right? And I heard Yolanda saying that she'd missed you since school let out. People do like you, Claire. You just don't want to believe it."

Emily grabbed another chip. "So, you really didn't get a car, huh?"

"Nope. I was hoping Mom was just trying to make me *think* that she was leaving me stranded, but I got a pair of sapphire earrings from her this morning, so I think she's serious." Claire rolled her eyes. It wasn't like they couldn't afford for her to have her own car. Her mom just didn't think she needed one.

Claire's ears itched like they were on fire, just like her hands, and she pushed back her shiny brown hair so she could rub them.

"What are you *doing*?" asked Emily. "Matthew is totally watching you! Act normal!"

Claire dropped her hands, feeling the tingle of a flush in her cheeks. Matthew Engle gave her a little wave, and rolled his eyes in the direction of the giggling group sitting behind him. She smiled at him, and he grinned back. A shock of electricity shot through her as he motioned for her to come over. Besides being one of only two guys in the entire school who wasn't an immature jerk, he was cute. Really cute. Turn-your-brain-to-mush cute.

"It's not like I have a chance with him, anyway," Claire said, turning back to Emily.

"Of course you do! You're smart, you're funny, and you look totally amazing in that bikini. You definitely need to go talk to him."

"Only if you come with me."

"Oh, *fine*. But you don't need me. You'd be okay on your own." Emily grabbed her soda and pulled Claire to her feet.

Claire took a deep breath and strolled over to Matthew.

"Hey." *Wow, Claire, way to impress him with your conversational skills.*

"Good party," he said.

A shriek erupted from the other side of the circle of deck chairs, buying Claire time to think of something half-intelligent to say.

"Oh, ewwww! I am so serious—I don't want to hear any

more." Yolanda Adams slapped her hands over her ears and turned away from the group.

"What?" Claire asked.

Dan Maxwell glanced at her. "The last guy who got killed by the werewolf? Turns out it crushed his skull. One of the other ER nurses told my mom about it. His brains were oozing out all over."

"Dude, shut *up*." Matthew shook his head. "Didn't you just hear Yollie say she didn't want to hear about it anymore?"

"Right," said Emily. "Like there's anything else to talk about in this town."

The werewolf was all over the news—in the last month alone, it had killed three people. No one went out after dark anymore. Werewolf attacks were the sort of thing that happened once in a while in Eastern Europe, maybe, or rural Japan, but in the United States they had become as rare as an outbreak of cowpox.

Emily turned to Dan. "Even if Yolanda won't listen to your gory details, I'm always up for insider information." She grabbed a handful of pretzels and arranged herself next to Dan. Emily made it look so easy. Claire watched her best friend flirt effortlessly with a guy who wasn't even her type. Emily only got serious about guys who wore a lot of black, looked sort of unwashed, and were totally into art.

Claire turned back to Matthew, wishing that she had

Emily's confidence around guys. She glanced at the empty plate beside him.

"So, um, have you tried the salsa yet? Lisbeth makes it from scratch."

"No, but that sounds great. Come on, I need another drink, anyway."

Matthew grabbed Claire's hand and pulled her over to the food table. The press of his warm skin against her palm made Claire dizzy, even after he'd let go.

"You probably hear enough about werewolves at home, huh?" she asked him, scratching her earlobe. Again.

He shrugged. "Dad's spending so much time at the lab and on TV, he really hasn't been around much. He's dying to get into Lycanthropy Researchers International—he's been getting a lot of crap from the media about how he's not as qualified as the other members of the Federal Human Protection Agency. He's convinced that this new case is going to be his 'big break.'" Matthew sounded irritated.

Claire raised an eyebrow. Dr. Engle was leading the hunt in Hanover Falls for the werewolf. It was part of his job for the FHPA—the whole agency was all about researching werewolves and stopping attacks on humans. Claire had seen him on TV a ton, especially lately. He always said the same thing during interviews: "I am honored to be able to help my own hometown in its hour of need. Hanover Falls is currently the FHPA's top priority, and I will make sure it stays that way until this situation has been resolved." Then he would adjust his tie. Every time. He creeped Claire out.

"My mom isn't home much, either," she offered.

Matthew looked at her, his warm brown eyes locking onto hers.

"Yeah, she just had that big shoot in Greece, right?" he asked.

Claire nodded, amazed that he'd remembered. Her mother spent at least one week every month, usually more, traveling for her photography. Travel magazines, art-book publishers, galleries—they all wanted Marie Benoit behind the camera. Claire didn't mind all the trips. Things were actually easier, more relaxed, when her mom wasn't home.

"Okay, everyone, time for cake!" Claire's mom called, sticking her head out one of the back doors.

She stepped out, holding the door for Lisbeth, the latest in the long line of au pairs who stayed with Claire while her mom traveled. No one else had lasted more than a year, but Lisbeth had been with them since Claire was thirteen. Claire loved Lisbeth, even though she wished her mom would realize that she was too old to need someone around all the time. It was one thing for Lisbeth to be there when her mom took long trips, but surely Claire was old enough to come home to an empty house in the afternoons. But if her mom didn't think that sixteen was old enough to get a car, then she probably wouldn't listen to Claire's ideas about how much supervision she needed from Lisbeth, either. At least having Lisbeth meant not having to ask her mom's permission all the time, and Lisbeth wasn't nearly as strict.

Lisbeth walked onto the patio carrying a giant chocolate cake with *Happy 16th Birthday, Claire* in white icing. A ring of candles burned around the top.

Everyone turned to look at Claire, breaking into a half-hearted rendition of "Happy Birthday to You." Claire forced herself to smile, even though she was completely mortified.

Claire leaned over and blew out the candles.

"Did you make a wish?" Matthew asked.

"Yeah." Claire nodded, unable to look him in the eyes, since her wish totally revolved around him.

The patio door burst open and Claire looked up, relieved for the interruption. Dan's mother tore into the yard wearing bloodstained hospital scrubs.

"Mom?" Dan sounded confused and annoyed. Mostly annoyed.

"Get your stuff," she panted. "We're going."

Claire's mother stepped forward. "I'm sorry, is something wrong?"

"Yes. The news just came over the police dispatch at the hospital—someone thinks they spotted the werewolf at the edge of the woods. *These* woods." She gestured over the brick wall that surrounded the Benoits' backyard. Her hand shook as she pointed. "In broad daylight. The police are patrolling until the FHPA squad comes. I'm sorry, Ms. Benoit, but I can't let Dan stay here. It's too dangerous." She looked at the rest of the group. "It's too dangerous for all of you. You all need to go, *now*."

Right on cue, several cell phones around the pool started ringing.

Emily looked up at Claire, her phone glued to her ear. *It's on the news*, she mouthed. *My mom's freaking*.

Cars screeched into the sweeping drive of the Benoits' house and the guests grabbed their stuff. Claire scratched at her hands and shivered as she watched everyone stream into the house. A strong hand gripped her upper arm and she jumped.

Matthew stood behind her. A grin played across his face as he pulled her behind the pool house. He was so close, Claire could feel the heat from his skin.

"Aren't you scared?"

"Nah. Why should I be? The chance of a werewolf attacking in broad daylight—it's practically zero."

"But that's why everyone's freaking out, right? Because if someone actually saw a werewolf during the day, it might mean it would actually strike before dark?"

"Claire! Come inside, please," Claire's mom called from the back door.

The thread of electric energy running between Claire and Matthew faded.

*Argh! No!*

He stepped back, tucking a lock of Claire's hair back behind her ear.

"I'd better go," he said. "I had a great time. A really, really great time."

She nodded. "O-okay. Thanks." Her voice shook. "Be careful getting home."

"Don't worry about me—I'll be fine. Call you later!" He smiled and darted around the pool house.

Claire leaned against the wall, dizzy with happiness. *Oh my God! He said he'd call! Oh my God!* She wrapped her arms around her damp bathing suit and twirled around.

"Claire," her mother called from the door. "Everyone's leaving. Claire?"

After the party, Lisbeth was too freaked about the werewolf to deal with the mess outside, but, of course, Claire's mom was too bothered by the mess to let it be. She cleaned it up herself, her lips pursed, while Lisbeth hid in the kitchen doing dishes. By dinnertime, the tension in the house was thicker than the frosting on the birthday cake.

Claire sat at the kitchen island between Lisbeth and her mom. Half-eaten sandwiches lay in front of them—rare roast beef for Claire and her mother, and a vegetarian-friendly grilled cheese for Lisbeth. The news was running another special expanded edition about the werewolf sighting, which was pretty much just them saying, *"We don't know anything else, but we'll tell you as soon as we do. In the meantime, here's everything we do know, again,"* over and over and over. Claire ignored it, but her mom's eyes were glued to the screen, watching as a police sketch artist held up a rendition of what they thought the wolf might look like.

Lisbeth picked at the remains of her sandwich and patted the back of her sunburned neck. "I'm worn out. I'm gonna slather on some aloe and go to bed," she announced. She leaned over and pecked Claire on the head. "Happy Birthday, sweetie. Sixteen. Wow." She sighed. "I better hurry up and find a guy to sweep me off my feet, or you'll head off to college and I won't have anyone to take care of but your mother."

It sounded like she was joking, but Claire could see the concern that crinkled up the corners of Lisbeth's eyes.

*Guess the thing with that guy from her yoga class must have flopped.*

"Nah, you can come with me and fold my laundry in the dorm." Claire stuck her tongue out at Lisbeth. Next to Claire, her mother snorted.

Lisbeth rolled her eyes. "I'll let that go because it's your birthday." She leaned into Claire. "See you in the morning."

"'Night." Claire stopped scratching the backs of her hands against the rough underside of the granite countertop. She snaked one arm around Lisbeth for a quick hug.

Marie tore another bite out of her sandwich and nodded

at Lisbeth without taking her eyes off the news. Claire felt Lisbeth stiffen beside her—just a little—before she turned and left the room.

Claire fished an ice cube out of her glass and held it against the prickling itch in her ear.

"Are you still mad at Lisbeth about the cleaning thing?"

Her mother's jaw stopped midchew and she looked away from the replay of another interview with Dr. Engle. Claire's chest tightened under the full force of her mother's dark eyes.

"No, of course not. I'm angry at that ignorant, pompous quack. He's the reason Lisbeth was too scared to be out earlier." She ripped off another corner of her sandwich and chewed fiercely. "He's appointed himself judge, jury, and executioner—testing that stupid 'cure' of his without even confirming that his subjects really are werewolves. Ruining lives so that he can hurry to impress a group of scientists and hiding behind the government to do it—he makes me sick!" She threw the remnants of her sandwich onto her plate and strode over to the kitchen door.

Matthew's dad was working on a drug that supposedly cured lycanthropy. It somehow ate the disease out of the werewolf's brain so that it couldn't transform anymore. During a TV interview Claire had heard Dr. Engle explain how it worked, but it had been way technical and confusing—even the interviewer looked kind of lost. All she really got was that it had to be administered at the full moon, but when they were in human form.

No one really cared how it worked, just that it did. Once a werewolf had been treated, it stayed in human form, forever. The Austrian werewolves he had tested it on were left in a permanent coma. They were still in some locked wing at the Vienna University Research Center, but pretty much everyone agreed it was a well-deserved punishment for attacking humans.

"But the Austrian attacks stopped after he injected the werewolves," Claire pointed out. She glanced over at the television. Dr. Engle had the same golden-blond hair that Matthew did, but his face was sharper—all planes and angles.

Marie gripped the doorframe. Tension rippled across her back. "And you assume that there is no other explanation for that?" She spoke without turning.

Claire swallowed the wad of sandwich she'd stuffed into her cheek. "I, uh, hadn't thought about it. I guess there could be."

"That, my love, is his trap. Many fall into it. I hope that you won't make the same mistake. I am going to have a bath now. Please put your dishes in the sink when you're finished."

Claire's mother slipped up the steps while Claire toyed with the crust of her sandwich and listened to the mindless drone of the newscaster. Dark spots the size of pinpricks sprang up on the backs of her hands. She scratched at them with the tines of a plastic fork.

Claire sighed and trudged upstairs to find the cortisone cream.

A hand shook her shoulder.

"Claire. Claire!"

She cracked open one eye.

"Mrrrhmph," she mumbled, as Lisbeth shook her again.

"I brought you up a tray. It's nearly noon."

Claire pulled the covers over her head and nestled farther down into the bed. She heard Lisbeth walk a few steps and waited for the door to close, already sinking back into sleep. That is, until the covers were jerked off her. Lisbeth stood at the end of the bed, her arms full of fabric and a grin spread across her face.

"Your mom will be home in an hour—you need to be up and dressed by then. She wants to take you shopping." Lisbeth sat down on the end of the bed and snatched a triangle of toast off Claire's plate. Claire watched Lisbeth examine it for any sign of contamination from the strips of bacon before she crunched into it.

"Hey, I thought that was for me!" Claire sat up and made a halfhearted grab for the toast.

"Hey, yourself." Lisbeth took another bite. "Cook's treat. You're lucky I brought it up here at all, missy." Her face turned serious. "I figured you'd be tired after the commotion yesterday. I'm sorry your party ended that way."

Matthew's promise to call her echoed in Claire's memory. *Actually, I think it ended pretty well.* "Yeah, well, at least everyone came in the first place, right?"

Lisbeth ruffled her hair. "That's very positive of you, Claire-bear. Ya gotta go with the flow, right?"

Claire rolled her eyes. "Oh my God, Lisbeth, no one says 'go with the flow' anymore. You sound like some long-lost hippy. And don't call me Claire-bear."

Lisbeth stuck out her lower lip and pretended to be hurt. "I bring you brunch in bed, and all I get is abuse. Fine, I'm going back downstairs." She leapt off the bed.

Claire threw a pillow at Lisbeth, who ducked it expertly and laughed as she slipped out of the room. *Mom will be here in an hour.* Claire sighed. Nothing like being at the beck and call of someone who barely remembered you were alive.

Her mom was gone so much, and even when she was home, Marie spent most of her time locked in her darkroom, or pacing her office while she negotiated an even more astronomical salary for her next shoot. Still, it would be worth getting out of bed if it meant going shopping. Claire picked up a piece of bacon and nibbled at it, then tossed it back on the plate and walked over to her closet. She threw on a pair of shorts and a tank top, then hurried into the bathroom to get ready.

She was running the flat iron through her hair one last time when muffled music started floating out of her laundry basket.

"Crap!" Claire yelped. She dug through the pile of dirty clothes until she found the jeans she'd been wearing yesterday morning. Plunging her hand into the pocket, she yanked out her cell phone, glancing at the caller ID. Her heart pounded as she flipped open the phone.

"Hello?" She blushed at how breathless she sounded.

"Claire? Sorry, were you still asleep?" Matthew asked.

"No, I'm up. I just couldn't find my phone." *Oh, way to go, Claire. Now he thinks you're a ditz.*

"Cool." He paused. "So, I was wondering—do you maybe want to come over later? We could hang out here and watch a movie or something."

Claire bit her lip to keep from squealing.

"Yeah," she said, "that sounds good. What, uh—what time?"

She did a celebration dance around the room while they made plans. As soon as they'd hung up, she tore down the stairs and slapped, barefoot, across the marble floor into the kitchen.

"Lisbeth!" She called.

A blond head peeked around the corner. "What? You'd better be ready, your mom'll be here any minute."

"You have to drop me off at Matthew's house later, okay? I mean, I can go, right? To watch a movie?"

Lisbeth grinned, but a little worried line appeared between her eyebrows. "Matthew? Isn't he older than you are?"

"Only by a year."

Lisbeth put her hands on her hips and cocked her head at Claire. "Isn't he a Pisces? They're not very compatible with Geminis, you know."

Claire rolled her eyes. "Oh my God. Enough with the astrology crap. Just—can I go, or what?"

"Okay, you can go, but when he gets all emotional, don't say I didn't warn you." Lisbeth shook her head. "Now go upstairs and"—she stopped midsentence—"hey, why are your hands so red?"

Claire shoved them deep into her pockets. Overnight, the pinprick rash had gotten worse—it was on her ears, too. The scratchy denim hem rubbed against her wrists and it felt like heaven. "I think it's poison ivy. I already put some stuff on them."

The back door swung open. Claire's mother stepped into the house, her satiny-dark hair damp with sweat. "It's scorching out there, again." She looked at Claire. "Are you ready to go shopping?"

Claire nodded, kissed Lisbeth on the cheek, and hurried into the cool interior of her mother's waiting Mercedes. "Thanks for taking me."

"Of course," her mother said. "Your sixteenth birthday— it's important. A mark of change. We should celebrate."

# Chapter Two

THREE STORES AND four big shopping bags later, Claire and her mother slid into a booth at one of the restaurants attached to the mall. It was like the world's most upscale diner—hamburgers and tuna melts, but made with Black Angus beef and ahi tuna, served on ultramodern plates. The waitress took their order—two hamburgers, rare, with fries—and glided back to the kitchen.

Under the table, Claire scratched furiously at her hands.

"So, do you have any plans this weekend?" her mother asked, sipping at a glass of iced tea.

Claire played with the straw that the waitress had set next

to her Diet Coke. She'd nearly told her mom about going to Matthew's—no less than five times since they'd left the house, but her mom hated Dr. Engle so completely. . . .

*Lisbeth'll just tell her if I don't.* Claire swallowed hard.

"I'm going to Matthew's later to watch a movie," she said as casually as she could.

The waitress appeared next to their table and slid two plates in front of them. Her mother looked at the food in silence. To stop herself from saying anything else, Claire stuffed a huge bite of hamburger in her mouth. She couldn't bring herself to look at her mother's face. Instead, she stared at the hamburger bun, watching as the juices from the meat turned the bread rose-pink.

"Claire." Her mother sighed. "I don't think that's a very good idea. The Engles—"

"Mom!" Claire interrupted her. "Matthew's not like his dad, okay? You don't even know him. What about what you said last night? All that giving-people-a-chance-to-prove-themselves junk?"

Her mother dipped a French fry into a tiny dish of gourmet ketchup. "I see you feel strongly about this, *chérie*. Fine, then, you may go this time. But if you see Matthew's father, I want you to keep your eyes open and your mouth closed. And I will warn you—we must have a very serious discussion when you get home. Now, eat your lunch before it gets cold. I have film that needs to be developed this afternoon, and the day is slipping away."

Claire nodded and bit into her hamburger, smiling as she chewed. In a few hours, she'd be with Matthew, and right then that was all she really cared about.

Emily sat on Claire's bed, pawing through the shopping bags that Claire had tossed on top of the covers. Claire had called her the minute she'd walked in the door, and as soon as Emily heard the words "Matthew Engle" and "date" in the same sentence, she'd hurried over. Claire had heard Emily's car start before they even hung up.

"So, um—I'm sorry your party ended the way it did. That was pretty awful. Are you doing okay?"

"Are you kidding? I'm doing great."

"I figured that Matthew asking you out would make up for everything else. How did it all happen, anyway?"

"Matthew sort of caught me while everyone else was making a run for it. And then he called this morning and asked me to come over and hang out."

Emily grinned at her. "See, I told you things would work out. I knew he liked you—I knew it! Oh, I'm so excited for you." She pulled a bottle of pink nail polish off the bedside table and held it up to her toes experimentally. "So, what are you going to wear?"

"I don't know." Claire leaned against her closet door and kicked at a pile of shoes. "It's gotta be something with long sleeves, since I've got this stupid rash on my hands that I do *not* want him to see. What do you think?"

"It needs to be something sexy but not obvious. I mean, it should make him want you without being *sure* that he can have you, right? What about . . . hmm . . ."

Emily hauled herself off the bed and walked into Claire's closet, flicking through the tops that hung near the back.

"What about this?" She held out a red scoop-necked shirt. "You could wear it with that pair of jeans with the rip in the knee? That would be perfect, as long as you won't die of heatstroke."

"You're a genius. I totally forgot I even had that top. And I don't think heatstroke's much of an issue in the Engles' basement." Claire rummaged around in her closet, digging out the right jeans from a pile on the shelf. "Any other advice, oh-dating-guru-who-is-also-my-best-friend?"

"Don't chew gum. If he tries to kiss you, then you'll just have to swallow it, and that can get really awkward. Put some mints in your pocket instead and you can pop them if you need to."

"Mints. Got it."

"Oh, and one other thing . . ."

"Yeah?"

"He's not actually a god, Claire. He's a cute guy. And he's *lucky* that you're coming over. Just relax and have a good time, okay?"

Claire groaned. "I'll try, but I'm not making any promises. Listen, I'm actually leaving in about an hour, so—"

"Then why am I still here?" Emily interrupted. "Go finish getting ready—I'm already gone. God. Matthew Engle. Do you swear to call me tomorrow?"

"Sure." Claire grinned. "I'll give you the complete rundown."

Emily gave her a hug and headed downstairs. Claire went into her bathroom, hoping a shower would calm her down. Emily mentioning the possibility of Matthew kissing her had made her all jittery.

"Ow! Crap!" Claire jumped as the searing-hot plate of the flat iron grazed her neck. She pulled back the silky-smooth section of hair and inspected the damage. A tiny pink mark rose on her neck—not too bad. Not nearly as bad as the forest of red pinpricks that dotted her ears. At least her hair would hide them. Her hands were a whole other problem. Claire pulled on the Emily-endorsed red shirt. The ends of the sleeves came nearly to her knuckles, and she'd coated her skin with concealer and powder, which made the itching worse, but they looked a lot better. *If Matthew notices this stupid rash, I'll die.*

"Claire?" Lisbeth's voice echoed down the hall. "We're going to be late!"

"I'm coming!" Claire grabbed her cell phone, shook her hair back over her ears, and licked her lips. She hurried into the car. Lisbeth was already there, dressed in a sparkly purple tunic. Silver bangles chimed against one another on her wrists, and her lips shone with gloss.

Claire looked her over. "You're dressed up."

Lisbeth shrugged. "I have some plans."

Claire climbed into the car. "Fine then, be all mysterious."

A peony-pink flush spread across Lisbeth's cheeks. "I am allowed to have a private life, you know."

"Okay, okay. Sheesh. Don't smear your lip gloss."

When Lisbeth pulled up in front of the Engles' house, Claire tried not to notice that it was smaller than hers. Then again, most houses were smaller than the Benoits'. Claire's mother liked privacy as much as she liked nice things, and their huge house perched on several acres of land.

Matthew's house was the picture of normal—cutesy garden in the front, shutters painted, and a stained glass oval with a cross hanging in the front window. Claire leapt out of the car.

"I'll pick you up at nine," Lisbeth said. "And I mean on the dot—I don't want to be out after dark!"

Matthew opened the door before she could knock.

"Hey." He stepped aside and motioned her into the house. "C'mon in."

"Thanks," Claire said.

"My dad made popcorn." Matthew rolled his eyes. "Why don't we go grab the bowl and some sodas? Then we can escape to the basement."

"Sure," Claire said, tugging her sleeves as far down over her hands as they would go. She could see the kitchen from the front hall, and it was bright enough to do surgery in there.

Matthew's dad was leaning against a counter in the kitchen, drying his hands on a paper towel. He looked just like he did on the news, only he wasn't wearing a tie, and the sleeves of his dress shirt had been rolled up.

"You must be Claire." He extended a damp hand in her direction. "It's a pleasure to meet you."

Claire shook his hand as quickly as she could, then tucked her itching fingers behind her back.

"Your mother is a remarkable photographer," Dr. Engle said.

"Yeah, that's right," Claire said. Something about the look in his eyes—and her mother's warning: *mouth closed, eyes open*—kept her from saying anything else. It was like he was saying one thing but meant another, and Claire couldn't figure out what he was actually thinking.

"Marie Benoit . . . such a *fascinating* woman. Unique. And very outspoken, as I recall."

"Uh, I guess." Claire looked over at Matthew. He yanked open the fridge and grabbed two cans of soda. With the bowl of popcorn balanced on top of one of the icy cans, he jerked his head toward the stairs.

"If we don't start the movie, we won't have time to watch it before dark," Matthew said. "Thanks for the popcorn, Dad. I'll, um, let you know if we need anything."

"You do that."

Dr. Engle didn't take his eyes off Claire. She quivered under his unblinking gaze and followed Matthew down the carpeted stairs.

"Don't pay any attention to my dad. He's just weird like that."

"It's no big deal," Claire said, looking at the shelves of books that lined the basement walls. The thick spines were covered with gilded letters. Titles like *Vivisection and the Human Condition* and *Lunar Phase Sensitivity* glimmered at her in the dim light. *Spending all your time reading that kind of stuff would make anyone weird.*

"Your dad's really into his job, huh?"

"Yeah, I guess."

Claire looked over at Matthew and raised her eyebrows. He'd gotten touchy when the topic of his dad had come up at her party, too. "Touchy subject?"

"Kind of." Matthew sat back on the couch and cracked open one of the sodas. "It just gets old. Everyone else only sees one side of him. They get so excited because he's on TV so much. But he can't talk about anything except his 'cure.' He didn't even make it to a single one of my soccer games last season, you know?"

"Really? That sucks." Matthew was an incredible mid-fielder. Claire had heard someone saying he'd already been offered a bunch of college scholarships because of it. "Sometimes I think it's better, for me at least, when my mom's *not* noticing me—like when she's gone."

Matthew looked at her, surprised.

Claire shrugged. "I mean, that's when things seem normal. Lisbeth and I just—*are*. But when Mom's home, everything's all about her and when she needs to work or what she wants to eat, and Lisbeth tiptoes around the house like she's hiding from a burglar or something."

"Huh. Actually, that makes sense. My mom and I are the same way—when Dad's home, everything's about not bothering him. We practically can't breathe without it interrupting his thought process or whatever. I never thought about it that way, but you're totally right."

The intrigued look in his eyes made Claire's palms damp. She shrugged.

"Of course, my dad's not out-of-town gone like your mom is. I mean, he deals with werewolf attacks all over the world, but mostly he just does that over the phone from his lab, like consulting with other governments and scientists and stuff, trying to get them to try his cure. He's having an easier time talking people into things, now that he's on the FHPA. Anyway, enough about my dad. He's not half as interesting as you are." Matthew dragged the popcorn closer to the couch and put one of the sodas on Claire's side of the bowl.

His words sent a sudden rush of heat through her that made it hard to talk. Claire sank onto the couch, leaving a half-cushion length between her and Matthew. *Close enough that he can reach me but not close enough to look desperate.*

Matthew held up a DVD case.

"Is this okay?" It was some sort of action movie. The cover featured a sports car midexplosion.

Claire nodded. She didn't care what they watched—she was too hyperaware of Matthew sitting next to her. As casually as she could, Claire left her hand, palm up, on the cushion between them. The rough nub of the fabric felt good against the back of her itchy hand. Matthew shifted like he was just changing positions, but when he settled back, he was at least six inches closer to Claire than he'd been before. His arm was stretched across the back of the sofa, behind Claire but definitely not touching her.

Claire's breath caught, and Matthew looked over at her. She wanted to move closer, to be touching him. But wasn't he supposed to make the first move?

*Oh my God, this is so stupid. I don't* care *who's supposed to start things.* Claire scooted over and leaned into Matthew. He stiffened slightly and Claire's heart froze in her chest. *Oh, crap. Crapcrapcrap.* She started to sit up, to pull away.

"Not a chance." Matthew wrapped his arm firmly around her shoulder.

Claire didn't think he could see the enormous smile that spread across her face.

*Score one for the rule breaker.*

While cars flashed by on the television and police sirens blared from the surround sound, Matthew traced a pattern on Claire's shoulder with his fingertips, which made her shivery in a distinctly not-cold way. The movie—which she hadn't really been watching, anyway—became just a blur of images on the screen. All she could focus on was Matthew's touch.

When the closing credits popped up on the screen, Matthew turned his head toward her. "Claire?" he asked.

"Yeah?"

His face was inches from hers. In the dim light, his eyes flashed. "This is okay?" His voice was low, beckoning.

Claire swallowed hard. "It's very okay," she whispered.

"Good." He leaned toward her, his mouth hovering close enough to hers that she could feel the heat of his skin.

The door creaked open at the top of the steps. Claire pulled away from Matthew, but he caught her hand, keeping her close. The look of pained frustration on his face was so obvious that Claire had to fight back a giggle.

"Claire?" Matthew's father called down. "Your—er, someone is here to retrieve you."

"We'll be right there," Matthew shouted back. He looked at Claire, and a slow smile spread across his tanned face. "This is the only day in a month he's been home. Next time, he'll be bugging some reporter, instead of us."

"That sounds . . . better." *Next time! He said "next time"!*

"Or we could hang out at my house. Lisbeth's not, like, overly invasive, or anything."

Matthew glanced up at the open door and sighed. He reached over and traced the line of her jaw with his thumb. "I'll call you, okay?"

Claire floated out to the car.

"I told you nine on the dot," Lisbeth said. "The sun's already set."

Claire looked out at the streaks of pink and orange spread across the sky like fire. "I know," she sighed. "Isn't it gorgeous?"

Lisbeth snorted. "Ahh, young love," she teased.

"So, how were your *plans?*" Claire shot a meaningful look at Lisbeth.

"Successful." Lisbeth picked a fragment of dead leaf off her sleeve. A little smile twitched at the corners of her mouth. She obviously wasn't going to say any more about it.

"Well, good for you, Miss I-have-a-private-life." Claire rolled her eyes and turned up the volume on the car stereo. She scratched her hands against the fabric of the car seat, and wished they were home already.

Late that night, Claire tossed and turned in bed. Her ears and the backs of her hands were driving her crazy, even though Lisbeth had coated them with Calamine lotion after dinner. She dozed fitfully, waking with a start as the door of her room swung open. Her mother crept in, shutting the door behind her. Claire sat up in bed and blinked at the long mane of fine black hair that hung loose and wild around her mother's face. Her mom never wore her hair down—it was always up in a sleek bun, so that it wouldn't get in her way when she worked.

"You're up," her mom said as she lowered herself onto the bed.

Claire nodded. "I guess I had too much Diet Coke," she said. "And I'm itchy."

Her mom smiled, picked up Claire's hand, and pressed it between her cool palms.

"I'd forgotten about the itching," she said in a faraway voice.

Claire frowned. "You—what?"

Her mother let go of Claire's hand and pushed back her hair.

"Oh, *chérie*, I'm not even sure where to begin." Her mom sighed, staring out the window at the wide expanse of moon-lit lawn spread out below. "Now that you're sixteen, things— things are going to start changing. I—I have been waiting a long time to discuss this with you."

Claire felt hot blood rush into her cheeks. *Oh, God*, she thought, *she wants to have The Talk. Ew. What does she think happened at Matthew's, anyway?*

"Mom, it's okay," she mumbled. "We already did all this in Health class."

Her mother's eyes flew open wide. "What? How—oh. *Oh.*" She began to laugh. "No, Claire, that's . . . that's not what I meant."

Claire drew her knees up into her chest and wrapped her arms around her legs. "What, then?"

Her mother leaned back against one of the big carved posts at the end of the bed and smoothed the collar of her shirt. Claire stared at her mother. A middle-of-the-night, mother-daughter chat was way out of character for her mom. Something was definitely up.

Her mother sighed. "Our family is not like other families. Your history, your lineage—it's something I want you to be proud of."

"What, because you're French?" Claire struggled not to laugh. "I guess we could start celebrating Bastille Day."

"That's not what I mean." Her mother's voice was sharp. She closed her eyes and took a deep breath.

*Man, it's easy to push her buttons,* Claire thought.

"You come from a long line of proud women. Women who have survived, who have passed down a secret from mother to daughter." She twisted the sheet around her fingers.

Claire crossed her arms and waited.

Her mother's eyes darted up to meet Claire's. "Like me, like your grandmother before me, and her mother before her, you are what we call *loup-garou.*"

Claire cocked her head to the side. She hated it when her mother slipped back into French.

"A werewolf, *chérie.* You—we—are werewolves."

# Chapter Three

CLAIRE'S MOUTH FELL open, then snapped shut as she hurtled off the bed and headed for the door. *She's insane,* she thought. *It's not true. It can't be.*

Her mother caught her by the arm and whirled her around, her gray eyes sparking.

"Claire, I know this is difficult news. But it is the truth—that is why you have been itching, your hands, your ears. It is the beginning of your transformation."

Claire sank down onto the carpet, rocked herself into a tight ball, and covered her prickling ears with her hands. "You're crazy! You're wrong—there's no way I'm a werewolf! I would know—I would have known." She dug her fingernails into her earlobes so hard that her eyes watered from the pain.

"I wanted to tell you all along, but no one is ever told before her sixteenth birthday. Take a deep breath, Claire, breathe! It's going to be okay."

Claire inhaled sharply. "It's just not true. Werewolves, they kill people and I—I don't want to hurt anyone." Her voice rose.

"Sssshh!" Her mother cautioned her. "You mustn't wake Lisbeth."

She scooped Claire up, lifting her easily onto the bed. *How can she be strong enough to lift me?* Claire's teeth chattered.

"Why not us? It must be someone. Think about it, Claire. Why do you think we have always had an au pair? Someone to care for you when I am not here? Sometimes I am gone for work. But I sometimes leave for other reasons. One truth hides another. I know it's hard to accept—I know, I remember."

"But I don't want to hurt anyone. I don't want to hurt anyone. I don't," Claire whispered, her knees hugged against her chest.

"The television news is not always right, Claire. We prey upon other animals, yes, but so do most men. Killing humans for sport is not allowed."

"So why does everyone say that werewolves kill people?" Claire challenged.

Her mother's lips pressed into a thin line. "One of our kind sometimes strays from our laws—the same way men stray from theirs when they kill one another. But it is not our nature. It is not our way. Those *loup-garou* who kill humans are shunned by the rest of us."

"I don't believe any of this. If I, if *we* were werewolves, you would have told me before now!"

"No, I wouldn't have. I couldn't. Children are never allowed to know. They don't understand the danger involved. They are unable to keep their identity secret. Not revealing the truth until a child begins to change has been our tradition for many generations. Before we began doing it this way, many more of us were caught. And killed."

Her mother threw open the walk-in closet and strode to the back. "Get dressed," she said. "Something dark-colored. We're going out."

"O-out wh-where?" Claire stammered. She caught the pair of black pants her mother tossed at her.

Her mother turned to face her. "We're going to the woods. I didn't believe my mother until I had seen it, either." Her voice softened. "I will explain everything to you, when the time is right."

"When the time is right?" Claire squeaked, the edges of her vision growing fuzzy. "You're telling me we're going into the woods so that I can turn into a wolf, but it's not the right time to talk about it?"

"Not tonight. It takes three moon cycles for a New One to transform fully. I, though—I must transform. Do not be frightened, Claire. Nothing tonight will hurt you, I promise. You need to trust me now, and do exactly as I say." She pressed an old shirt into Claire's hands. "We must hurry. It will look bad if we are late."

Claire pulled on the shirt and crept down the hall behind her mother. She wasn't sure what scared her more—the idea that her mother had lost her mind or the possibility that she was telling Claire the truth.

They went out the side door, sliding into the empty night. Her mother moved so quickly through the shadows that it was all Claire could do to keep up. A painful stitch knotted her side. *God, I've never seen anyone move this fast.*

When her mother came to a sudden stop, Claire nearly collided with her. In front of them was an ivy-covered patch in the wall that separated their land from the forest.

"Here is the entrance," Marie whispered. She nodded toward the top of the wall. "That chipped brick up there—it marks the spot." She knelt down and pulled aside the ivy, revealing a large hole in the bricks. She eased herself through the hidden opening.

The woods were inky black, and Claire stopped just inside the brick wall, unable to see anything. She felt totally numb—no matter how hard she tried, she couldn't make herself move forward into the darkness.

*I wonder if I'm going into shock.*

"I can't see anything. Maybe I should go back."

"Your eyes will change soon enough," said her mother. She gripped Claire's hand and began to pull her along through the trees.

Twigs and leaves crunched under Claire's feet as they rushed through the woods. Something crashed through the underbrush on Claire's right, and her mother yanked her behind a tree, pulling her down onto the mossy forest floor.

Claire crouched behind the tree. Her mother made a warning noise, a low rumble that echoed deep in her throat. She sounded like an animal.

"What was that?" Claire whispered.

Her mother sighed. "I don't know," she admitted. "Perhaps it was one of the others."

*The others?* Before Claire could force the question out of her mouth, Marie jerked her to her feet and took off through the forest, her hand an iron band around Claire's wrist. Far ahead, in the deepest part of the woods, a dull orange light flickered. Claire blinked hard, trying to see through the thick branches while she ran. Her lungs burned as she gasped for air. They drew closer to the light, which waved and flickered. *It's a fire,* Claire realized. Her skin crawled when she saw the five figures surrounding it, their shadows coal-black in the fire's glow.

*Five of them. Oh, God.* She yanked her hand out of her mother's grip, shocked and sickened by her own sudden strength. Her mom grunted in surprise.

"There—there are *six* of you? Here, in Hanover Falls?" Claire stammered. She shivered hard in spite of the heat.

Her mother caught Claire's face between her palms. "Seven, *chérie*. There are seven of us. Come. I will introduce you."

Claire slunk into the circle behind her mother. The five sharp-eyed women seated around the fire stared at her. Marie pulled her forward, into the bright, hot light of the fire.

"This is Claire," she said. Marie turned to the old woman sitting on the ground near Claire. "Beatrice, I greet you."

The old woman smiled, her face cracking into a web of wrinkles beneath her cloud of frizzy gray hair. "Marie, I greet you," she replied. Her bright eyes raked over Claire. "Happy Birthday, little Claire," she added.

Claire stared at her, dazed. It was too much to take in all at once. She still hadn't seen anything that proved that her mother was telling the truth, that they really were werewolves—but the possibility made her legs wobble underneath her.

Claire felt her mother's elbow dig into her side. "Um, thanks," she said to Beatrice, who sat with a patient smile on her face.

*How did she know it was my birthday?* Marie's elbow stayed planted in Claire's ribs. "I, uh, I greet you, too, Beatrice."

The old woman clapped her hands delightedly. Claire's mom turned to a much younger woman, sitting with her arm around Beatrice.

"Victoria is the daughter of Beatrice," she said to Claire. "Victoria, I greet you."

Victoria smiled, tossing her straw-colored hair over one shoulder. "Marie, I greet you. Claire, I greet you, too."

Without thinking about it, Claire smiled back, calmed by how bright and normal Victoria seemed. "I—I greet you," she said.

*"Say her name,"* hissed her mother.

Claire winced. "I greet you, too, Victoria. Sorry."

"S'okay," Victoria said. "It's a lot to learn all at once. You'll catch on."

Claire's mom pulled her around to face the next woman in the circle. She was pale and thin, with coarse, iron-black hair.

"This is Zahlia. Zahlia, I greet you."

"And I greet you, Marie." She licked her lips and nodded at Claire. "Claire, I also greet you."

"I greet you, Zahlia," Claire said, more smoothly this time.

They went through the same ritual with the last two women, Judith and Katherine, two middle-aged women who both greeted Claire without even really looking at her. Claire's mouth went nervous-dry at the same time that her jaw clenched in irritation. It was like being paraded around in front of some of her mother's important clients—their eyes skimmed over her politely, but it was obvious that they couldn't care less about meeting her.

*It's not like I asked to be here.*

The dark-haired woman—Zahlia—caught Claire's eye and gazed pointedly at Judith and Katherine before rolling her eyes. Claire fought to keep the smile off her face. Okay, so not *everyone* thought she was just some dumb drag-along of her mother's.

Marie caught sight of the amused expression on Claire's face and gave her a sharp look.

"Sit." Her mother pointed to an open space next to Victoria, the blonde. "And listen."

Claire sank down onto the dirt next to Victoria. She wrapped her arms around her legs and squeezed out the desire to run back through the woods, go home, crawl into bed, and pretend none of this had ever happened.

Beatrice stood up and shuffled close to the fire. She raised her arms and began to chant in a clear, youthful voice that surprised Claire. *This can't seriously be happening. Maybe it's just some really screwed-up dream I'm having.* Claire pinched her palm with the nails of her left hand. *Crap. Not a dream.* Victoria scooted closer and grabbed Claire's hand, making her jump.

"It's okay," she whispered. "I was scared at first, too. Don't worry."

Claire's mom shot them an impatient look and Victoria fell silent. Claire couldn't understand most of the chant, and it seemed to go on forever. She heard something about the wind and the Goddess, and heard Beatrice calling each of their names . . . except for Claire's.

"Close your eyes," said Victoria. "It'll be easier."

Claire shut her eyes and leaned forward, resting her forehead on her knees. The crackle of the fire filled her ears. A low moan moved through the circle. It changed and grew until it became a howl—*no,* Claire realized, *six howls.* She opened her eyes with her forehead still on her knees. On the ground next to her, she saw two brown paws, bigger than any dog's, in the exact spot where Victoria's sandaled feet had been. A cold, wet nose nudged Claire's ear.

Claire lifted her head and jumped when she saw the enormous, mottled brunette wolf in front of her.

An anxious whine rattled the wolf's throat, somewhere just above Claire's head.

*It's okay now. It's over.*

As a wolf, Victoria was bigger than Yolanda Adams's St. Bernard—almost the size of a pony. Everyone knew that werewolves were larger than regular wolves, but Claire hadn't really grasped just how big they really were. Claire spun around. In the spot where her mother had been stood a silvery-gray wolf. She was a little taller and darker than the two next to her, who must have been Judith and Katherine.

"Mom?" she squeaked.

*Yes, Claire?* The silvery wolf's mouth stayed shut tight, even as her mother's voice rang in Claire's ears. Claire blinked.

*I'm—reading her mind? Werewolves have ESP?*

*Not exactly,* her mother said, sniffing the air. *You are reading my body language, the same as I am reading yours. And you* can smell the chemical changes that come with shifting emotions. *You're just translating it in your head, the way I do from English to French. It's part of the heightened senses that you will have from now on—even in your human form.*

A low growl interrupted them.

*We are already late. It is time to hunt.* Zahlia's pure-black fur shimmered against the flat dark of the forest shadows. She was huge—the same size as Marie, with pale flashing eyes.

Claire's mother nodded. *Zahlia is right. Claire, you must stay here with Beatrice. We will be back as quickly as we can.*

"But—" Claire started to protest, but Zahlia stepped in.

*Oh, Marie, why not let her come? She might as well start learning.*

Claire's mother gave Zahlia a look that could've frozen lightning. *You know that training does not begin until after one's transformation is complete.*

Judith sniffed. *Beatrice must make the decision. And I'm getting hungry.*

Zahlia shrugged her dark-furred shoulders, tilting her head slightly to one side in a gesture that clearly said *Whatever you want.*

They all turned to Beatrice.

*Marie is right.* Beatrice sat tall and still on the ground next to the fire. *This is not the right time. Go, the five of you, and hunt. Claire and I will wait here.*

The five werewolves streaked off into the woods. Claire

looked over at Beatrice, whose wolf-form looked almost exactly like Victoria's, only thinner, and with white fur streaking her muzzle and ears. Her ribs showed.

Beatrice padded over and eased herself down on her haunches next to Claire and nudged Claire's arm around her neck. Tears flooded Claire's eyes, and Beatrice pressed her flank close against Claire's leg.

*It'll be okay, child. Your mother—after you finish your transformation, she will be able to explain things better. I know it's hard to believe, but she's as nervous and afraid as you are, Claire. Maybe more. When Victoria had her change, I was so proud, but at the same time my heart broke for her. Our life—it's a wonderful one, but it's also a heavy burden to bear, and Marie knows it. Did your mother tell you that she is second only to me?*

Claire shook her head.

*Someday, she will be the Alpha of our pack. You must trust her, Claire. She knows our ways—she knows what she is doing. Things will be fine, really.*

Claire buried her face in the soft fur of Beatrice's shoulder. Her breath came in short, ragged gasps. *If this is what I have to be, things will* not *be fine. I want to go home*, she thought. *I just want to go home, I want to go home. And how the hell could she not tell me any of this for sixteen freaking years?* Before her tears could begin to flow in earnest, she heard a strange sound, like something heavy was being dragged through the woods.

"What's going on?" she whispered.

*It's the hunt.* Beatrice began to pant.

Victoria bounded into the clearing ahead of the others.

*I hope you're hungry,* she said, butting her head into the side of Beatrice's neck. *We got a buck!*

Claire looked over in time to see her mother and Katherine dragging an enormous deer into the clearing. The silvery fur on her mother's chest was matted with blood. The buck kicked once, sending a wild hoof in Katherine's direction.

"Oh," Claire cried. "Oh—it's not even dead!" She scooted back and cowered against the trunk of a tree.

Zahlia clamped her jaws around the deer's neck and squeezed until it lay still. The six wolves gathered around the animal. Claire shut her eyes and tried to block out the sounds of ripping deer hide, and chewing.

There was a soft *yip* that sounded familiar, somehow. Claire looked up and cringed.

Her mother cocked her head to one side. *Are you okay?*

In spite of herself, Claire glanced over at the other werewolves crouched around the mutilated deer. Its wounds glittered in the firelight. To her horror, Claire felt a band of hunger squeeze around her stomach. Her mouth flooded with saliva and she swallowed hard.

Claire's mom blinked at her. *Do you want me to bring you some?* Her ears flicked in Claire's direction. *Your teeth—human teeth—won't work.*

Claire shook her head. In spite of her watering mouth, she couldn't eat that. She wouldn't. *I'm not an animal,* she thought. She forced herself to look away, gazing down at her hands. The sight of them made her gasp. A coat of silky fur, the color of a storm cloud, covered the backs of her hands. Slowly, she reached up and brushed the same sort of fur as she traced the outlines of her ears. They had lost their usual seashell curve. They were flatter, more pointed. An inhuman whine whistled through her teeth.

Claire's mother padded over to her and sat on her haunches. Marie ducked her head low so that they were almost face-to-face. *The hunger will get stronger and stronger for you, and it will bring more changes each time it comes. Each month, your transformation will be more complete. In three full moons, Beatrice will call your name in the ceremony, too. This is the way of our world. The sooner you accept it, the easier things will be.*

Claire's chin trembled. She pushed her palms hard against her eyes, trying to force back the tears, and shook her head. The fur on the backs of her hands was like a blanket. Her skin underneath felt hot, smothered. She heard her mother sigh and pad away across the clearing, back to the deer.

While the others ate, Claire huddled against the tree and ignored the growls coming from her stomach. She closed her eyes and waited while the minutes crawled by. Finally, Beatrice stood over the remains of fire and gave a strange, gurgling howl. As the noise died away, so did the flames, and since the moon had long since dipped below the tops of the trees, the clearing was left in darkness.

Judith and Katherine left for home together, still in their wolf-form. Beatrice slipped silently into the trees while Victoria and Marie dragged the remains of the deer back into the deep woods. While they were gone, Claire felt a snout nudge her. She looked up at the round, gold-flecked eyes that stared down at her.

*You kind of look like you're freaking out.* Zahlia flopped down next to Claire and stretched out her legs, licking at the blood spattered along the fur of her shins.

Claire shrugged.

*Well, it's nothing to be ashamed of. Your mom's really smart and all, but she expects a lot of everyone. You especially. Just 'cause she thinks this is normal doesn't mean you do, you know?*

Claire nodded, her clenched teeth opening the smallest bit.

Zahlia's mouth opened in a wolfish grin. *When my mom dragged me into the woods on my sixteenth birthday, I totally panicked and ran halfway to the interstate before Beatrice caught up with me. And then I didn't speak to my mom for almost a month. The fact that you're here and not tearing through the woods like a screaming lunatic tells me you're doing pretty damn great.*

"How long did it take before it didn't freak you out anymore?" Claire whispered.

*A year, maybe? I guess it's different for everyone. I'm nineteen now, and this all seems more normal than being human ever did. So, you know, there is hope.*

Claire managed a tiny smile. "So, where's your mom?"

Zahlia looked into the fire. *Gone. It's a long story. Anyway. The pack—it's all about tradition and rules and history, right? But sometimes that stuff doesn't give you what you really need. So . . . you let me know if you need something, okay?*

"Um, okay. Thanks." Claire could hear the confusion in her own voice. She didn't know what Zahlia was talking about, but she was obviously trying to be nice.

Victoria and Marie slipped back into the clearing. Claire could see the surprise and suspicion that crossed her mother's expression when she saw Zahlia sitting with her, but she couldn't tell what her mother was thinking. It was like Marie had intentionally blocked it, somehow.

*Claire, it is time to go,* her mother said.

Claire nodded and got stiffly to her feet. Finally. She was dying to get out of here—to get home. Claire's mother shook her silvery fur and sighed. Her form shimmered and stretched, patches of skin appearing over her pelt. Claire tried to look away, but a horrible fascination kept her eyes glued to her mother. Until she realized that her mom was naked. Claire's cheeks burned and she turned away. Out of the corner of her eye, she saw her mother stretch out a pale, elegant arm and grab a bundle from underneath a shrub. In a flash, she'd pulled on clothes and twisted her dark hair into its usual tight bun.

The firelight skimmed over her mother's high, pale forehead and straight nose. It was the face Claire had always known—what still seemed like her mother's real face. Claire scratched at the back her hand, startled and relieved when her nails clawed across smooth, hairless skin. They were back to normal—both of them.

"Thank God," she whispered. "I changed back!"

Her mother leaned close to her. "From now on, you should really say 'thank Goddess,' *chérie*. And you are not yet able to change back on your own." Her mother's low, barking laugh disappeared into the undergrowth. "So impatient. I pulled you back with my own transformation. Mothers can do this for their children—it is a protection. To change back, you must hold your breath and feel yourself being pulled in, like putting your fur back under your skin, like stuffing a blanket back into a drawer. But there will be time to learn that later, after you have completed your *devienment*, your 'becoming.' For now, you must learn to wait."

Behind her mother, Claire saw Zahlia roll her eyes while she adjusted the collar of her shirt.

Marie continued. "The most important thing, Claire, is that you must never say anything about who you are. To anyone. Obviously."

Claire bristled. She hadn't given her mother any reason to treat her like a six-year-old. "I'm not a moron. I wasn't exactly going to run off and post it on the Internet."

Marie pursed her lips. "Mistakes have been made before. I am just trying to keep you safe."

Claire stared numbly at her mother. "You have blood on your chin," she said.

Her mother rubbed her shirtsleeve across her chin.

"You seem distressed. Are you all right?" She brushed the twigs and dirt from the front of her shirt.

All right? Was she *all right?* A flame of anger licked at Claire's insides. Her mother had just turned her world completely upside down and she didn't understand why Claire might be upset. Was she serious?

Marie waited, her arms crossed in front of her.

"I, uh—didn't think about the clothes," Claire finally stammered.

Her mother nodded. "One must always take off the first outfit before putting on the second, yes? This is the same thing"—she paused—"only different." She shrugged. "A body is just a body. Now. Let's go."

Claire trailed through the woods behind her mother. They crawled back through the hole in the wall, sneaked back across the yard, and then they were safe inside the house. Her mother flipped the bolt on the kitchen door and turned to Claire.

"Go upstairs and put your clothes where Lisbeth won't find them. Then you must shower and go straight to bed. We will talk more tomorrow." She smoothed back a hair that had escaped her bun. "You did well tonight, Claire. I'm proud of you."

Claire watched as her mother slipped up the back staircase. She sighed. When she was little, she'd wished her mother were around more, that they could spend more time together. This wasn't what she'd had in mind. And even worse—there didn't seem to be any way out of it. The sudden feeling of being trapped wrapped itself around Claire so tightly that she had trouble catching her breath. She forced herself not to think—to walk up the stairs one step at a time and get into the shower like nothing was wrong.

When she'd washed away the smell of the campfire and stashed her filthy clothes, Claire crawled into bed. The sky was already streaked with pink, predawn light, and she fell into an exhausted sleep as soon as she tugged the comforter around her shoulders.

# Chapter Four

IT WAS THE only house on the block without a porch light on, the only one with enough darkness to hide in. She'd hoped to get one of the Engles' neighbors, not just someone who lived on the same street. Still, it would be enough to rattle some teeth, shake some bones . . . wake them up. She wondered if they would notice if she took a little memento. The house felt cool against her flank when she pressed into the siding. Inside, everyone was breathing the breath of sleep.

She opened her jaws and keened so high and thin that only the dog—the one she could smell sleeping at the foot of the bed—could hear. The barking was sudden, frantic, afraid. She snuffled with *pleasure. Dogs. Smart enough to be scared, stupid enough to lure the humans to their sharp-toothed end.*

*She huddled by the back door. When it creaked open, she watched the fool dog streak out into the yard. Watched the human step out after it. And then she sprang. His body held the door open nicely. She stepped around his twisted-necked form and padded inside.*

"Claire? It's time to wake up—c'mon, sleepyhead."

The memory of the night before bubbled to the surface of Claire's mind, and her heart sank before she'd even opened her eyes. *Welcome to My Life As a Monster, Day One.* She swallowed hard.

"Are you feeling okay?" Lisbeth frowned. "You look sort of . . . green."

"I'm fine. I just didn't sleep very well," Claire lied.

"You could've fooled me, since you slept till noon. Anyway. Your mother—she asked if you would meet her in her darkroom."

Claire's mouth fell open. No one was allowed in Marie's darkroom. Ever. Not even Claire.

Lisbeth shrugged. "It surprised me, too."

"Yeah, well, thanks for waking me up." Claire stretched.

Lisbeth headed over to Claire's closet. "I'm doing a load of darks—I'm gonna grab your dirty stuff to fill it up."

"No!" Claire jumped up, throwing off her sheets. She'd stuffed her smoky clothes underneath a massive pile of shopping bags, but Lisbeth had a nose like a bloodhound.

Lisbeth put a hand on her hip and stared at Claire. "What? Why?"

Claire took a deep breath. "I don't think I have any dark stuff dirty, that's all. Anyway, I should probably start doing my laundry myself, you know? I mean, I'm sixteen—I don't need someone else to fold my T-shirts."

A little wrinkle of suspicion grew between Lisbeth's eyebrows. "You're sure there isn't maybe something in your laundry you don't want me to find?"

Claire swallowed hard. She stalked over to her closet and yanked out the laundry basket. With her heel, she nudged the door shut.

"You want to go through my pockets? Fine. There's nothing there, Lisbeth. I can't believe you don't trust me." She was wound so tightly that it made her voice shake. She thrust the basket at Lisbeth.

"Okay." Lisbeth held up her hands like a surrendering criminal, leaving Claire holding the laundry. "Sorry. After three years of pulling wadded-up tissues and Diet Coke bottle tops out of your jeans, I'd love a break. It just seemed sort of sudden, that's all. I'll be watching the news if you need help."

*That was too close. As soon as she leaves I'll find a better spot to—*

Something in Lisbeth's voice stopped Claire midthought. "The news? Is something going on?"

Lisbeth looked at Claire, her eyes scared and sad. "There

was another . . . attack last night. Three doors down from the Engles' house. That—that monster killed some guy by his back door and then snuck into the house and killed his wife." She shook her head. "I don't for the life of me know why people don't just stay inside with the doors and windows shut like the City keeps telling us to. Anyway. It's been on the news nonstop all morning. The police don't know what to do, and the FHPA just keeps saying that it's an 'ongoing investigation,' whatever *that's* supposed to mean.

"When I think how close we were yesterday . . . we drove *right by it.* I just hope they catch that thing, and soon."

Claire watched the door long after Lisbeth had left. How could there have been another attack? Who could have done it?

*It couldn't have been anyone in the pack. We were all together last night.* Claire yanked a pair of shorts out of her dresser. On her vanity, her cell phone lit up. Claire picked up the phone and looked at the screen. Matthew. Her thumb hovered over the SEND button. *What am I going to say to him?—Yeah, I'm fine, glad it was the neighbors and not you? I had a great night, and guess what, I'm a werewolf?—Oh my God, no wonder my mom hates his dad so much! Dr. Engle's freaking* hunting *her.*

The voicemail alert flashed, and then the phone went dark in her hand. Of course, Emily would probably call any second, looking for details about her date with Matthew. Claire dropped the phone back onto her vanity and pulled on her clothes, throwing her hair back into a messy ponytail. At least her ears had quit itching. They were as smooth and pink and normal as they'd been every other day before her sixteenth birthday. Which just made everything she'd seen last night seem even more like a bad dream.

She hurried into the hall, headed for the back stairs that led down to the basement—and the darkroom.

Claire knocked on the thick oak door as softly as she could. Her mother appeared, her hair slicked back into its usual tight bun. A tiny, cupboardlike room was all Claire could see behind her mother—and another door, this time painted black, like the walls and ceiling. Overhead, a dim red bulb glowed, like a warning.

"Come in," her mother said and stepped back into the tiny room. "And shut the door behind you."

Claire crowded close to her mother and did as she was told. The room was so small that the doorknob poked into her back and its little twist lock dug into her spine. Her mother led her into a huge room, lit entirely by the same ruby light. Rows of metal tables lined the walls. Wire shelves held bottles and jugs of the chemicals that smelled so familiar—her mother's scent. Some moms wore Chanel, Claire's mom doused herself in developing fluid.

Claire spun around slowly, staring at the vast room. Camera equipment covered the wall behind her. Lenses and cases, camera straps, tripods, and, of course, the cameras themselves, lay cased in gray foam.

Marie gestured to a tall wooden stool. "You may sit."

Claire perched on the edge of the seat and dragged one toe across the concrete floor. A million questions all crowded together in her head, but being in the darkroom was like going into a country where she didn't know any of the customs. If what she said wasn't right—if she asked the wrong thing—she might get kicked out. The quiet settled over her, surrounding her. She felt trapped.

Her mother picked up a pair of tongs and swirled a blank sheet of glossy paper down into its first chemical bath. "I suppose Lisbeth has already told you what happened last night— the Engles' neighbors?"

"Yeah." Claire swallowed hard.

Marie sighed and dropped the tongs back onto the table with a clatter that made Claire jump.

"Our pack—we have been trying to find the cause of these horrible deaths. But we must not be exposed while we do it. It makes searching . . . difficult. And the longer these things go on, the more dangerous our lives become. The constant chattering of those *people*"—she spat out the word—"on the television . . . It just makes everything worse."

Claire was pretty sure that by "people" her mother meant Dr. Engle.

"This is not the first time that our kind have been

threatened. We will find out who—or what—is causing this. You do not need to concern yourself with this. There must be other things you're wondering about? Questions you have?"

"So, Lisbeth really doesn't know about any of this?"

Marie shook her head sharply. "Of course not. Lisbeth knows I have a job that takes me away at a moment's notice— a job with odd hours, strange comings and goings. I couldn't leave you here alone when I was off in the woods, any more than I could when I went to Dubai. Lisbeth . . . filled in the gaps. I know it will be hard for you to keep this from her, but you must find a way to do it."

The reality of the situation slammed into Claire. It was like being kicked in the chest. Claire forced back the moisture that crept into the corners of her eyes. She hated lying to Lisbeth. And now she was going to have to do a lot of it. Anger flooded through her, drying the tears that clung to her eyelashes.

"You've been hiding this from her, from us, for years." Claire's voice shook.

Marie shrugged. "You know I am not close with anyone. I find it easier that way. Not everyone does. But werewolves and humans—we were not meant to be friends, Claire. I believe things go better for those who remember that." She turned away, reaching for another jug of fluid.

Claire clenched her fists. "How can you act like this is no big deal? First you tell me I'm a—that I'm not even freaking *human.* And now you want me to lie to everyone, and I'm not even supposed to care?"

"I do not appreciate that tone. I know this has come as a shock to you—"

"Well, *that's* the understatement of the century." The words came out soaked in sarcasm.

"Enough!" Marie's calm exterior finally gave way. "This is not a death sentence. It is an honor. And if you cannot stop the sass long enough for us to discuss it, then this conversation is over."

"Fine!" Claire slid off the stool with a *thump.* "I'll just get out of your freaking *space,* then." She slammed out of the darkroom and stormed up to her room.

Claire yanked on the first bathing suit she found and raced out to the pool, throwing herself into the deep end. The taste of chlorinated water pushed the flavor of salt tears out of her mouth, and she began to swim, clawing furiously at the water. She went back and forth across the pool, until she lost count of how many laps she'd completed. She swam until her arms ached—until exhaustion slowly overtook the rage that glowed in her chest.

When Claire finally crawled out of the pool, her legs shook underneath her. She collapsed, dripping, onto one of the lounge chairs and lay there panting. Eventually her breathing slowed and she drifted into a half doze.

* * *

A warm hand shook her awake.

"Claire?"

Claire opened one eye. It was her mom.

"What?" She sounded more sullen than she'd meant to.

"I want to apologize. I am so accustomed to things that it all seems—well. I should have been more prepared for your reaction. I am sorry."

Claire squirmed. "I didn't mean to freak out on you. But I *am* freaked out."

"I know. And I am sure that you have many questions."

Claire nodded, picking at the woven fabric of the lounge chair. "So, are there any others—you know, like us, around here?"

Her mother toyed with her watch. "No. There are no other packs nearby. In fact, Judith and Katherine come all the way from Rochert every moon, because we're the closest to them. Occasionally, we can scent that *une seule,* a wolf without a pack, has traveled through. But they rarely stay more than a few days."

All the images from the night before flashed through Claire's mind. The memory of Matthew's arm wrapped around her shoulders sent a rush of heat through her. It also sent a question sailing out of her mouth.

"So, how come there are no men werewolves in our—uh, pack?"

Her mother's head snapped up. "Oh, *chérie,* I thought I had—" She sighed and leaned back against the patio table.

"There aren't any males of our species. Anywhere. There never have been. All werewolves are women."

Claire's eyes shot wide-open. "But—they've caught them before. I've seen it! Those Austrian werewolves that Dr. Engle tried his cure on were male."

Her mother shook her head sadly. "Innocent, all of them. Everyone is so anxious to believe in a cure that they believe his claims. Have you never realized that he has no photos of his 'patients' in the form of a wolf? He has evidence of misshapen teeth, of chests with enough hair that they seem furred." She sighed. "Mortal men misunderstand the symptoms. They misdiagnose. People expect such strength, such . . . bestiality to be the realm of males. This ignorance has helped us to stay mostly hidden for so many generations."

"But then how do we, I mean . . ." Claire felt the heat of blood rush into her neck, crawl up her cheeks, kiss her hairline. She stared at the ripples on the surface of the pool, unable to meet her mom's gaze. "Werewolves must, uh, reproduce, somehow?"

Her mother laughed. "Do not be embarrassed. It is a normal question, one I asked my own mother. We mate with human men."

Claire twisted uncomfortably in her seat when her mother said the word "mate."

Her mother sighed. "It is a weakness. Because we need men to create another generation, we must live near them. It creates a great risk for us. Our, er, relationships are often short-lived. That is the safest way."

Claire's heart thudded in her chest. It took all of her willpower to ask the next question. "So, my dad . . . ?" The stories flashed through her head. All her life, her mother had told her that her father had been a kind man, a scientist, killed in a plane crash two months before Claire had been born.

"For that I must apologize. I had to explain somehow. I knew your father only a few weeks, but because of the morals, the beliefs of the human world . . . The depth of our relationship . . . It was a lie. In this world we werewolves are driven to lie a great deal, Claire. More than most humans do. I am sorry."

Claire's stomach twisted, and she tried to swallow back the bile that filled her mouth. She scrambled to her feet.

"Are you all right, *chérie*? You look pale."

"I think I'm going to be sick." Claire ran into the house.

She stumbled into a seldom-used bathroom. Hunched over the toilet, Claire reeled. All the lies her mother had told her spun through her head. That there weren't any pictures of her father because he couldn't stand to be photographed. That his family had disowned him, and wouldn't speak to Claire or her mother. None of it had ever been true. The hole in her heart every Father's Day, the little ache she felt every time she saw Emily's dad joking around with her—it had all been for nothing.

The reality settled around her like a cage. The silky gray

fur on the back of her hands last night, the warm blood of a fresh kill—this was her identity. And, really, it always had been. Claire leaned her head against the cool marble of the bathroom wall. Nothing she'd believed about her life had ever been true. *So when I was with Matthew last night, was that just another lie?*

Still shaking, Claire crawled back up the long staircase to her room. She flopped down on the little cushioned bench in front of her vanity and stared in the mirror. The wild, freaked-out look in her eyes just made her feel more like an animal. *Which I am,* she reminded herself. *I'm a werewolf.* She couldn't get enough air. Her heart started to race as she struggled to fill her lungs. Sweat beaded her forehead and slicked her palms. The itching she'd felt yesterday came back worse than ever and she stared in the mirror, horrified to see fur slowly pushing its way out of her skin, covering her ears and the backs of her hands.

"Oh, no. Nonono," Claire moaned.

*This can't be happening. It's not even night!* Anger surged through Claire as she stared at the thick fur. *I will not let this happen. I don't care what family I was born into, I'm not doing this.* She leapt to her feet, knocking over the bench. Her mother had never shown up to dinner covered in fur—there must be something she hadn't told Claire—some way to hide it. *How could she leave out the fact that I might randomly turn into a fur-covered freak? It's not the full moon anymore! Oh my God, this is going to happen to me all the time, isn't it?*

*Fine. I'll go back down there and* make *her tell me exactly what I'm supposed to do about this.*

Claire spun around and headed for the door.

"Claire?" Lisbeth knocked gently. "Everything okay in there?"

*Damn.* Claire glanced at the doorknob. Unlocked. *Damn!* "Uh, yeah, Lisbeth. I just knocked something over." Claire hurried over to her bathroom, anxious to get another door between the two of them.

"All right, if you're sure." Lisbeth sounded doubtful.

"Yep, just getting in the shower," Claire called, slamming the bathroom door behind her and locking it. She slumped against the wall, relieved. She took a deep breath, and thought about what her mother had told her the night before—that she had to pull herself back into human form, like stuffing the fur back under her skin.

She closed her eyes and tried to concentrate. After a few seconds, she cracked open an eyelid and looked at her hands, which were still covered in fur. *It's not working!*

Claire's gaze fell on the razor sitting on the edge of the tub. *I said I was getting in the shower. Maybe I'm not such a liar, after all.*

Shaving the fur off the backs of her hands was easy, but her ears still had dark patches when she was finished. If she kept her hair down over them, they looked normal enough. Claire wadded up the damp clumps of fur in a pile of toilet paper and buried them in the trash can. She stared at herself in the mirror. *It's not perfect, but it's better than nothing.*

Claire stomped downstairs, looking for her mother. On her way to the darkroom, she ran into Lisbeth, her arms full of laundry. The pile of clothes flopped out of her grip, landing on the floor. On top was a lavender T-shirt of Lisbeth's, spattered with dark stains.

Lisbeth blinked twice and then looked at Claire. "I hope those wine spots come out in the wash." She gathered up the clothes and held the bundle to her chest.

*Wine?* Claire wondered. *Lisbeth never drinks.*

"So," Lisbeth said, her voice breezy. "Off to storm the castle?"

"I'm going to go talk to my mom, actually."

"Not right now you're not. She just left to go meet with some potential clients—said she wouldn't be back until late."

"What? How could she go when I just—" Claire barely caught herself in time. Not telling Lisbeth what was going on was harder than she'd thought it would be.

"When you just . . . ," Lisbeth prompted.

"Never mind." Claire turned around and headed back upstairs. *I'll just wait until she gets home. I can be patient. And then as soon as she comes in, I'll* make *her tell me everything she left out—like how to keep from turning into a wolf in the middle of the freaking afternoon.*

"Hey, Claire?" Lisbeth called after her.

"Yeah?"

"Your ears look sort of funny. Is that rash back? Maybe I should call Dr. Abramowitz and get you an appointment."

Claire's hand crept up to cover the mark. "It's nothing. I just burned myself with a flat iron."

Lisbeth frowned. "Oh, okay." She didn't sound convinced.

Claire bounded upstairs and slammed her bedroom door. The cell phone sitting on the edge of her vanity caught her eye. The screen flashed at her—four new messages.

Claire flipped open the phone and speed-dialed her voice-mail. The first message was from Matthew. His voice sounded shaky, and Claire could hear other people and cars in the background.

"I just wanted to make sure that you got home okay, since—well. Since what happened at the neighbors' last night. Call me, okay?"

Claire deleted the message. The next two voicemails were from Emily. She demanded details about the night before—what had they watched, had the outfit worked, had they kissed? Claire was dying to talk to Emily but not about Matthew. She wanted to tell her best friend that her mother had ruined her life last night. But she thought about the dead-serious look on her mother's face when she'd told Claire not to say anything. And also she didn't really know how Emily would take that sort of news. Claire sighed and deleted Emily's voicemails. The last message was blank. Claire checked the missed calls list—it had been Matthew, again.

There was no way she could talk to Matthew right now. It sucked that he was worried, even though it sent a little ripple of happiness through her middle to think that he had called—*twice*—just to check on her. The phone buzzed in her hand and Claire looked down at the screen. Emily. Claire shut her eyes and answered the phone, throwing herself down onto her unmade bed. She braced herself for Emily's inquisition.

"Hello?" Claire tried to make her voice sound normal.

"Hey." Emily's voice held none of its usual excitement. She sounded sort of depressed, actually.

"Are you okay?" asked Claire.

"Not really." Emily's voice trembled. "Mom and Dad freaked out about the Engles' neighbors. They're talking about making me go stay with Aunt Masie until school starts. On the stupid *farm*. I am so, so pissed off right now. I don't even think they get cell phone reception out there. Oh my God, Claire, I'm going to *die* if they send me away for the rest of the summer!"

*If they send her away, at least I won't have to think of a way to hide this from her, too.* Her best friend was about to be shipped off and her first thought was "great"? Guilt filled Claire's throat. It choked her when she tried to talk. "Emily—that's horrible. I know your parents are sort of paranoid, but this is really over the top."

"I know. I swear to God, Claire, they're actually *trying* to ruin my life." The thought of Emily leaving made Claire ache.

She'd never been away from her best friend for more than a week. Now they would have to spend the whole summer apart if they couldn't think of a way to stop Emily's parents from going off the deep end.

"Emily, breathe. They're just worried about what happened to Matthew's neighbors. My—my mom's totally freaked out, too." *That's only sort of a lie, right? She said that the pack is worried about what's happening. . . .*

Claire hadn't ever hidden anything this big from Emily. And it sucked.

"Oh my God, I didn't even ask you about yesterday! What happened? How was it? Did he kiss you?"

Claire bit her lip. She didn't really want to talk about Matthew, but she couldn't bring herself to lie to Emily about everything. "Almost. He would have if his dad hadn't interrupted us."

"Oh my God, didn't I *tell* you he liked you? Were you so mad at his dad?"

"Not as mad as Matthew looked," Claire admitted. The memory of Matthew's frustrated expression made her smile.

"Well, next time for sure. There is going to be a next time, right? Have you talked to him today? I mean—has he called you?"

"Uh, yeah, he called, but I haven't called him back yet. I just got up a little bit ago, and then my mom wanted to talk to me and stuff."

"Then why are you still talking to me? Get off the phone and call him! I have to go beg my parents to see reason, anyway. Call me later, okay? And do you wanna hang out tomorrow?"

"Sure, tomorrow sounds great," said Claire. "I'll call you. Good luck with your parents."

Emily groaned and hung up the phone without saying good-bye. Claire caught sight of her face in the mirror and it stopped her cold. *It's because of me. Emily's parents are going to send her away because they're afraid of* me. . . .

# Chapter Five

IT WAS WELL after dark before Claire could bring herself to call Matthew. "Hello?"

"Um, hi, Matthew."

"Claire!" Relief flooded his voice. "Are you okay?"

"Yeah, I'm fine. I'm sorry about your neighbors. Things must have been pretty nuts around there today, huh?" She hoped that he would just think she sounded shaky because she was upset about the murders.

"Totally. My dad's in hyperdrive, and if the news guys aren't in our living room, the cops are. He doesn't think it's a coincidence that it was our neighbors who were attacked, so he's taking it way more personally than usual. Mom and I are just trying to stay out of his way."

Claire's head spun. She sat down on the edge of her bed and drew in a deep breath.

"Claire?"

"Yeah, I'm here. So, your dad—he thinks this was like, some sort of warning?"

"I guess. Or taunting, more like. Like that *thing* thinks it can't be caught, that my dad'll never get him." He laughed. "It was like waving a red cape in front of a bull. He's more determined than ever to find the werewolf. Then he'll be able to use his cure—like Superman saving his own town, you know?"

Claire managed a weak chuckle.

"Do you want to meet at the club tomorrow? It's too hot for anything but swimming, anyway."

The thought of Matthew standing at the edge of the Brookshire Country Club pool in his swim trunks made Claire's fingertips tingle. She swallowed hard.

"I—I can't. I have to keep the day open for Emily tomorrow, in case she has to leave." It sounded lame, even to Claire, but there was no way she could see him right now. Not when there was a chance she might sprout fur with no warning. "Maybe some other time," she added, before she could stop herself.

"Oh, yeah, sure."

"Listen, I've gotta go, but, um, I hope things settle down over there soon, okay?"

"Yeah, thanks."

Claire could hear the confusion in his voice. *This is so unfair! Someone like Matthew Engle is actually interested in me, and his stupid dad is ruining it. Well, that and the fact that I'm the spawn of the wolf-woman. There's no way I can see him until I figure out how to keep the werewolf crap in check.* Her head throbbed. She could be as sarcastic as she wanted, but it was still true, and it still sucked.

"Okay, well, uh, I'll talk to you soon."

"Okay," he said, his voice brightening considerably.

They hung up and Claire stared at the phone in her hand. She just had to avoid him for a little while, that's all, until she had a better handle on what was happening.

That night, Claire lay awake for hours, waiting for her mother. As soon as Marie got home, Claire was going to confront her. Make her explain why fur had just appeared on her like that, and how to keep it from ever happening again. She listened for the sound of the Mercedes speeding up the drive, but it never came.

She watched the late news, and then the *Late Show*. With each minute that passed, she got angrier and angrier. It was so like her mom to just disappear at a time like this. And Claire didn't even know how to find any of the other women she'd met last night. When a rerun of the news started, she checked the clock—two a.m. She threw off the covers and padded across the room. The door creaked when it swung open and she winced. She poked her head out and peered down the hall. Lisbeth's door was shut and Claire could hear her snoring even more loudly than usual.

She wandered down into the kitchen and opened the refrigerator. She pulled out a plate of steak left over from dinner.

"Still awake, *chérie*?" Her mother's voice came from the darkened dining room, making Claire jump. The plate of food tipped in her hand, and she barely managed to hang on to it.

"Jesus, don't *do* that. When did you get home? I didn't even hear you come in. God." Claire's heart thudded away in her chest, and the sharp smell of adrenaline wafting up from her body made her eyes water. *Why can I smell that?*

"There is no God, Claire. I thought I had explained that."

"It's just a figure of speech, Mom." She sniffed the air—as her heart slowed the sour tang faded. In the dark her mother smiled approvingly.

"Your sense of smell is developing. That's good."

"Something else you forgot to mention, I guess," Claire muttered.

Her mother tensed. "Is something the matter?"

"Oh, no, not at all." Claire couldn't keep the sarcasm out of her voice. "Not only am I a freak of nature, but it turns out that it's not just once a month. I could sprout fur at any second. It'll probably come in real handy in the winter. Except that it might make it pretty awkward to be with, you know, *people*, I guess. Man, I just can't *wait* to find out what other superfabulous things are going to happen to me next." Tears brimmed in her eyes, making the food in front of her seem to waver. She knew she'd get in trouble for talking to her mother that way, but right then she couldn't have cared less. *How could things get any worse, anyway? What's she going to do, ground me?*

A look of surprise crossed her mother's face. "It is very unusual that you should transform like that. Most who are as new as you don't have the ability to change on their own. They need the strength of the full moon to do it."

"So I'm strange even for a monster? Great."

"You are not a monster, Claire. Stand still." Marie put a firm hand on Claire's shoulder. "We *must* transform at the full moon. The Goddess, the One who created us, makes our true natures so strong on that one night that we must reveal them. But once a werewolf matures into her powers, she is able to change at any time."

Under her mother's grip, Claire's skin felt tightened, pulled, and her senses dulled.

"There. Returned to your human form," her mother said.

Claire could still smell her mother's surprise. She could hear the filament buzzing in the lightbulb above the sink.

"If I'm human, how come I can still smell and hear so much?"

"Because you are truly a werewolf, Claire. This skin is just a disguise. You have passed the first moon of your transformation and from now on, your senses, your strength—they will always be more sensitive and intense than a human's. Even when you look the same as everyone else. I understand that this is new, and that it is not easy, but you must try to be patient."

"Patient! You left me on my own, looking like Grizzly Adams. Was I just supposed to hang out looking like that until you got home? I didn't know how to get rid of it! What if Lisbeth had seen me?"

"It is not like regular hair. It is a mark of the Goddess, and no human invention can permanently remove it. Not even a razor." A trace of amusement laced her mother's words.

"How did you know?" Claire crossed her arms.

"I didn't imagine you had transformed back into a human on your own this afternoon. And," she admitted, "I could smell your embarrassment and also shaving foam. It *is* a gift, Claire. What we are. And as soon as your transformation is complete, you will learn all you need to know—how to do everything we are able to do. In the meantime, there is no need to panic. What happened today is unlikely to happen again. It was probably because we were still so close to the full moon."

"Oh, yeah, don't panic. No problem. I'll just keep some Nair in my purse," Claire sniped. "Is there anything else I should be carrying around? A file for my claws? A dog brush?"

"That is enough," Marie said sharply. "I have told you that you will learn what you need to, and at the proper time. We have been training New Ones for many generations. Our traditions, our methods, are not without reason."

Claire scowled.

Her mother watched her evenly. "I know it is difficult for you right now."

"Really? Because you're sure not acting like it."

"Claire, stop. I think you should go to bed now. When you are fully transformed, you will be better prepared to learn. Until then, you must be patient, and watchful. That is the best way to keep yourself—to keep all of us—safe." Her mother moved noiselessly across the kitchen toward the stairs. "It will get easier, Claire. You must trust me."

Without even saying good night, her mother glided up the stairs, leaving Claire alone in the kitchen.

Claire shoved the plate of leftovers back into the fridge, her appetite gone. She stared across the lawn, her gaze traveling over the brick wall at the edge of the property. The thick woods beyond the wall twitched in the night breeze.

If her mother wasn't going to teach her anything, then maybe she would just go figure things out for herself. After all, no one had said she shouldn't do anything, just that they wouldn't show her how yet. She leaned against the counter, thinking. It sure as hell hadn't felt like it was the moon that made her change today. When the fur had come, she'd been thinking hard about being a werewolf. That could have been what triggered the change. Maybe her mom wasn't giving her enough credit. Maybe she could transform on her own, if she had a chance to try.

*Well, there's no time like the present to start.*

She just needed somewhere to practice where her mom or Lisbeth wouldn't walk in on her. Somewhere big, and private.

Somewhere like the woods.

Outside, the humidity pressed against Claire's face like a wet handkerchief. A film of sweat popped out on the back of her neck. She turned to look up at her house. The windows were all dark.

A warm breath of air tickled her ear and she spun away from it, dropping down into a crouch on pure instinct. The space where Claire had been only a moment before was empty. She blinked at the vacant yard, surprised at how fast she'd moved.

From inside the pool house, she could hear the faint, chirrupy whisper of the ceiling fan. Crap. She'd left it on again. If Lisbeth saw it, she would freak about how much energy Claire had wasted. She hurried over to the little building, and then stopped short. A squeak escaped her mouth before she could stop it.

*Oh my God, I could hear that all the way from the back of the house?*

She'd known her hearing was better than it had been, but this was crazy.

Realizing she'd made a noise, she looked back up at the house. All the lights were still off.

Claire hurried across the lawn, wondering if her mother was going to realize she was gone—if she was about to come and stop her. The nerves in her fingertips tingled in time with her breathing as she tiptoed through the yard. With every step the smell of the grass being crushed beneath her feet flooded into her nose, carrying with it the sharp scent of chemical fertilizer. When she eased through the opening in the brick wall, the more natural, less uniform odor of the forest washed over her like cool water, and she sighed in relief.

Her nose twitched. She could smell *everything*. The squirrel hiding in the fir tree. The dry dirt and pine needles on the forest floor. And—her mother. She could smell her mother.

*Crap.*

Claire ducked under the low branches of the evergreen next to her and held her breath. How could she have missed the fact that her mother had followed her? She waited, frozen, her heart thudding against her ribs. The squirrel above her took off through the trees and Claire let out her breath.

When she breathed in again, she realized that the scent was faint and stale.

*Oh my God. It's from last night! I can smell where she walked last night.*

She slid out of her hiding place and tried to shake the jumpiness out of her shoulders.

She took a deep breath. If she was going to be stuck like this, she was damn well going to learn to control it.

She focused on the nearly invisible tree trunks in front of her. They shimmered the tiniest bit, like ink on black paper. *Huh. I can see in the dark? That's . . . helpful.* She tried to concentrate, to remember the feeling in her hands and ears when she'd changed before.

The thick fur blanketing her hands and ears was so strong in Claire's mind that it may as well have already been on her. A wave of dizziness swept over her. Unable to keep her balance, she reached out to grab the closest tree, misjudged the distance, and landed hard on her knees with her fist empty and her head spinning. Her gut ached and her lungs burned, like someone had punched her in the stomach.

As quickly as the feeling had come, it passed. She reached out one shaky, fur-blanketed hand and stroked her ear. The silky fur slid underneath her fingertips. *I just shaved it off this afternoon—but damn, it doesn't feel like I ever even touched it.*

Still, it was not horror that she felt when she looked at her fur this time—it was relief. *I did it. I can control it. Oh, thank God, uh, Goddess, I can control it.*

Success glowed in Claire's chest like an ember. She checked to see if she was any different than she had been last night, but everything looked the same. Furry ears, furry hands, and human-looking everywhere else.

But still, she needed to be able to change back. And she'd

done that before only with her mother's help. Now she had to figure out how to do it on her own.

She sat down, folding her legs underneath her, determined not to be knocked over by the force of turning human, the way she had been when she tried to become a wolf. She sucked a breath deep into her lungs, smelling a deer somewhere to her right, deep in the forest. The surprise of the scent—so clear and so far away—shook her concentration, and she let the breath slip back out in a quiet *oh*.

Claire twisted to face a thick stand of trees. She could see the individual grooves in the bark of each tree. The sharp, musky scent of a scared doe wafted out between the branches. It was definitely in there.

Claire clenched her fists. A desire to hunt swelled in her chest. It blotted out everything else. She could barely keep herself from slinking off into the trees, following the deer's scent. Her stomach grumbled.

She forced herself back onto the ground. Without meaning to, she had risen up onto all fours, ready to run. *What the hell am I doing?* She shook her head, clearing it, and pulled in another deep breath. If she was hungry, she'd go home and get a snack like a normal person. *Jesus. I was actually going to chase down a deer. . . .*

The most important thing now was getting rid of her fur. Drawing herself in was trickier, but she held her breath and focused on being normal—being with Emily, hanging out with Lisbeth, hearing Lisbeth laugh at something she said.

". . . right now, no . . . I *can't*. Think how suspicious that would look!"

Lisbeth's voice rang in Claire's ears and she gasped, opening her eyes and staring wildly at the trees around her. It had sounded tinny, like a bad phone connection, but it hadn't been in her head. It wasn't the same echo of Lisbeth's voice that Claire heard when she left the water running while she brushed her teeth, or when she threw her clean laundry in a pile on the floor.

She had actually heard Lisbeth. Talking. Here.

*What the hell?*

Claire closed her eyes again. Had she made that happen, somehow? She'd been focusing so hard on Lisbeth, on hearing her. She kept the sound of Lisbeth's voice fixed in her mind. It felt sort of stupid—but then, it *had* happened before.

"You know I didn't mean for things to go like this! But it's too late. I can't go back and change—"

Excitement flooded through Claire and her concentration wavered. Lisbeth's voice was gone again, but she didn't care. She could *hear* her.

Immediately, she wondered if it would work on anyone else. She tried to think about Emily the same way she'd been thinking about Lisbeth. She wrapped her arms around her knees and listened hard. Nothing happened. Well, it was the middle of the night—Emily was probably asleep.

"Oh. Shit." Her voice sounded loud in the quiet forest.

If Claire couldn't hear someone unless they were actually saying something, then that meant Lisbeth was awake, which put Claire one bed-check away from being in deep trouble. Who on earth was Lisbeth talking to at this hour, anyway?

*Oh, God, what if she's talking to Mom? Okay. This is not the time to panic. All I have to do is change back and then get home. It can't be that hard to transform. It just can't.*

Claire pressed her fur-covered hands against her eyes. She focused on the memory of the skin, smooth as an egg, that she'd worn every day for sixteen years. She wanted it—wanted to be back to normal. To be human.

The feeling of coming back into her skin was claustrophobic, like wriggling into a dress that was too small. The smell of the deer faded and she couldn't see as clearly. The trees were just shimmers in the black night. Claire could tell she'd changed back, but panic rose in her chest. She didn't feel like her usual self. Being in her regular body didn't feel better than being a wolf. It was just as uncomfortable, only in a different way. Tears welled up in her eyes.

How could anyone adjust to this? Her breath hitched painfully, and her lungs felt slow and thick in her chest. Maybe this was why her mother was always so closed off. Maybe that made it easier.

A tear slipped down Claire's cheek and she brushed it away. She didn't have time for this now. Once she'd gotten home without Lisbeth catching her, she'd have all the time in the world to cry.

Claire pulled herself to her feet. Her muscles ached and her stomach was rumbling. As she hurried home, she listened with her human-dulled ears to the tiny pops and cracks of the bracken that crunched beneath her feet. When she squeezed back through the wall onto her own lawn, the ache in her chest eased. The lights were off—Lisbeth must have finished her conversation and gone back to bed. The house was quiet. The ceiling fan still buzzed in the pool house. Claire crept over and turned it off. Surely if Lisbeth had discovered she'd been missing, there would be lights. Noise.

Claire had snuck out and gotten away with it. Relief coursed through her, washing away the sadness she'd felt in the woods. A grin spread across her face.

She slipped into the silent house and walked to the refrigerator. If Lisbeth heard her in the kitchen, who cared? She was allowed to get a midnight snack if she wanted. Claire pulled out the plate of leftover meat, picked a limp slice of steak from the plate, and put it in her mouth. Before she could stop herself, she thought how much better the deer would have tasted.

# Chapter Six

*THE YAWN WAS jaw popping. Lung cracking. Exhaustion ringed her thoughts like smoke, making everything hazy and indistinct. Morning had come so soon. It had been too much in one night—hunting for food, and then stalking the youngest one, the brand-new wolf. Tracking her while she stumbled through the woods like a human. She'd gone home so proud of herself. Fool enough to think that because the lights were off, she hadn't been seen. Been caught.*

*Too young and stupid to think there might be other eyes watching her.*

The phone rang six inches from Claire's ear. She rolled away from it, throwing the covers over her head. Who the hell was calling at—she cracked an eye and checked the alarm clock—9:33 in the morning?

As soon as the voicemail picked up, the phone started ringing again. Emily's number flashed across the screen.

"Jesus God, Emily, it's too *early*. Something had better be wrong."

There was a loud sniff on the other end of the phone.

"Well, it is. They're dead-set on sending me away next week, Claire. To the *farm*." Emily didn't so much say the last word as wail it. "Are you up? Can I come over? If I have to look at my mom for one more second right now, I'm going to freak out. I am so pissed off!"

Claire rubbed her hand across her eyes. "Wow. I mean, of course you can come over. I'm sorry, Em, I'm not totally awake yet. That's really, really crappy, though."

"You're the best. I'll be there in a few minutes."

Claire stretched and rolled out of bed. She wandered downstairs, looking for Lisbeth. A note sat on the counter, pinned underneath a clean coffee mug.

Claire-bear,
Good morning! Don't forget, I'm at an all-day yoga retreat and your mom's gone to Chicago for the day. If you go anywhere, please leave me a voicemail, okay?
See you around six!
Love,
Lisbeth

A whole day without anyone looking over her shoulder? That was more than okay with Claire.

She put a pot of coffee on and sat at the island while it brewed, staring out the window. Last night had been so bizarre—but in a much better way than the night before had been. At least now she didn't feel so out of control, like she was just supposed to sit on her hands and hope everything was okay. If she randomly started to sprout fur, she could fix it. Hell, if she thought someone was talking about her, she could listen in.

*Huh.*

Could she do that in her normal body, or did she have to be changed?

Claire focused the same way she had the night before, trying again to hear Emily.

Nothing happened. Claire couldn't hear anything except the coffeepot burbling as it finished brewing.

She thought about transforming and trying again. No one was home, so it wasn't like anyone would come walking in on her—it would probably take Emily another fifteen minutes to drive over, anyway.

Claire decided to go for it.

Just as she'd closed her eyes, the front door rattled.

"Claire?" Emily's voice echoed off the marble floors in the entryway.

*Shit.*

"In the kitchen!" Claire called, silently vowing never to do anything else that stupid. How would she have explained it if Emily had walked in on her while she was covered in fur? To cover the fact that she was totally flustered, Claire got up to pour herself a cup of coffee.

Emily wandered into the kitchen. "Hey. Thanks for getting up early for me."

"No problem. You must have driven like a bat out of hell to get here so fast," Claire said, focusing on filling her cup to exactly the right level. Her hand was still shaking.

"Yeah, well, I had to get out of the nightmare that is my house."

Claire turned to offer her the coffee. Emily's eyes were red and puffy, and her lips looked pale.

"Do you want a cup?"

Emily shook her head and went to the refrigerator. She pulled out a Diet Coke and popped it open. "What am I going to *do*? If I have to spend the rest of the summer on the farm, I'll miss everything! I'll be so out of the loop by the time school starts that my parents might as well send me away permanently."

Claire took a long sip of her coffee and tried to push away the feeling that it was her fault that Emily was so upset.

*I haven't done anything wrong. Just because I'm . . . what I am, this isn't my fault.*

"We'll figure something out, Em. Seriously. What have you tried?"

Emily ticked it off on her fingers. "I promised them I wouldn't leave the house after dark, that I'd leave my cell's GPS on all the time, and that I wouldn't go anywhere outside alone. Which is, like, the equivalent of putting myself in jail all summer. But practically no one else is allowed to go out after dark, so it's not like I'd be missing that much. And at least I'd be *here*. But they won't listen!" Emily flopped down on one of the bar stools and sighed. "I don't know why they think the stupid farm is any safer than here, anyway. I mean, there's way less people out there. If something attacks us on the farm, I'm one of three people for it to pick from. Isn't that, like, basic statistics?"

Claire smiled at her best friend's logic and sat down next to Emily.

"Well, that's about all you can do, isn't it? I mean, unless you swear to stay in your room all the time, and that's as bad as being sent off to your aunt's place."

Emily laid her head on the table. "You're not helping, Claire."

Guilt slid through Claire like an oil spill. Maybe she wasn't trying hard enough. There was a little part of Claire's brain that was whispering to her that it would be a lot easier to lie to Emily over the phone. And that Emily couldn't walk in on her midchange while she was on the farm.

"Maybe things will settle down. If I were you, I'd play up the whole 'the farm is dangerous, too' angle. Make them panic that you'll be too far away, that they can't keep an eye on you. Can you get your aunt to agree to some crazy-late curfew or something?"

"Huh. That's not bad, actually. I can't say anything else today or they'll know I'm just fishing to get out of it, but it might work."

Claire chewed on a ragged cuticle. "It's worth a try, at least."

"Yeah. Okay. So here I am, being totally self-centered. What's new with you, huh?"

Claire stopped the laugh a millisecond before it hopped out of her mouth. "Um. Not, uh, not much."

Emily shook her head. "That is *so* not the truth, Claire. Don't even try to lie to me."

Claire's mouth went dry. She resisted the urge to pat her ears, to make sure Emily hadn't seen anything that had made her suspicious. Did she know, or could she just tell that Claire was hiding something?

"Um. I don't—" Stalling for time, Claire lifted her mug and took another drink of coffee, even though her stomach twisted in protest.

"Come on. Matthew. Engle. What's going on with that, huh?" A smile played at the corner of Emily's mouth.

"Oh. *Oh.*" The adrenaline flooding her body left Claire's fingertips tingling. Okay, Matthew she could talk about. God, hiding things from Emily was hard. They'd just come up with a solution for Emily's problem. Claire could have used the same sort of help. A lot of help, actually. "Yeah, Matthew. It's just—it's really weird, you know? I didn't really think we'd have much in common, but we had a great time the other night. He's so easy to talk to."

"And? Are you seeing him again?" Emily didn't look nearly as depressed now that they were talking about guys.

"Probably. He wanted to get together today, but you and I had plans, so I put him off."

Horror flashed through Emily's eyes. "Oh my God. Claire, you are totally, totally nuts. Why would you do that?"

Claire shrugged. "I mean, I really like him, but I'm not sure it's a good idea for me to see him." As soon as the words left her mouth, Claire realized that she'd maybe been a little too honest with Emily. She wasn't used to censoring herself around her best friend.

Emily looked at her, dumbfounded. "Why on earth would it not be a good idea? You've liked him forever. He obviously likes you. What's the problem?"

Claire took another sip of coffee. Maybe she could ask Emily about this, as long as she worded things very, very carefully.

"Well"—she set the cup down on the counter—"I mean, I know he likes me now, but what if . . . what if he gets to know me, the *real* me . . . and he hates what he sees? That could ruin everything. And I mean, really, everything. Wouldn't it be better just to stop things now, before anything gets screwed up?"

"Claire, be serious. You're already the real you. That's why you hate flirting. It's why you feel awkward at parties. You don't know how to pretend to be someone you're not. Trust me. If he likes you now, and he does, then you're not going to come up with some huge new side of yourself that's going to shock him into shunning you."

Claire rubbed a hand across her eyes. Emily had no idea how wrong she was, and there was no way to tell her the truth. "I'm not so sure about that, Em. But I appreciate the pep talk."

"You'll feel a lot better when you see him again, you know. Why don't you call him and tell him I bailed on you? See if he still wants to hang out."

Claire shook her head. "I'll call him later, maybe. Right now, I kind of want to hang by the pool for a while. Interested?"

Emily sighed. "Of course. If I'm really going to be exiled to the farm, I want as much time with you as I can get before I go. But I still think you're nuts. And I have to be home for lunch, so I only have a little while."

"Great. Let's get changed."

For the next couple of hours, Emily's chatter and the glitter of the hot sun on the surface of the pool kept Claire mostly distracted. Still, her mind did wander—wondering about what had happened in the woods last night. What else could she do besides hear people talking miles away, and hunt? She wished there was someone she could ask. Someone who would talk to her.

"Helloooo." Emily waved a handful of polish-wet fingernails in front of Claire's face. The sharp, chemical smell did as much to snap Claire out of her thoughts as Emily's irritated voice. "Are you even *listening* to me?"

"Um, no, actually. Sorry. I got sort of distracted."

Emily searched Claire's face. "You're thinking about Matthew, aren't you?"

"Yeah." The lie rolled off her tongue like a marble. "Sorry."

"Don't be sorry. I'd be distracted too." Emily checked her phone. "I've gotta go anyway. The last thing I need is to give my parents any reason not to listen to me, you know?"

Claire nodded. "Call me and let me know how things go, yeah?"

"Of course." Emily sighed and slid on her flip-flops. "It's gonna be a dicey couple of days."

*Yeah. You can say that again.*

Claire stayed by the pool after Emily left. The treetops were motionless in the thick, hot air. Her brain felt fried, short-circuited by too much thinking and too much heat. She stood up, thinking that maybe a quick swim would clear her head. Before she'd even taken a step toward the crystal-clear water, her phone rang.

An unfamiliar number flashed across the screen.

"Hello?"

"Hey. Claire. I'm glad I caught you." The voice was familiar but not recognizable.

"Um, yeah. Sorry—who is this, again?"

A low, throaty laugh echoed on the other end. "It's Zahlia. Sorry. I should have said."

"Oh my God. No, it's fine. I'm glad you called. Actually, I'm *really* glad you called." Claire sank down onto the scorching-hot concrete at the edge of the pool and dangled her feet in the water.

"I figured you might have some questions, and I heard that your mom went to Chicago. Not that she'd likely answer them, anyway."

"Yeah. Why is that, exactly?"

"Your mom is just really . . . traditional. So—has everything been okay?"

The fist that was clenched around Claire's sternum loosened. "Actually, everything's been pretty crappy. But I think I've figured out a couple of things." She heard the pride creep into her voice as she admitted that, but she couldn't stop it. "I—I was trying to change, you know, in the forest?"

"Good. Were you successful?"

"Yeah, I was. But the weird thing was that while I was trying, I heard Lisbeth talking. And she was at our house. Is that normal?"

There was a pause at the other end of the phone. "Not

everyone can do it, but yeah, long-distance hearing is one of the more common gifts."

"So, I could only hear half of the conversation. Can you hear more than one person at a time? Do you have to be a wolf to do it?"

"I can't do it at all, but I think Beatrice can hear multiple people at once. I'm pretty sure it's just a matter of practice. And yeah, even though you have heightened senses all the time, you have to be in your true form to use any of your actual gifts."

"Okay, I guess that makes sense."

"So—you said you were in the woods. Does your mom know that you're trying this stuff?"

A little butterfly-flutter of panic stirred inside Claire. "Um, no. You're not going to tell her, are you?"

Zahlia laughed. "No. I'm not. She wouldn't approve of it, and I don't agree with her about that. Why waste these three months? You'll be a better pack member if you know what you're doing when your transformation is complete."

"Okay. Good."

"So, listen, you'll have my number in your phone now, and if you need anything, you let me know. I remember how hard those first few months were."

"Yeah, I'll call you."

"I'm looking forward to it."

Claire hung up and swung her feet against the resistance of the water, making the surface ripple and burble. If she had someone who would actually help her—who *could* actually help her, unlike Emily—then maybe she could get through this after all. With a flick of her wrist, Claire tossed the phone onto the cushioned deck chair behind her and slid into the cool, quiet pool.

The conversation with Zahlia and a good set of laps in the pool had made Claire just calm and tired enough to think that calling Matthew was a good idea.

"Hello?"

"Um, hey, Matthew. It's Claire. How are you?"

"I'm bored out of my skull. Seriously. It's too hot to go for a run and my dad's getting ready for some sort of big meeting, so he's kind of taken over the house. I'm actually thinking of doing my summer reading assignment. It's that bad."

Claire laughed. "It must be bad if you're willing to do schoolwork."

"Yeah, it's pretty awful. But, *A Separate Peace* actually looks sort of interesting. And it's short."

Claire stretched, smiling. She'd guessed he was smart—not in a geeky, chess club way, but a quiet kind of smart. She liked that. She liked it a lot. "Well, Emily bailed on me around lunchtime and you don't hear me resorting to trigonometry," she teased.

"Hey, hey, hey, not so fast. I said *nothing* about doing math," he shot back. Claire could hear him grinning. "So, do you want to rescue me from my boredom before I resort to doing something productive? I could come pick you up, maybe grab a smoothie or something?"

Claire hesitated. There were plenty of reasons to say no—like the fact that his dad was hunting her family, that she might slip and give something away. But it was so easy to talk to him. And he was so cute.

"Sure," she said, trying to shut up the part of her brain that was second-guessing her even as she agreed to go. "That sounds fun."

"Great! A half hour from now okay with you?"

"Perfect." Claire was already halfway up the stairs, mentally scanning the contents of her closet. "See you then."

While she was dressing, Claire called Lisbeth and left her a message. She put on a little makeup and the sapphire earrings her mom had given her for her birthday.

*Pretty, but not as good as a car.*

She sighed and headed downstairs to wait for Matthew.

The outside of Matthew's car was coated in a thin layer of dust—almost everyone's was, because the drought had dried everything out so badly—but Claire was surprised to find the inside was really clean. No soda cans rolling around on the floor, no dirty soccer cleats stashed behind the seats.

"What?" he asked, clearly amused at the amazement on her face.

*Damn. I've got to be a little less see-through than that if I want this to work.*

"N-nothing. It's just—I didn't expect your car to be so, um . . . ," she faltered.

"Clean?" he offered, pulling out onto the street.

"Yeah."

Matthew shrugged. "I ruined a really expensive jersey once—it was behind the seat and I threw a soda can back there. Turned out, the can wasn't quite empty. Ever since then, I'm pretty good about keeping it clean."

Claire thought about the piles of clothes on her floor and the nest of covers on her unmade bed. Maybe they weren't as alike as she'd first thought.

"My room's another story," Matthew said. "It's usually a disaster."

Claire stifled the laugh that bubbled up in her chest. "Mine's pretty bad most of the time too."

They got to The Juice Junction and stood studying the menu.

"Are you ready?" Matthew asked, putting a hand on the small of her back. His touch sent a wave of fire through her and Claire swallowed hard. She managed to nod.

They got their drinks—Mango Tango for Claire and Strawberry Blast for Matthew—and sat at a sticky-topped table. Claire sipped at the sweet, frosty slush, trying to get her head back together. Her back still tingled where Matthew had touched her, and the memory of him almost kissing her on his couch was extremely distracting.

"So, what else is new?" Matthew wadded up his straw paper and stuffed it in his pocket.

Claire shrugged. "Emily's parents are freaking out about the werewolf. They're sending her to her aunt's farm for the rest of the summer, which *she's* freaking out about."

"That sucks. I mean, the killings are horrible, but still."

"Yeah, well, everyone's panicking about it, right?" Claire held her breath. If there was one thing she shouldn't be talking about, this was it. But somehow, she couldn't resist feeling him out. If he was the same sort of fanatic his dad was, she'd probably be better off finding out now.

Matthew sighed. "Yeah. I dunno. The whole thing kind of makes me uneasy."

Claire tilted her head to one side. "Uneasy how?"

Matthew fiddled with his straw. "This isn't something—with my dad being who he is, it's hard to talk about, you know? He doesn't exactly approve of what I think."

Claire snorted. "Trust me, I've got an extra serving of disapproving parent myself."

He stared at her, his brown eyes warm and serious in the afternoon light. "I do trust you, actually." He sighed and shifted in his seat. Their knees pressed together under the table and Claire's breath caught. "I guess that, for me, it's kind of the same thing that makes me not like the death penalty."

"I—okay, you're going to have to explain that."

"Well, it's not that some crimes aren't worth dying for. It's just that—sometimes they find evidence that says that the person on death row is innocent. So you have to figure that maybe some of the people they've executed were innocent."

Claire nodded. She'd heard that before.

"Well, what if it's the same with werewolves? What if the ones in the comas, the ones Dad's 'cured'—what if some of them are the wrong ones?"

Claire was trying not to shiver. "But aren't all werewolves killers?" she whispered. Was it possible that he could totally disagree with his dad? That he could actually *get* it?

Matthew raised an eyebrow at her. "I don't think that makes sense. I mean, bears can kill people, but not all of them do, right? Or lions? You hear about some lions turning into man-eaters, but not all of them do. Anyway. It's just a theory. And my dad gets freaking pissed if I even start to talk about it."

Claire's insides were dancing. She struggled to keep her face interested but not ecstatic. "Well, it makes sense to me," she said.

He met her eyes, and she could smell a wave of relief waft up from him, clean-scented, like fresh grass.

"You really aren't like everyone else, are you?" he asked.

Claire swallowed hard, not a hundred percent sure what he meant. She shrugged. "I like to think for myself, is all," she said. Which technically was not a lie, even if it was miles away from the whole truth.

She tried to take another sip of her smoothie and was surprised to find that she'd already finished it. Matthew rattled his straw against his own empty cup.

"Do you want another one?" he asked.

Claire shook her head. "I'd probably better get back, anyway. If we beat Lisbeth home, you can escape without her doing your horoscope."

Matthew stood up, grinning. "I dunno—that could be pretty interesting."

Claire rolled her eyes. "It loses its appeal after the fiftieth time, trust me."

As the two of them walked out to the car, Matthew slipped his hand into hers. Even though his touch sent little electric shocks through Claire with every step, it felt totally natural at the same time—like they'd been holding hands for months.

# Chapter Seven

IN THE WOODS, *the sunlight rippled across the undergrowth. The leaves flashed and turned. Behind her, she could hear some stupid little animal scuttling around the base of a tree. Her stomach growled, but this wasn't the time for a snack. She had bigger things to do. Plans to make. Unsettled by the wait, she licked at an invisible spot of dust on her foreleg and watched as the wet patch of fur glittered in the sun.*

*Finally, there was a flurry of movement in the open parkland below her vantage point. The man walked out into the grassy expanse, all jiggling thighs and fat-padded shoulders, focused on walking over the uneven ground. Her mouth watered and she*

*rose into a crouch, brushing against a low-hanging branch. As her*
*muscles bunched to spring, the man was joined by two women and*
*another man, shouting at him to wait. A third man straggled out*
*into the clearing behind them, lugging a giant backpack.*

*Damn. Too many. Everyone had forgotten about the so-called*
*"daytime werewolf sighting." Which hadn't even been her. She'd*
*wanted to prove that she could kill in daylight—take away the*
*false safety of the sun—but this was asking for failure.*

*Keeping the rumble of frustration and disappointment that*
*vibrated in her chest to a whisper, she sank back down onto the for-*
*est floor. The angle of the light against the trees increased her frus-*
*tration. She'd run out of time—they'd be expecting her back, soon.*
*What a waste. Still, maybe she'd have time to try again tomorrow.*

When Matthew and Claire pulled up in front of Claire's
house, it was only a little after five thirty. Lisbeth's note said
she'd be home around six, so they had close to half an hour
before she'd be back. Half an hour in an empty house.

"Do—do you want to come in?" Claire asked.

Matthew twisted in his seat so that he was facing her. He
reached up and tucked a strand of hair behind her ear, and
Claire took a breath. Matthew's scent filled her nose, and she
resisted the urge to sigh.

"I want to come in more than anything," he said, and the
rough catch in his voice told Claire that he meant it, "but I don't
think that Lisbeth would love coming home and finding me

here. And I really want Lisbeth to like me, because I'm hoping to be around a lot more, and it'll be a lot easier if she does."

Claire gave in with a sigh. "You're right."

"Still, we *do* have a few minutes." Matthew cupped her face in his warm hands and leaned close. Claire blinked up at him, but when he brushed his lips against hers, her eyes fell closed. His mouth was gentle but insistent. Her lips parted and Matthew's hands slid down to her shoulders, pulling her closer. The happiness that bubbled up in her chest when his arms slid around her was like nothing Claire had ever experienced before. After the last few days, when she'd felt uncomfortable everywhere, in every form, she'd finally found a place where everything seemed right.

It seemed like only seconds later that Claire heard Lisbeth's car coming up the long gravel drive. She pulled away from Matthew, straightening her hair and taking a deep breath.

"Is something wrong?" The worried look on his face made Claire want to kiss him again.

"I heard a car coming," she explained.

"Really?" he looked out his window. A few seconds later, the rumble of tires on gravel got louder and Lisbeth's car pulled into view.

"Wow. I guess I wasn't paying enough attention."

*Or I wasn't paying enough attention. God, I was so focused on kissing him that I didn't even think that I'd be able to hear something like that way before he could.*

Claire nudged him with her knee. "You didn't hear me complaining," she said.

"So, do you want me to stick around and say hi?"

Claire shook her head. "Maybe next time." She opened the door and slid out into the heat. "I'll talk to you soon, okay?"

"I'm counting on it." He smiled at her.

Matthew drove past Lisbeth, waving to her as he went.

Lisbeth got out of the car, looking a little out of sorts. She pulled her yoga bag out of the passenger seat and walked over to Claire.

"So, how was your date?" The note of teasing in Lisbeth's voice fell flat.

Claire felt her cheeks start to burn. "It was nice," she said, lifting her chin. She was allowed to date. She'd called Lisbeth to let her know where she was going. There was no reason for Lisbeth to make a big deal out of this. "How was your workshop?"

Lisbeth glanced at her bag and an unreadable expression fluttered across her face. "It was pretty good. I'll be sore as anything tomorrow, I bet." She turned to walk into the house. There was a dried leaf caught in the back of her hair and Claire plucked it out.

"Were you guys doing yoga outside?" she asked.

"Um, a walking meditation, yeah. It was hot as Hades. Why?"

Claire held up the leaf. "This was in your hair."

"Oh." Lisbeth brushed a hand over her head. "Well, thanks."

"No problem. So, what's for dinner?"

Lisbeth groaned. "Anything that can be delivered. I just want to take a shower and find a soft place to sit for a few hours. That okay with you?"

"Sure. Whatever." As long as Lisbeth didn't plan to grill her about Matthew, Claire couldn't care less. The two of them headed inside, and Claire made a beeline for the kitchen drawer where they kept the delivery menus. Even though she was pretty sure that the twisty feeling in her stomach had as much to do with Matthew as it did with being hungry, Claire browsed the China Palace menu and listened to the distant thrum of the shower. Outside, the whistle of a breeze through the treetops called to her, sharpening the hunger in her belly and bringing with it a desire to run.

Claire stared out at the woods and wished that a jog around the neighborhood would satisfy her. Somehow, she knew it wouldn't.

Lisbeth went to bed when it was just barely all-the-way dark outside. Claire tried to call Emily—she wanted to know if her parents had come to their senses yet—but it went straight to voicemail. Claire flopped down on the couch. She flicked through the TV channels until she couldn't stand the pinpricks of restlessness in her legs anymore. She had to get out of the house. She was dying to get into the woods, to stretch her legs and run, to see what else she could do. She might as well go practice. Maybe if she learned to control the were-wolf stuff better, she'd be able to focus on something normal again.

It was just after ten when she slipped out into the back-yard and hurried across the lawn to the hidden opening in the wall. She knew that it was risky to sneak out two nights in a row, but with Lisbeth sleeping like the dead and her mom still in Chicago, it was too good an opportunity to waste.

The forest seemed less strange tonight. The invisible paths that wove between the trees looked familiar, and the scent of leaves and dirt smelled heavenly. It was easy to find the same spot where she'd practiced the night before: the two huge pine trees surrounded by scrub oak. Claire sank down onto the ground and let the feeling of fur slide over her hands and ears. Willing it to come.

Even though her eyes were closed, Claire knew she'd transformed—the sounds of the crickets and mosquitoes were suddenly twice as loud. Her senses might have been sharper than a normal person's before, but in her wolf-form, they were almost painfully sensitive. Everything seemed very close to her, sharp and immediate. She could feel the texture of the ground beneath her through the cotton of her workout pants. *I should probably start taking them off when I transform. One of these days, I'm going to grow a tail and rip right through them.*

The thought of having a tail made her a little queasy, and she took a deep breath.

The forest scents were strong enough to make her dizzy. Leaning forward, Claire rested her head on the cool ground and closed her eyes, trying to acclimate to this new world where nothing was hidden.

*Maybe I should take this just a little slower.*

A sludge of disappointment sat in the pit of her stomach, weighing her down. Since she'd already done it once, she'd somehow expected that changing would be easier. Instead, she was just as uncomfortable as she'd been last night.

When the assault on her senses had stopped making her nauseous, Claire sat up again. Her fur went a little farther up her arms tonight. She reached up and felt her ears, which were larger than before, and pointed at the tips. Her feet had transformed into something a little more cramped and pawlike. Mostly, though, she still looked human.

Getting unsteadily to her feet, she walked a little way into the woods, wondering if she could find the clearing where she'd met the others. She wove her way through the trees, surprised at how many landmarks she remembered. When she'd come here with her mom, it had seemed like she was just stumbling through the forest, too dazed to really notice anything. But there was the big fallen oak they'd climbed over. And a little ways farther on, the gnarled tree whose trunk twisted into the shape of an *S*.

Finally, the smell of a burned-out fire tickled her nose, and Claire followed the bitter, almost hollow scent all the way to the clearing. She sat on a fallen limb and wiped the veil of sweat from her forehead. It was cooler here, in the deep part of the woods, but the humidity was still thick.

Without the fire or the rest of the pack, the clearing seemed oddly normal. Like any other part of the forest. Claire stared up at the patch of sky visible directly overhead and sighed. There was nothing special about this place, and she couldn't figure out what had made it seem like such a good idea to come all the way out here, anyway. She didn't want to practice in the clearing—it felt too exposed, even this deep in the woods. She'd be better off walking back to the pine trees. Claire stood and stretched. She had just turned to slink back into the trees when the voice spoke behind her.

"Don't freak out," it said.

Claire backed across the clearing as fast as she could, nearly falling over the well-hidden remains of the fire in the process, and ducked behind a tree. Her mouth was open, but some primitive instinct kept her scream locked in her lungs. If she screamed, they'd find her for sure.

A thin figure slid through the trees, walking into the shaft of moonlight that struck the clearing. "Claire?" Zahlia called, her pale features scanning the trees.

Claire stepped out from her hiding place, her heart thudding. "Jesus! You scared the crap out of me," she breathed.

"Sorry." Zahlia folded herself down onto the same fallen limb where Claire had been sitting. "I didn't mean to."

"No, it's fine. So, uh, hey."

"Hey, yourself. What brings you to the clearing when it's not a full moon? Is your mom around?" Zahlia asked, her eyes glittering in the bluish light.

Claire shrugged. "No, it's just me. I felt sort of like practicing, so I came out to the woods, and then I kind of wandered over, I guess. I didn't even know if I'd be able to find it." She felt heat rise into her cheeks. "My mom doesn't really know I'm out. Am I not supposed to be here?"

"You're allowed to be in the gathering place. And of course I won't tell your mom that you were here. It's just that usually I'm the only one who ever comes, other than when we all meet. It's a good place to think."

Claire sat down across from Zahlia. "Yeah, I can see that. It didn't seem like a very good place to practice, though."

"Really?" Zahlia cocked her head to one side. "Why not?"

"It just felt too . . . sort of out in the open, or something."

Zahlia grinned. "That's a great sign."

"It is?" Claire sounded startled, even to herself.

"Sure," Zahlia said. "Not wanting to be seen while you're in your true form—it means your instincts are strong. And the stronger your instincts, the easier it is to learn, to be good at the things we can do."

"Oh. Well—okay then." Being good at being a werewolf

was better than nothing, right? Claire wiped the moisture off her temples and winced as the perspiration matted the fur on the backs of her hands.

"You look hot." Zahlia smiled. "There's a way to fix that, you know."

"Uh, no. What do you mean?" Claire sat up, interested. Sweat trickled down her spine and pooled in the small of her back.

"Close your eyes and think of something really cold. Snow, ice—it doesn't matter what."

The icicles that clung to the edge of her window every winter popped into Claire's head. The way they hung there like a set of uneven, shimmering teeth . . .

"Do you have something?" Zahlia asked.

Claire nodded.

"Okay, so this is where it gets a little tricky. You have to sort of pull that idea around you, like a cloak, and hold it there."

The cool air that slid through her fur surprised Claire, and her eyes flew open. *Holy crap.* The heat rushed back over her.

Zahlia laughed. "We're not done yet. You have to stay focused. That was only the first step. Why don't you try again?"

Claire squeezed her eyes shut and pulled the cold around herself, shivering a little against the sudden chill.

"Great," Zahlia whispered. "Now you've got to let it in. Hold it under your skin, the same way you keep your wolf-self hidden."

Claire felt the cold slide under her fur. It was like the jolt of diving into icy water on a hot day—shock and relief at the same time, and the tiniest edge of pain that disappeared as her body adjusted to the change. She opened her eyes and stared at Zahlia in disbelief.

"That's amazing," she breathed.

Zahlia nodded. "I love that one, especially. It really comes in handy when you're hunting—keeps the temperature from being a distraction. Go on, move a little—give it a try."

Claire ran a little way into the woods, experimenting. An hour ago, even a short run had left her panting and drained. Now, the heat of her exertion was whisked away by the cold inside her. Claire let out a *yip* of pleasure. She could run for miles, for hours, like this. Without the thick air pressing down on her, she was filled with new energy. It tingled through her, and she shivered happily as she made her way back into the clearing.

"So—I can do this to stay warm, too?"

"Sure. You can keep either heat or cold beneath your skin, but only as a werewolf. In your human form, you've gotta listen to the weatherman, just like anyone else. You'll get hot and cold like the rest of the humans."

Claire nodded, grateful. "Thank you so much for teaching me that. It's just—it's nice to have these extra things, you know? It kind of helps make up for everything else."

Zahlia wrapped her arms around her legs and stared at

Claire. "Being a werewolf isn't a curse, Claire. It's hard, but it's got more benefits than drawbacks, I promise. Wait until the first time you get to hunt with the whole pack. It's amazing—like you're everywhere at once, and totally unstoppable. Humans don't get to feel that. The Goddess has given only us that honor."

Claire rubbed a hand across her forehead. "Yeah, okay." She wasn't really convinced about the whole honor-of-the-hunt thing yet—she'd still trade it in if she could be normal again. She took a deep breath. "So, what else can we do?"

"Oh, lots of stuff, as long as you're in your true form. Fire will do your bidding. Some of us can open locks with our thoughts. Things like that."

Claire's mouth fell open. *Well, that's a hell of a lot better than just being able to hunt in the off-season.* "When can I learn them?"

"Soon enough." Zahlia stood up and brushed the dirt off her pants. "I've gotta go if I'm going to able to drag my butt out of bed tomorrow morning."

"Oh—sorry. I used up all your thinking time, huh?"

Zahlia smiled at her. "Are you kidding? I'm happy I could help. I just wish I could stay longer, show you some more stuff. Really, Claire, the sooner you master all of this, the faster you'll realize that your old life is nothing to mourn, that being human is boring."

"Maybe." Claire shrugged. Most of the humans she knew

had lives that seemed a hell of a lot simpler than hers did. There was something to be said for that.

Zahlia laughed. "Give it a little time, New One. If you want, we can meet again next week, work on some things."

"That would be really great, actually. I'd like that."

"Good. You'll have an easier time getting home if you stay in your true form. The scent trail will be easier to follow." Zahlia jumped over the log where she'd been sitting and strode to the edge of the clearing. "See you next week."

"Yeah," said Claire, heading for the faint path that had brought her through the woods. "Thanks."

Only a few yards into the forest, Claire started to get tired. With each tree she passed her fatigue grew, like she'd finished the hardest workout of her life and the adrenaline rush had finally faded. The sight of her practice spot sent a wave of relief through her, and she nearly lay down and slept on the spot.

Instead, Claire forced herself to transform. She crept back across the lawn and into the house, took the quickest shower in history, and fell into bed with her hair still wet.

The relentless clanging of pots and pans forced its way into her dream, waking Claire. She lay blinking at the clock on her bedside table. It was only eleven thirty, for crying out loud. Did Lisbeth really have to make that much noise in the kitchen?

Still half-asleep, Claire stumbled into the bathroom and

stared at the mass of snarled hair framing her face. That's what she got for not drying it before bed.

While she picked through the mess of tangles, Claire called Emily.

"Hey," Emily answered, her voice glum.

"Hey, yourself. How'd things go with your parents last night?"

"Ugh. I mean, *ugh*. They weren't listening at all. And my mom wants to go shopping with me later—"

"Well, that might be good, right? Some time to talk?" Claire interrupted.

"You didn't let me finish. She's taking me shopping for luggage. *Luggage!* Like I'm going on some sort of old-lady cruise or something."

Claire winced. "Oh. Ouch. Maybe you won't find anything you like?"

"Ha. I don't think that's going to stop them, but nice try. How about you? Did you do anything fun yesterday?"

"Actually, yeah, Matthew and I went to The Juice Junction."

"You did? That's awesome. How was it? What did you talk about? Did he kiss you?"

"Um, you know . . . we just talked about random stuff."

*Stuff I can't really tell you about, that's all.* Emily would kill to hear the specifics of the conversation, but Claire had promised Matthew she wouldn't say anything. And she'd meant it.

"Fine, you talked," Emily teased impatiently. "But what about the kissing? C'mon, you know I'm living vicariously through your love life right now."

"Yeah, we kissed," Claire said, tingling with the memory of it. "And yeah, it was amazing. But that's all I'm saying."

"Okay, I can take a hint. I'll change the subject. So, um . . . anything else exciting happen yesterday?"

An image of the trees flashing past her as she ran through the woods popped into Claire's mind.

"No, not really." God, it was starting to feel like there wasn't anything she could talk to Emily about. It was weird and uncomfortable and it made Claire want to get off the phone. "Listen, I've gotta get downstairs for lunch before Lisbeth gets ticked. Call me later?"

"Yeah, sure." Emily sighed. "I'll tell you all about my fabulous matching suitcases."

After they'd hung up, Claire stared at the phone in her hand and let out a long, slow breath. Friends weren't supposed to lie to each other, but what other choice did she have?

# Chapter Eight

CLAIRE STARED AT the ringing phone, chewing the last bite of her toast while Matthew's number flashed on the screen. Since his soccer practice schedule had picked up and Lisbeth still didn't want her out after dark, it had been nearly a week since she'd seen him, though they talked almost every day. She swallowed, winced, and answered.

"Hello?"

"Claire, hi!"

"Hey, Matthew, what's up?"

"Not much, actually. Sore quads and memorizing plays, mostly, since practice is cancelled this afternoon."

"Really? That's frustrating, huh?" Hope made Claire fluttery. He had an afternoon off?

"Not so much, since it gives me some time to see you . . . except . . ." He paused.

"Except what?"

"Well, see, here's the thing—my dad has this rally scheduled this afternoon, and I have to go, but I really want to hang out with you."

Claire hesitated. She was dying to see Matthew, but at a rally for Dr. Engle?

"Listen, it's going to suck, but it would suck a lot less if you went with me. I know it's not exactly dinner and a movie, but—," he hesitated.

"Well, why not? I've never been to a rally before," she said. *And it's not like anyone will know that I'm a werewolf, right?*

"Great. I'll pick you up at two thirty."

There were more people than Claire had expected. They'd set up folding chairs and tables with bakery cookies and damp bottles of water that glistened in the sun. Kids ran through the crowd, their T-shirts emblazoned with the outline of a howling wolf, partly hidden behind an enormous red *X*. Some of the people milling around the tables held signs with the same image, others had posters that said SUPPORT THE NEW P.A.C. The heat had left everyone flushed and sweating, anxious for the rally to begin in earnest.

A beefy man sporting a sweat-stained ball cap clapped Matthew on the shoulder. "Hey! I seen your picture in the paper—you're Dr. Engle's son, right? You must be pretty proud of your pops, huh?"

"Uh, yeah," Matthew stammered, blushing as several people turned to look at him curiously. "He's been working real hard on all this."

Claire couldn't stop the grin that inched across her face while Matthew squirmed under the attention of his father's admirers.

"Good man, Dr. Engle. We're lucky to have him." The man caught sight of someone behind Matthew. "Hey! Jim! You need a hand with the rest of those signs?"

Matthew grabbed Claire's hand and pulled her to the back of the crowd. "Ugh, it never *stops*," he complained. He dropped his voice. "It's not like he ended world hunger, or anything. He's only trying to get everyone fired up because he's worried that Lycanthropy Researchers International is losing interest in the case. And if he doesn't get into the LRI, he might not get to stay with the Federal Human Protection Agency."

*Huh. So Dr. Engle doesn't have everyone dazzled, after all.*

At the front of the crowd, a stage had been erected. Someone had draped it—crookedly, Claire noted—with red and blue bunting. There was a podium in the center with a microphone poking out of it. Behind the podium Dr. Engle stood, adjusting his hair, his wilting collar, and the microphone in quick succession. He tapped the mike and a stream of feed-back squealed out of the speakers. A collective groan rose from the crowd, but they all stopped talking and turned to face the stage.

"I'd like to thank you all for coming out in the heat to support us today." The sun glinted off his expensive-looking teeth when he talked. "I know you'd all like to get back to the air-conditioning, so I'll keep this brief. We here in Hanover Falls have been living for too long under the twin shadows of fear and uncertainty. The fine, upstanding citizens of our community do not deserve to have their activities cut short by the arrival of darkness—they do not deserve to have their nights plagued by the apprehension that something might be lurking outside their windows. It's not fair, and I for one will not stand for it one more second."

Even from the back of the crowd, Claire could see Dr. Engle's knuckles turning white as he squeezed the edges of the podium in his long hands. All around her, people strained forward like flowers leaning toward the sun.

*Because they want me dead. And he's holding their hands and telling them that they're absolutely right.* The realization hit Claire like a slap. *They don't even care what the truth is. They're scared, and they're mad, and they want someone to pay for that.*

She forced herself to look over at Matthew. His features didn't hold the same slow-burning anger that shone on everyone else's face. But he didn't look disgusted by his dad's rhetoric, either. *He's been listening to this for seventeen years,* Claire reminded herself. *He's probably immune to it by now.*

Dr. Engle leaned into the microphone, his voice booming over the crowd. "It ends today. This is Day One of a new era. It gives me great pleasure to announce the formation of the P.A.C.—the Protective Action Council. This community-based group will work in conjunction with Federal Human Protection Agency and the local police. Your cooperation will allow us to take every measure available to us to capture the beast that lurks, unwelcome, in our midst."

Claire shivered, glad he didn't know just how accurate his words were.

"Anyone who would like to volunteer their services . . . and we need everyone, from those who can stuff envelopes to those of you who are skilled and experienced hunters"—Claire blanched—"can sign up before you leave here today. The time for action has come, and I am counting on each of you to answer the call. Thank you, and God bless."

The crowd erupted into cheers. They thrust their signs into the air, whistling and applauding. The table where the sign-up clipboards lay already had a line snaking around the parking lot. Claire stared, unable to pull her gaze away from the stream of people who, one after the other, signed up for the privilege of killing a werewolf.

Matthew slid his arm around her shoulders. "You're not thinking of joining, are you?" he asked.

A strangled laugh slipped out of Claire's mouth. "Uh, no." *Way to blend in, Claire.* "But your dad's a really good speaker. Everyone seems really excited." *I hate him, but yeah, he can fire up a group of morons, all right.*

Matthew rolled his eyes. "It sort of loses its oomph when you've heard him practicing in front of the bathroom mirror for two days. Come on, if we don't get out of here soon, I'll get stuck shaking hands for the next hour." He steered Claire toward the cars. With trembling fingers, she opened the door, slid into the oven-hot car, and leaned her head back against the seat.

*This is the worst date I have ever been on.*

Matthew's car couldn't get cool fast enough for Claire—between the heat and the panic, she felt faint.

"You look flushed." Matthew's voice was worried. "Why don't we go get some ice cream? Cool off a little?"

"Can I take a rain check?" She hated how shaky her voice sounded. "Right now I just want to go home and take a shower. And maybe lie down for a little while." The urge to get home, to sort through what she'd just seen, was too strong to ignore.

"I'm so sorry, Claire."

Matthew turned the air-conditioning vents on his side of the car toward her. Since they were still blowing hot air, it didn't do much good, but it was still sweet of him.

"I should never have dragged you out in this heat to stand around with a bunch of self-righteous morons."

She reached over and took his hand. "I liked being there with you." The last two words made it true.

Matthew pulled up in front of her house. "Do you want me to walk you inside?"

She shook her head. "I'll be fine. Thanks for dropping me off."

He leaned over and kissed her, just a quick, light pressure of his mouth against hers. "Call me later and let me know how you're doing."

"I will." Claire slid out of the car and walked into the house.

She dragged herself upstairs, worn out from the heat and the crash from the adrenaline high she'd been on at the rally. She pushed open the door to her room and cringed to see her mother sitting on her bed.

"What are you doing in here?" Claire thought of the journal hidden under her mattress, and the shirt—the one she'd taken from her mother's closet without permission—that lay in a stained lump in the bottom drawer of her dresser. There were secrets stashed all over her room. *If she's been snooping around in here, I'll die.*

Claire's mother pursed her lips. "I'm waiting for you, obviously."

"Couldn't you just wait in the kitchen?" Claire complained. She edged into the room and sat down on the bench in front of her vanity.

"No. I want to talk to you, and it is not a conversation that I want to have an audience for." Her mother glanced pointedly at the door.

Claire got up to close it, rolling her eyes once her back was to her mom. She sat back down on the bench and waited. Marie eyed Claire like an apple she suspected of having a worm.

"Did you have fun at the rally?"

Claire leaned against the vanity behind her. "I had fun with Matthew," she said carefully.

"I imagine his father delivered quite a speech." Marie fiddled with the strap of her watch, straightening it against her wrist.

"Yeah." Claire shuddered. "I guess you could say that. He's forming some sort of werewolf extermination squad. People couldn't sign up fast enough. It was crazy."

Her mother let out a long breath. "I assumed it would be something like that. It's good that you went. That you saw firsthand what people think of us, what they would do to any one of us if we were exposed."

"I know how to keep my mouth shut." Claire huffed. "I don't have a death wish and I'm not an idiot. God."

"Goddess," her mother corrected.

"Whatever. Fine." Claire crossed her arms in front of her chest, unwilling to give her mom the satisfaction of hearing her say it.

"I'm not trying to start an argument with you, Claire. Please. This is important, and I need you to listen."

Claire cocked her head to the side. "I'm listening."

"Very well. Most of us have a relationship with a human at some point that is about more than reproduction. It does not often last long. There is too much to hide, and too many lies are told. But it is allowed. The need for companionship is understandable."

Claire swallowed hard. *I really don't think I want to know where this is going.*

"Mom—"

Her mother held up a hand, silencing her. "But. Matthew Engle is not just any human. His father is a danger to us. And you are at a very vulnerable time in your transition. It is a bad combination, a risky one. Because of this, I must forbid you from seeing him. You are welcome to find another boy to date, but from this point on, Matthew is off-limits."

Claire stared at her. "You have got to be joking."

Marie stood up and straightened her shirt. "I would not joke about this. I am your mother and you will do what I tell you."

The ice in her mother's voice made Claire stiffen. Her mom headed for the door.

"It smells like dinner is almost ready. I'll see you downstairs."

Claire stuck out her tongue at the closed door, crossed the room, and turned the little lock on the doorknob. She didn't want her mother coming back in to make any additions to her new "rules."

Claire sighed and unlocked the door.

*It's not like a little twist lock is going to keep a werewolf out.* The words turned in her mind, forming a new thought. *It's not like it can keep one in, either.*

Her mom didn't trust Matthew because she didn't know him. But Claire did. And since her mother was gone so much, she'd never know if Claire saw Matthew or not. At least, not as long as Claire was very, very careful.

Claire was still asleep when Matthew called the next morning. She dug her cell phone out from under the pillow next to her and looked at the clock.

"Hello?" She cleared her throat. *God, I sound like an eighty-year-old with a Marlboro habit.*

"You're still asleep?" Matthew teased.

"So I'm not a morning person. Sue me," Claire grumbled.

"Lawsuits aren't really my style. How 'bout I take you to lunch instead?"

Claire bit her lip. Being with Matthew was the only time she felt really *good* anymore. But she'd have to make sure that she could get there—and back—without her mom knowing.

Crap.

"Hang on a second." She stuck the phone under her pillow and walked to the door. "Mom?" she hollered down the stairs.

"You missed her by an hour—she won't be home until dinner," Lisbeth called back. "Do you need something?"

"Um, no."

Claire crawled back into bed with a smile on her face. With her mom gone, she just had to get around Lisbeth, which wouldn't be too hard. She dug the phone out from under the pillow. "Yeah, lunch sounds good."

"I'll be there in an hour, okay?"

"Okay," Claire agreed, struggling out of bed. She snapped the phone shut and headed for the shower.

When she got downstairs, she told Lisbeth that she was going out to eat with some friends. Which wasn't a lie.

Lisbeth's eyes lit up, which wasn't the reaction Claire had expected. "If you don't need me to make you lunch, then I'm going to go practice my forward bends for a while."

"Ooooh, thrilling," Claire teased, trying to hide the fact that she was jumping up and down inside. This was easy. This was *too* easy. She hadn't expected Lisbeth to be so excited to get rid of her.

Right on time, Matthew pulled up in front of the house and honked the horn. Claire winced, hoping that Lisbeth hadn't heard. She'd seen Matthew's car before, and if she looked out the window to see who it was, Claire's luck would be over.

In the six seconds it took Claire to cross the driveway, tiny beads of sweat had already sprung up on her forehead.

She practically leapt into the cool interior of the car.

Matthew grinned and turned the air-conditioning up even farther. "It's ridiculous out there, huh?"

"Oh my God, it's insane." Claire leaned forward into the stream of cool air and sighed. "So, hi."

"Hi, yourself." Matthew's smile widened. "You hungry?"

"Always." Claire leaned back in the seat, twisting around to look at her house. She didn't see Lisbeth hovering behind any of the windows. So far so good.

"Yeah, I know that feeling." Matthew turned out of the drive. "Is Louie's okay?"

"Sure." Her hunger faded at the mention of Louie's. The diner was always full of people from school. Pretending that she was normal in front of Matthew wasn't so hard, but the idea of being surrounded by people she knew, of having to hide what she was in the wide-open like that—it made her want to sink down into the car seat and disappear.

*But I was already changing at my birthday party, and no one noticed anything. 'Course, it's a lot easier to keep a secret if you don't know what it is.*

To hide her nerves, Claire flipped through the stack of CDs that Matthew had stuffed below the car stereo. She held up a disc. "You mind?"

Matthew glanced at it. "Are you kidding? That's pretty much my favorite band right now."

Claire smiled at him and put in the disc. When she sat

back, Matthew reached over and slid his hand into hers like it was the most natural thing in the world. The tingly feeling that zipped through her made Claire catch her breath.

The third song had just started when they pulled into the parking lot. Claire took a deep breath.

"You okay?" Matthew stroked the back of her hand with his thumb.

"Just don't want to get out of the air-conditioning," she lied.

"I can help with that." Matthew pulled up to the front door. "Go on inside. I'll just go park and I'll be right there."

"Oh, uh, thanks." Claire climbed out—he'd stopped so close to the diner's glass entrance that she had to be careful not to bang it with the car door.

She stepped into Louie's and shivered. It wasn't the rush of cold air—it was because nearly every person in the restaurant turned to look at her. Everyone always looked when someone walked in to Louie's, watching for people they knew, but the scrutiny sent panic clanging through Claire's chest. The crowd at the rally hadn't bothered her—after all, no one there had known who she was. Standing in front of a roomful of people who were rating her social status while she watched was totally different.

A couple of people waved and she forced herself to smile.

Matthew walked in behind her. Relief washed through her when he wrapped an arm around her shoulders and steered her toward a booth. Several people looked surprised to see the two of them together, which just increased Claire's desire to slide underneath a table.

She'd never been wildly popular. Being the center of so much attention would have made her uncomfortable last year, too. *But at least then I thought I was the same species as everyone else.* She scowled at the menu.

The waitress appeared and tapped her pencil against her order pad. "You all ready?"

Once they'd ordered and were alone again, Matthew leaned back against the cushioned banquette and draped his arms across the top. He looked comfortable, familiar. He looked like he belonged.

Across the diner, a tableful of girls that Claire recognized from the show choir stared at her and Matthew. They looked horrified. With her pulse thudding in her fingertips, Claire reached up and touched the rims of her ears, checking for fur. Her skin was smooth.

*Oh my God. They're not looking at me because they know what I am. They're acting like that because Matthew's here with* me.

Claire picked at her cuticles under the table and glanced around the diner. The show choirettes weren't the only ones staring. Near the back of the room, Claire spotted Yolanda Adams. Claire hadn't seen her since her birthday. Yolanda raised a hand and waved at Claire, grinning. Claire smiled back, feeling relieved and pathetic all at once.

"So, uh, how's soccer going?" It was the only question Claire could think of. *Lame, lame, lame!* She fiddled with the paper from her straw, tearing it into tiny shreds.

Matthew shrugged. "It's not, really. Coach cancelled our two-a-days. I guess the school board thinks we're going to get heatstroke or something. I'm pretty worried about it, actually. If we don't get some serious practice time in soon, we're going to suck when the season starts."

Claire winced. "Sorry, but I, um—when does the season start again, exactly?"

"Two days after school starts. Why would you be sorry?"

Claire shrugged. "It just seems like something I should have already known." Matthew reached across the table and squeezed her hand. The murmuring at some of the tables across the diner picked up. "There's no reason you should have known that. Did anyone ever tell you you're too hard on yourself? Seriously, though"—Matthew locked eyes with her—"it would mean a lot to me if you came to the opening match."

Claire's heartbeat echoed in her ears. "I wouldn't miss it for anything," she whispered.

The waitress appeared out of nowhere and dropped two plates between them. Claire pulled one of the plates closer to her, picked up the burger, and took a bite.

A worried crease appeared between Matthew's eyebrows. "You okay? You seem kinda quiet today."

"Yeah, I'm fine," Claire said. "Just a little tired, I guess."

*Oh, and my mom said I couldn't see you anymore and also I'm pretty sure Kate-Marie Brown just took a picture of us with her cell phone.*

The waitress brought the check the instant the last fry disappeared from their plates. Claire reached for the cash she'd stuck in her back pocket, but Matthew snatched up the bill before she could get to it.

"Not a chance." He smiled and shook his head.

Claire shifted uncomfortably. "Matthew, I can pay my share."

"I'm sure you can. But this is a date, and I'm buying."

"It's not a date if I buy?" Claire fired back, arching an eyebrow at him.

He considered that. "I dunno." Then he grinned. "I'll think about it while I go pay this." He slid out of the booth and walked over to the cash register.

Claire dug a piece of gum out of her pocket and headed for the front door. The stares that were drilling holes into her back didn't even bother her. Let them look. She could pretend to be normal, right? *What do they call it? Hiding in plain sight? Guess I'm gonna have to get pretty freaking good at that.*

# Chapter Nine

THE SMELLS COMING *from the Dumpster were almost too much to bear. The wasted, rotten food. The toxic plastic of the trash bags. The bitter scent of a bottle of that must have been pitched before it was empty. Still, it was the best hiding place—in the darkest corner of the alley, but close enough to the back door of the apartment building for easy access. She breathed slowly, ignoring the stench, and forced herself to be still.*

*The suburbs were too easy, but this—an exclusive building downtown, where the idiots felt safe—this was perfect. It was even better than a daytime kill.*

*Two women wearing impossibly high heels and too much perfume breezed down the alley and into the back door of the building, arguing about whose turn it was to clean the bathroom. She tensed, once again checking the angle of the security camera above the door.*

*Finally, she saw the streetlight at the end of the alley catch his blond hair. Looking rumpled after a long day, he walked down the alley toward the building. He paused in front of the door, patting his pockets of his suit coat like he was looking for a key.*

*She leapt without hesitating and closed her jaws around his neck, crushing his windpipe before he even thought of screaming.*

A few days after Claire had been to Louie's with Matthew, the editor of the *Hanover Falls Post* turned up dead. Every TV station was blaring the story, and the paper had devoted the entire front page to him. He had been young and handsome and important, which had made everyone even more upset about his killing than they had been about the others.

Claire found Lisbeth at the kitchen counter, mug in hand, staring at the newspaper.

"Emily called—she said you weren't answering your cell."

"I don't usually answer my phone when I'm sleeping," Claire pointed out. "What did she want?"

"She wanted to meet you at that coffee shop on Fourth. If you want to go, I can take you over in an hour or so."

"That'd be great." Claire grabbed for the remote, already tired of the repetitive news show, but Lisbeth snatched it away from her.

"It's just tragic." Lisbeth said, sipping her tea. There were dark circles under her eyes and the frown on her face made her look pinched.

"The editor?" Claire asked, hopping up to sit on the edge of the counter.

"Of course the editor!" Lisbeth snapped. "And don't sit on the counter. You know your mother hates that."

Claire *thunked* back onto the floor. "Fine. Geez. If I'd known you were so *tense* I wouldn't have said anything. Where is Mom, anyway?"

"Meeting with a potential client. She'll be back later this afternoon. And you're right. I am tense. I didn't sleep very well last night." Lisbeth walked around Claire and put her tea mug in the sink. "Maybe I'll go do some breathing exercises and see if I can control myself a little better." She gave Claire a forced smile. "See you in a half hour, okay? We'll leave after that?"

"Sure." Claire snagged the remote and pointed it at the TV, wondering how Matthew was doing. If Lisbeth was this stressed about the situation, Dr. Engle must have gone freaking nuclear. "Have fun breathing and stuff."

Claire sat at one of the little tables in the coffee shop's front window, sipping a mocha and waiting for Emily. The shop was mostly empty. Claire closed her eyes and leaned her head against the window, enjoying the quiet. The little bell above the door chimed, and Claire opened her eyes, expecting to see Emily.

Instead, Victoria walked in. She looked over at Claire, recognition and then caution flashing across her face in quick succession.

"Um, hey," Claire said carefully.

"Hey. Nice to see you, Claire. It's been a while." Victoria smiled, but her voice was guarded. She nodded at the counter. "Do you come here often?"

"Sort of. Yeah. I'm meeting a friend." Claire squirmed in her seat. It was like running into one of her teachers, or something. She didn't know what to say—everything she knew about Victoria was a secret. Claire couldn't exactly ask her for fur-grooming tips in the middle of a public place.

Victoria nodded. "Well, I'd better get going. Tell your mother I said hello."

The door opened and Emily came flying into the coffee shop, her car keys in one hand and her phone in the other.

Claire waved Emily over, then looked back up at Victoria. "I'll tell her."

Victoria shot her a tiny smile and headed for the counter.

Emily flopped into the chair across from Claire. "Who's that?" She kept her voice low, but Claire knew Victoria could hear them.

"Someone my mom knows." Claire shrugged. Out of the corner of her eye, she saw Victoria glance over and give her a lightning-quick nod of approval. "So—what's going on? Your message this morning was . . . odd."

"Sorry. I wasn't exactly free to talk. My mother's been closer to me than my own damn shadow ever since they decided."

The word made Claire's mouth go dry. "Decided"?

"It's over, Claire. My parents are taking me to my aunt's house tomorrow. I thought I'd convinced them to let me stay, but after what happened to that Dave McKinney guy, they totally panicked."

Claire leaned back in her seat, tension knotting her shoulders. "Wow. I . . . wow. Do you think you can calm them down again?"

Emily let out a bitter, choked-sounding little laugh. "No chance. They both had that look on their face when they told me—the one that means they don't care if they *are* wrong, they're doing this anyway."

"Yeah, I know that look." Claire sighed. "So, what are you going to do?"

Victoria headed past them, a paper coffee cup in each hand. She winked at Claire over the top of Emily's head. Distracted, Claire twitched her fingers in a tiny wave.

"I guess I'm going to pack." Emily sniffed. "Will you come help me?"

"Of course." Claire pushed away her drink—she felt too awful about Emily leaving to finish it. And even worse than that was the fact that deep down, she was a little relieved. *It'll be so much easier to hide things from Emily if she's hundreds of miles away.* It made Claire sick that she was thinking things like that . . . even if it was true.

She ran a hand through her hair and forced herself to focus on Emily's resigned-looking face.

"So, when are we packing? I need to call Lisbeth and tell her."

"Now, if you can." Emily looked over at the counter. "I'd better go get a cup of civilized coffee while I still can."

Claire picked up her phone and dialed Lisbeth.

Emily held up a sequined tank top and stared at it regretfully. "I can't imagine I'd have a single reason to wear this on the farm. You'd look great in it. Wanna borrow it while I'm gone?"

"Sure," Claire said, putting down the magazine she'd been paging through. "Thanks."

"No problem. I'm sure Matthew will love it."

Claire rolled her eyes and Emily wadded up the shirt and threw it at her.

"What?" Claire smiled. "I just think sequins might be sort of . . . scratchy as far as Matthew is concerned."

"Oooooooh." Emily's eyes lit up. "Are you telling me you've done more than just kiss him?"

Claire felt herself blush. She'd never really had a boyfriend before, and though she'd always been willing to listen to Emily's play-by-play of her make-out sessions, she really didn't feel like telling Emily everything about her and Matthew.

"It's not—uh . . ." Claire paused.

"Oh, come *on*. We tell each other everything, right?"

Claire winced. That used to be true. Now all of a sudden, she wasn't telling Emily anything. She didn't want to talk about Matthew, and she wasn't allowed to talk about being a werewolf. Having so many secrets from her best friend felt totally abnormal, but what choice did she have?

"Well," Claire conceded, "I will say that he's an amazing kisser." That much she could say without feeling squicky about it.

"He's not one of those tongue-down-your-throat guys?"

Claire squirmed. "Um, no."

"Well, that's good. Jesus, do you remember Darren from last year?"

Claire's embarrassment faded. "Oh, yeah. The one who kept licking your teeth?"

Emily nodded and shuddered. "Yep. God, I should never have kept dating him after that first kiss. I mean seriously, why didn't you stop me?"

Claire settled back against the pillows. Now they were back on safe ground, subject-wise.

*I just have to keep Emily talking about herself, that's all. Like, for the rest of our friendship.*

Claire re-sorted Emily's piles of clothes as they rehashed Emily's last two relationships. She felt totally fake—like an interviewer on TV trying to keep some movie star talking—but at least Emily seemed happy. That was something.

Sort of.

That evening, Claire lay on her still neatly made bed, exhausted. She'd spent the rest of the afternoon making sympathetic noises while Emily crammed things into her suitcases and vented about her parents. It had been a relief when Lisbeth finally came to pick her up, especially since Lisbeth was in a much better mood.

Claire's cell phone rang, and she closed her eyes, hoping it was Matthew. But it wasn't. It was Zahlia.

"Hello?" Claire answered, sitting up.

"Hey, Claire, it's me. Is this a bad time?"

"No, I'm not busy. What's going on?"

"I was wondering if we were still on for practicing tonight? It's not that long until the next full moon, you know. If you're up for it, I was thinking we could meet in the clearing, around eleven?"

Claire started figuring backward in her head. It wouldn't work. She'd have to be ready to go by ten thirty, and there was no way her mom would be asleep by then. And she wasn't exactly planning to tell her mom where she was going.

"It's actually a little early. Is midnight okay?"

Zahlia laughed. "I take it Marie's still not too keen on you learning things ahead of schedule."

"I sort of haven't told her about it," Claire admitted.

"That's probably smart. She'd just freak out, and then you'd be stuck waiting until you were fully transformed before you could so much as chase your own tail."

Claire blinked. "Um—when will I get a tail?" Her voice sounded strangled.

"Dunno. Maybe this moon, maybe next. I was just using it as an example."

"Oh. That sounds, uh . . . interesting. Yeah. Well, I'll see you in the clearing, then."

"Sounds good." Zahlia hung up without saying good-bye.


Claire leaned against a rough tree trunk, still in her wolf-form, and panted into the darkness of the forest. She couldn't even begin to smell the trail she'd been following. She'd lost the deer. Again. Behind Claire, Zahlia shuffled her feet.

"You seem like you're having trouble concentrating."

At the sound of Zahlia's human voice, Claire jumped. She hadn't expected her to transform back. Claire slumped against the bark, exhausted. They'd been hunting for hours, but Claire hadn't caught so much as a squirrel.

"I know." The misery in her voice embarrassed her. "I'm sorry."

Zahlia pulled on the running shorts and tank top that she'd been carrying through the woods. "Why should you be sorry? You're still new to all of this. That's the whole point of practicing. You'll get better, I promise. You just need someone to help you. That's what friends do, isn't it?"

Claire thought of Emily, her best friend in the whole world. Who couldn't help her because she didn't have any idea what was really going on. A whole lifetime of never being able to tell anyone the whole truth spread out in front of Claire and it was depressing as all hell.

"Are you all right?" Zahlia stepped closer.

Claire shrugged. "I guess." She bit her lip. "It's just hard."

Zahlia cocked her head to the side. "We're not talking about hunting anymore, are we?"

Claire shook her head.

Zahlia shrugged and sat down. "I promise you it gets better. You have the pack—we don't have to keep secrets from each other."

"I just can't believe that no human ever knows, you know?"

"Well—" Zahlia hesitated. "There is occasionally a human who does."

Excitement slid up Claire's spine. "Really?"

"It's extremely rare. Every once in a really long while, some bizarre circumstances will come up, and we reveal our identities to a human. Maybe we need something from them, or maybe one discovers us accidentally. If they're willing, they become a secret-keeper, a *gardien*. I haven't ever known one, but they do exist. I think your great-great-grandmother or some such belonged to a pack back in France that had a *gardien*, but you'd have to ask your mother about that."

Claire crushed a dried leaf to powder in her fingers, thinking. "So, were they, like, friends with her?"

Zahlia shook her head. "That would be extremely unlikely—too risky for everyone. Plus, what would they have in common, really, besides the secret? I mean, a secret-keeper is *human*. So. Who is it you wish you could tell?"

Claire blinked, startled. "How did you know?"

"Because everyone feels that way at first."

"Yeah. I guess that makes sense. It just seems like this would all be a lot easier if I could talk to my best friend about it." Claire shoved down a wave of emotion. It made her chest feel tight.

"You know you can't, right? It doesn't work that way. And think, Claire, how burdened this secret makes you feel, in spite of the benefits and abilities that come with it."

Claire couldn't stop them any longer—the tears fell.

"Hey, don't cry. Come on, think about it. Besides the fact that it's forbidden—that it would be an enormous risk to our pack—would you really want your friend to suffer like you're suffering? Telling wouldn't just be dangerous, Claire. It would be hugely selfish."

Claire's jaw tightened and her voice was little more than a breath. "I hadn't thought of it that way." She rubbed a hand across her weary eyes. "Can we just bag this for tonight? I'm totally exhausted."

Zahlia stood up and stretched. "Fine by me. I'm actually pretty tired, too. Want me to run home with you?"

Claire shook her head. "Nah, I got it. But thanks for meeting me and talking and everything."

Zahlia squeezed her shoulder. "I had a good time. You think for yourself, Claire, and I like that. I like it a lot."

The compliment made a warm spot in Claire's chest.

"I'll call you soon."

Zahlia transformed on the spot, her dark fur blending in with the night around them. Claire picked up the shorts and top Zahlia had worn and handed them to the wolf, who took them in her mouth and waved her tail once in thanks before streaking off into the woods like a shot.

Claire turned and limped home, exhausted in every possible sense of the word.

# Chapter Ten

WHEN MATTHEW CALLED the next day and suggested they go mini-golfing, Claire leapt at the chance for a distraction. Matthew seemed a little surprised when she wouldn't let him pick her up, but agreed to meet her there.

Her mom was going to be gone all afternoon looking at some new camera lenses. Claire just told Lisbeth that she was meeting some friends, and Lisbeth reluctantly agreed to drive her. In spite of the scorching heat, the Putt-Putt parking lot was crowded with families and couples, and Lisbeth was too focused on not hitting anyone to even wave good-bye, much less examine who Claire was meeting. Besides, you couldn't even see around to the front of the putter shack from the parking lot.

Claire leaned on the handle of her putter and watched as Matthew expertly tapped his ball through the windmill blades. She shaded her eyes with her hand.

"Another hole in one," she muttered, marking the humidity-softened scorecard with the tiny pencil. "If soccer doesn't work out, maybe you should go out for the golf team."

Matthew grinned. "No way. Have you seen the dudes on the golf team? Man, talk about uptight. Anyway, I'm only good at miniature golf. I suck at the real thing."

"I doubt that." Claire grinned back. They leaned against the split rail fence that surrounded the course and waited for the family ahead of them to finish the safari-themed hole that came next. Claire stifled a yawn.

"Up late?" Matthew asked.

Claire searched his voice for a hint that there was more to his question than small talk, but there was nothing else there. She forced her shoulders to relax. "Yeah, kind of. I was watching something and just sort of lost track of time." A true statement, but not incriminating in the least. So far, so good.

"Was it the *Late Show*?" Matthew asked, wiping the sweat off his forehead.

"Uh, no, it was something on TiVo." Claire shifted uneasily.

"A movie?"

She could tell he was just making conversation, but she didn't want to lie any more than absolutely necessary—it was too hard to remember, otherwise. It was easier to change the subject. "What'd I miss on the *Late Show*?"

"Oh, man, they had the funniest guy on there. He did this whole routine on the difference between guys and their dogs—"

"So what's the difference? Between the guys and the dogs?" Claire interrupted, eager to feed his enthusiasm for the new topic.

"Okay, so you know how dogs are always using their paws to scratch behind their ears?"

Claire nodded, then winced when Matthew delivered the somewhat questionable punch line.

"Well," he admitted, "it was probably funnier when the comedian did it."

She rolled her eyes at him. "Yeah, well, it's just lucky I don't like you for your joke-telling ability."

"I'm lucky you like me, period," he laughed, wrapping his warm hand around hers.

Claire cringed, sure he would be grossed out by her damp palm, but he didn't seem to mind.

It would be so nice to be able to control her temperature the way she could when she was a wolf. She was starting to hate the sticky-slick feeling of her human skin, hated the constant worry about how the heat was making her look, but she was stuck with it—at least until they could get back into Matthew's air-conditioned car.

With their fingers linked, they wandered up to the next tee. Matthew leaned forward and gave her a quick kiss before he bent forward to put his golf ball on the worn Astroturf. "And now," he announced, "prepare to be amazed."

Claire stepped back to give him some room. This felt normal. Being with Matthew felt *normal*. A bright bubble of happiness formed in her chest. She reminded herself that Emily was leaving for her aunt's house this afternoon. But it didn't make any difference in her mood. How could it? Matthew— the most beautiful guy she'd ever seen—had just kissed her in front of a ton of people.

"Yo, Engle!" The voice floated up the hill from one of the holes below Claire and Matthew. Matthew leaned over the fence, scanning the crowd.

"Doug! What's up?" he called back.

"You coming to my party?"

"Yeah, of course."

"Cool! You bringin' Claire?"

Claire peered over the fence. Doug, who she recognized from the soccer team, waved up at her.

"Hey, Claire." The smile on his face looked genuine.

"Hey, Doug," she said, unable to keep the pleasure out of her voice.

Matthew turned to look at her. "You don't mind do you?

It's a week from Friday—we can totally just stay for an hour and then go do our own thing."

"Yeah, sure, that's fine." She hid her wince. There had to be a way she could get there without her mother knowing.

Matthew leaned back over the fence. "We'll be there."

The older couple behind them started to look impatient, and Claire hurried up to the next hole. She and Matthew spent the next half hour teasing each other about missed shots and cheating on the scorecard.

It was the best afternoon Claire had spent with anyone in ages, and she was still half-floating when Matthew turned onto her street.

"Um, why don't you just drop me off at the end of the driveway?" she suggested.

Matthew glanced over at her. "Why can't I just take you up to the house? You have a seriously long driveway, and there's no reason for you to walk all that way."

"Um, it's just—it might be easier, is all." She could see her mailbox ahead. If he pulled into the driveway and Lisbeth noticed his car, Claire would be dead. She squirmed in her seat.

Matthew braked smoothly, pulling the car off onto the shoulder of the road just in front of Claire's driveway.

"Okay, babe. What's up? Seriously." He turned so that he was facing her.

Claire twisted her hands in her lap. She wanted to make

something up, tell him that the driveway was being repaved, or that Lisbeth had the plague. But when she opened her mouth, the only thing she could think of was the truth.

"It's my mom." She sighed. "She sort of told me that she didn't want me to see you anymore."

Matthew's eyes widened. "But why? She hasn't even really met me, except for at your birthday party."

Claire dropped her gaze and stared at the gearshift between them. She was afraid that if she looked him in the face, she'd end up telling him everything.

"Oh my God," Matthew whispered, and Claire glanced up at him in spite of herself. "It's my dad, isn't it? She's freaked out because of my dad—she thinks being with me puts you in danger," he guessed.

It was so close to the truth that Claire almost laughed. She bit her lip and nodded.

"Yeah, that's pretty much it," she said, relieved not to be lying, even if Matthew didn't know exactly what sort of danger his father posed to Claire.

Matthew sighed. "So that's why you wouldn't let me pick you up today."

Claire nodded. "Are you mad?"

Matthew put a hand on her cheek. "Of course not. Our parents' problems are—well . . . They're not our problem. I don't want you to get in trouble over this, though."

Claire leaned closer to him, breathing in his scent of

soap and sun. "I think it's worth getting in trouble over," she said, closing her eyes.

When Matthew spoke, his mouth was so close to hers that she could feel the vibration of his words against her lips. "Then we'll just be very, very careful."

Claire would have said something in agreement, but her mouth was much too busy. The kiss consumed her, drove out every thought that wasn't Matthew. They wound tighter together, and Claire shivered as his fingertips traced a path down her spine and around her waist.

The gearshift was jammed uncomfortably into her thigh, and when Claire tried to shift away from it, Matthew paused, leaning his forehead against hers.

"Okay, it's broad daylight and we're on the side of the road," he observed in a strained voice.

"It's a very private road," Claire panted.

He laughed a low, rumbling laugh that went straight to Claire's middle. "Still, this is probably a very bad idea." He kissed her again, his lips moving down to the edge of her jaw. "Can you really find a way to get to Doug's party?" His voice was full of concern. "I don't want to talk you into doing anything you're uncomfortable with."

"I wouldn't miss it for the world," she whispered.

"Okay." He straightened up and grinned at her. "Then get out of my car before we get caught, and I'll call you later."

Claire opened the door, fully aware that she had a

ridiculous smile on her face, and not caring in the least. "That sounds fabulous."

As she made her way up the shimmering-hot driveway, Claire heard his car drive away. When she opened the front door, Lisbeth looked up from the couch where she was sorting a pile of papers.

"Oh! I didn't hear a car," she said, surprise crossing her face.

Claire shrugged, not trusting herself to say anything.

"So, did you have fun?" Lisbeth asked.

"Yeah, we had a great time. But it was too hot. I'm gonna go for a swim, if you don't mind."

"That's fine. I may even join you when I'm done with this." Lisbeth went back to her papers and Claire floated up the stairs. She hadn't even had to tell Lisbeth outright lies. . . . It was just a matter of making people see a different side of the truth, that was all.

Claire was lying across the foot of her bed, flipping through the channels, when someone knocked. Her hair was still damp from swimming, and the chemical scent of the chlorine tickled her nose. "Come in," Claire called, thinking it was Lisbeth.

The door opened and her mother came in. She shut the door behind her. Claire swallowed hard.

"Hey," she said, trying to sound natural.

"We need to talk." Her mother sat on the bench in front of Claire's vanity.

*Oh, crap.*

Claire sat up and braced herself.

"You've seen Matthew again, haven't you?" The hard glint in her eyes made Claire shiver.

"What makes you say that?"

Her mother straightened the cuffs of her shirt. "This is no time for games. I know you left the house last night. You were not in your room until almost four in the morning. Explain yourself."

Relief rushed through Claire. Fine. This she could handle.

"You're right, I wasn't here. But I wasn't with Matthew."

Her mother stared at her, waiting.

"I was with Zahlia. She was helping me—practicing with me so that I'd be ready for the next moon. Call her and check if you don't believe me." Claire crossed her arms in front of her.

Her mother pressed her lips together. Claire could tell she was mad, but she could also smell confusion, bright and almost electrical, coming off her.

"You were practicing? But you haven't completed your transformation yet. What would you be practicing?"

Claire shrugged. "Hunting, a little bit. And some other stuff she showed me how to do. It's no big deal, Mom. I wasn't going to tell anyone else, but I don't want to look like a moron when I transform, and that's exactly what will happen if I don't know how to do anything."

"I told you that I would teach you when the time is right.

You should have listened. Zahlia is not the sort of influence that you should have guiding your transformation. I want you to see less of her. I cannot command you—only Beatrice can do that. But I'm concerned that you two have grown too close. This is not just about you, you understand. If our relationships become too close, it is a risk for our pack. The more we associate with one another outside of pack business, the greater our chances of being discovered."

Claire frowned. "Well, I just ran into Victoria while I was with Emily at the coffee shop and she didn't act like I was a stranger or anything."

Marie clenched her jaw. "Why didn't you tell me sooner? What happened? What did you say to her?"

Each question scraped against Claire's nerves. She was getting really tired of her mother's personal version of the Inquisition.

"I didn't think it was a big deal. She said hi, I said hi. I told Emily that Victoria was someone you knew, which wasn't exactly giving anything away, since you know pretty much everyone. Victoria didn't act like I'd screwed anything up, so I don't know why you're freaking out."

"I'm not 'freaking out,' as you so eloquently put it. I'm trying to protect you. Any pack interaction in the human world is an occasion for caution. What if someone overheard something? If they became suspicious, they could make a report to the FHPA. And that would be disastrous. You see? This is exactly why I don't think you should be close with Zahlia. It's too easy to make a mistake."

Claire narrowed her eyes. "But—what about Beatrice and Victoria? They're close."

Her mother laughed softly and leaned against the bedpost. "That is true. But, then, they are mother and daughter."

Something Claire hadn't quite put together before slid into place in her mind.

"Why isn't everyone's mom part of the pack? I mean, you and I are related, and Victoria is Beatrice's daughter, but Zahlia and Judith and Katherine are all by themselves."

"Judith and Katherine moved here years ago, after their own mothers died—the packs in their areas became too small to survive. Zahlia's mother used to belong to our pack." Claire's mother twisted the sliver bangle on her wrist, her eyebrows sinking low over her eyes. "Her mother was second to Beatrice in our pack, and Zahlia was right behind her. But then—well. Something happened, and she left the pack to become a lone wolf, *une seule*. Zahlia also paid for her mother's carelessness by losing her own position. I became the second."

Claire blinked in surprise. "Wow. She never told me any of that."

"I imagine there are many things Zahlia hasn't told you. Which would be yet another reason for you to distance yourself from her."

"But she's the only one who's even answered my freaking

questions. I can't do this all by myself, and you never want to help me! I mean, Victoria has Beatrice, but I—" Claire snapped her mouth shut, cutting off the rest of the sentence.

"We have never been close, have we?" A wistful look crossed Marie's face.

Claire shrugged, staring down at her hands. "I guess not."

"It is hard, raising another while always hiding. You are right—I am your mother, and whether or not you believe it, I do want to help you. But only when the time is right, Claire. And right now the best help I can offer is to advise you to distance yourself from Zahlia."

"But it's not an order."

"Not now. But if I have to go to Beatrice, I will. So. I hope you will be joining Lisbeth and me for dinner tonight?"

Claire frowned. "Yeah, I guess."

"Good. I'll see you then."

Her mother left the room and Claire rolled over onto her stomach, burying her face in the comforter. Sometimes, she really, really hated her mom.

Just before dinner, Emily's car pulled up to the house. Claire hurried down the stairs to meet her.

"You're here! I thought I was going to have to say good-bye on the phone!"

Emily grinned. "I told them if I couldn't come see you, I was going to do something horrible."

"Like what?"

"I dunno." Emily shrugged. "They didn't ask—they're too freaked out to be logical at this point. I can only stay for a minute, though."

Tears filled Claire's eyes and she sniffed. "I can't believe you're really going."

Emily looked up at the ceiling and blinked. "It's not like I want to. Oh my God, I am not going to cry. I have on way too much mascara to start crying."

Claire swiped at her eyes, fighting to control herself. "I mean, hey, it's not like we aren't going to talk, right?"

"I made my parents switch my cell plan to unlimited minutes." Emily said proudly. "Okay. I have to go. I just came over to give you a hug."

Claire wrapped her arms around her best friend. How much different would she be by the time Emily got back?

*What if things are never like this again?*

"Hey, I said 'hug,' not 'crack my ribs,'" Emily said, straightening up and forcing a smile. "Call me, okay?"

"I will."

"So . . ."

"Don't say it. Just go."

"Yeah, you're right. Better that way." Emily slid on her sunglasses and walked out to the car.

Claire watched her go, the lump in her throat getting bigger with every step Emily took.

She didn't want to watch Emily drive away. Taking the stairs two at a time, Claire bolted up the steps and into her bedroom, where she could fall apart in private.

Three days later, Claire stood in her room, sorting dirty laundry into piles. She'd actually made it out of bed before noon, since she'd been stuck in the house for almost seventy-two hours, trying to make her mom less suspicious. Lisbeth had been so excited to see her while it was still morning that she'd made pancakes.

The phone rang and Claire looked at the screen. *Crap*.

"Hello?" she braced herself.

"Thanks a *lot*," Emily huffed.

"Sorry?" As usual, Emily was going so fast that Claire couldn't keep up right away.

"Well, you should be. I've been stuck out here for almost a freaking *week* and you haven't called me once! What kind of best friend is that?"

Claire winced. "Sorry. The time just got away from me, I guess. Things have been pretty crazy around here."

"Thanks for rubbing it in. You're right there in the middle of all the excitement, and I'm stuck out in cow-pie central with no Internet connection."

*Right in the middle of all the excitement. Man, she has no idea how close she is to the truth.*

"It's pretty bad, huh?" Claire asked.

"Oh, my *God*, they have the Farmers' Almanac on the coffee table, like it's the damn Bible or something. My aunt cooks stuff in lard, Claire. *Lard.* Do you know what that *is*? And this morning," she sniffled, "there was a mouse in the bathroom."

Emily sounded so pathetic, but Claire couldn't help but think how minor her best friend's problems really were. Emily hadn't turned into an animal. No one was hunting her. And the biggest secret she had to keep was the fact that she had a pack of cigarettes hiding in the pocket of an old bathrobe.

It didn't matter how much Claire wanted to feel sorry for Emily—jealousy gnawed on her insides, eating up any room she might have had for sympathy.

"Claire? Hello? Are you there? Damn it!"

"No—I mean—yeah, I'm here. You've still got a signal."

"Thank God. I have to sit on top of the kitchen table and lean toward the window to get two stupid bars. I'll probably have to go a freaking chiropractor if my parents ever decide to let me come home."

"Any chance of that happening?" Claire asked.

"I don't think so," Emily moaned. "Not until they catch the werewolf, anyway. I swear, I hate that stupid thing more than Dr. Engle does."

Claire sagged against the bedpost. *She doesn't know what she's saying. If she knew, she wouldn't feel that way at all.* Claire struggled against the urge to tell Emily what was going on.

The only thing that stopped her was the memory of last year, when Emily ruined two separate surprise parties because she couldn't stand to keep a secret.

"So, is there anything at all about being at your aunt and uncle's that doesn't suck?" Claire asked, anxious to get away from the subject.

"Well," Emily hedged, "there might be *one* tiny thing."

"Might that thing have two legs and a dimple?"

"Yes on the legs, no on the dimple," Emily admitted. "His name's Dan . . . I dunno, Claire, he's so . . . wholesome. He's gorgeous and funny and we met because he actually opened the door for me, but . . . it's weird. I mean, when we went out to dinner last night, he had *milk* with his meal. Whole milk. And he calls my uncle 'sir.' I just don't know if he's really my type."

"But you like him?" Claire asked.

"Yeah, I like him," Emily sighed.

Even though it had been days since she'd talked to Emily, the next twenty minutes crawled by. Listening to her friend debate the pros and cons of getting involved with a guy who didn't know who Chagall was and had never had anything pierced was so far from everything that was going on with Claire that she couldn't think of anything to say. Which was especially strange, since the two of them had had this same conversation every time Emily liked a new guy. Claire hadn't felt this abnormal since the first night she'd transformed, and she paced around the room, trying to get away from the feeling.

"Claire, I've gotta go. My aunt wants to set the table, and I'm sitting on it."

Claire closed her eyes in silent thanks. "Sorry, Em. Keep me updated, okay?"

"Yeah, yeah, yeah."

Emily hung up and Claire flopped back on the bed, the tension draining out of her body. She sighed and sat back up to finish sorting her dirty clothes. No matter how badly she wished things were normal again, it just wasn't going to happen.

Almost a week went by, and Hanover Falls breathed a collective sigh of relief. No one else had been killed. It had been nearly a month since the editor's death, and on the evening news they spent as much time talking about the unprecedented heat wave as they did covering the unsolved murders.

Ever since their discussion about Zahlia, Claire had been avoiding her mother as much as possible, pretending things were fine, but later that afternoon, while Lisbeth was at the grocery store, Marie stopped her in the kitchen.

"We need to talk again, *chérie*."

"Hey, it's been ages since I even left the stupid house, much less seen someone you don't want me to. I haven't done anything wrong."

"I did not say that you had, Claire. There's no reason to jump to conclusions."

"So, what's up?" Claire asked. She was anxious to get out of the kitchen and away from her mother's probing gaze.

Her mother sat down at the island.

"You know what night next Tuesday is, yes?"

Claire's heart sped up. "It's the full moon."

"Yes. And I want to prepare you a bit for the gathering. It will be . . . somewhat different than it usually is." Her mother pulled an elastic hair band off the granite countertop and stretched it taut between her fingers. "It is time for our pack to expand. Victoria has had"—she cleared her throat—"she has encountered a man. She is pregnant. We find out on Sunday if she will have a New One." Claire's mother squeezed her shoulder.

"What do you mean? If she's pregnant, she's having a baby, right?" Claire stuck out her lower lip in confusion.

Worried creases appeared at the corners of her mother's eyes. "Not necessarily. If she is pregnant with a male, the fetus will not be able to withstand the stress of her transformation, and her pregnancy will end."

"You mean . . ." Claire let the question trail off.

"If it is a male child, then Victoria will lose the baby. If it is a New One she carries in her womb, then her pregnancy will proceed." Her mother twisted the hair band between her fingers.

"How long does it take after she changes? If it's a boy, I mean."

"It begins immediately."

Claire's mouth opened. *Jesus.* The idea that she might have to watch Victoria lose her baby sent nausea spiraling through her. She tried to cover her shock. "So, what's different if it's a girl? How does her body know?"

Her mother shrugged. "We can't be certain. Our legends say that the Goddess knows and protects Her own Unborn. But it is perhaps hormonal, chemical."

Claire thought for a moment. "Does everyone—I mean, do we all have to have a baby? Eventually?"

Her mother shook her head. "No. Many of us have a child. But not all. The Goddess has Her own plans for each of us."

The set of her mother's mouth and the stiffness in her shoulders said to Claire that the topic was closed for conversation.

"Well, thanks for telling me, I guess. Victoria must be really nervous, huh?"

"I'm sure she is. Well. I've got some work to do. Try not to leave an enormous mess in here for Lisbeth, hmm?" She slid off the stool and walked toward the stairs.

Claire leaned against the fridge and sighed. Things just kept getting better and better.

# Chapter Eleven

THE NEXT MORNING, Claire found Lisbeth outside by the pool, lying in the sun with an unopened book on the table next to her. When Claire sat down next to her, Lisbeth lifted her sunglasses.

"Hey, what's up?"

Claire hesitated, hoping that her new system of telling absolutely as much of the truth as she could would work again. "Not much. Well, something, actually. I got invited to this party on Friday night—at Doug Kingman's house? And I was hoping you could drive me."

Lisbeth squinted at her. "That name doesn't sound familiar."

"He goes to school with me. We didn't hang out much last year, but . . ." Claire trailed off.

"But?" Lisbeth raised her eyebrows and grinned. "Oooh—you like him, don't you?"

Claire couldn't stop herself from smiling. Lisbeth had just given her the perfect cover.

"Um, yeah," Claire said, hoping it sounded like a confession. And it wasn't like she *didn't* like Doug, she just didn't know him all that well.

"Matthew-schmatthew." Lisbeth giggled. "You got over him in no time, huh?"

Claire shrugged. If she said anything, she might make Lisbeth suspicious.

"So—will you take me to the party?"

"Yeah, I can do that. What time does it start?"

"Seven thirty." A smile spread across Claire's face.

"Will it be over before dark?" Lisbeth frowned.

"Well . . . no, but, Lisbeth, there'll be a million people there. And we'll be inside. I'll be as safe there as I would be here."

Lisbeth sighed. "Okay. I don't love it, but as long as you agree to be careful, I guess it's all right with me."

"I'll be careful," Claire promised. She stood up and half-skipped to the door. As soon as she got up to her room, she grabbed her phone and called Matthew. It went straight to voicemail, and Claire realized that he was probably at soccer practice.

"Hey," she said, "it's me. Guess what? I talked Lisbeth into letting me go to Doug's! She's dropping me off at seven thirty. Good news, huh? Anyway, I just wanted to call and say I'll see you there."

She hung up and headed to the closet, wondering what on earth she was going to wear.

*The soft tick of snapping twigs moved through the forest ahead of her. When would that fool ever learn to move silently? Her own feet made no noise as she wove through the trees, moving closer and closer to the edge of the woods. She stopped and doubled back. The scent trail hit her like a slap in the face. It reeked of determination, bitter somehow, with an edge of something almost like ammonia. The rich musk of self-importance cut through it, mixing unpleasantly with the first smell.*

*She allowed herself a small, victorious snuffle, almost inaudible beneath the ruffling leaves. Stupid, egotistical bitch. She deserved whatever happened to her.*

On Friday night, Lisbeth pulled up in front of Doug's driveway, which was packed with cars. Half the street was full too. Claire swallowed hard. She'd been so excited to see Matthew that she hadn't really thought about all the other people who would be there. Even though things had gone okay at the diner, it still made her nervous to walk into a roomful of incredibly popular people.

"Well, are you going or not?" Lisbeth teased.

"Yeah, of course." Claire opened the door and slid out. If she backed out now, Lisbeth might get suspicious. She'd just have to suck it up and hope that she didn't get laughed out of the room when everyone saw her walk in.

"I'll pick you up at eleven," Lisbeth called.

"I'll be ready." Claire shut the door, smoothed her hair, and walked up to the house. She knocked once, but there was so much noise inside that no one heard her. After a couple of deep breaths, she opened the door and stepped in. The living room was full of people huddled in small groups. In the corner, a CD player thudded away next to a table with bottles of soda and bowls of chips and pretzels. Claire hesitated in the front hall and took another deep breath. The smell of cheap alcohol tinged the air, and Claire realized that not everyone had soda in their red plastic cups.

Across the room, Kate-Marie Brown caught sight of Claire and curled her lip. She turned to whisper something to the blond girl next to her, and Claire felt her heart stutter in her chest.

*Okay, so this was definitely a huge mistake. I don't know what I was thinking when we were at mini-golf, because I really, really don't belong here.*

A warm arm wrapped around her waist and pulled her against a familiar body. "Hey, there," Matthew murmured in her ear. "I've been dying for you to get here."

Claire twisted around, looking up into his sparkling eyes. "It's really good to see you, too," she said, meaning every word.

She shouldn't be worried about Kate-Marie or anyone else. They were all just . . . *humans*, right? Claire caught her breath, startled by her own thought.

Matthew frowned, catching the sudden change in her mood. "Are you okay?"

"I'm fine. A little thirsty, maybe."

"Then let me get you something to drink. Do you want it spiked or unspiked?" He stepped toward the table with the cups and raised his eyebrows at her.

"Something diet and unspiked, please." She hoped her answer wouldn't make him think she was a total dork. Then again, he hadn't smelled like he'd been drinking, and she'd been plenty close enough to tell.

"No problem. I'll be right back."

Matthew worked his way across the room, stopping to slap a couple of guys on the back and to greet a cluster of girls that were staring at him. The girls practically fell over themselves flirting with him, and jealousy gripped Claire, squeezing her ribs until she couldn't breathe.

Her self-control was slipping, and panic rose in her chest. She could feel her wolf-form pushing against the too-thin layer of her human skin. What if she changed without meaning to, the way she had in her room that first day? She forced herself to unclench her hands. The backs of her hands were still smooth. Just because her heart was twitching against her ribs was no reason to freak out.

The smells around her suddenly intensified, and the urge to flee became too strong to ignore. She had to find some place to calm down, somewhere away from all these people. While Matthew's back was to her, Claire slipped out of the room and down the back hall. She opened the first door she came to and breathed a sigh of relief. It was empty. And decorated in princesses. She'd found Doug's baby sister's room. Claire closed the door behind her and sat down on the edge of the bed.

After a few deep breaths, the haze of panic started to clear. Claire stood up and ran a hand over her hair. A few more seconds, and she'd be ready to go back out there.

The door opened and Matthew poked his head in. He had a cup in each hand.

"Hey—I wondered where you'd gone. Everything okay?"

Heat rushed into Claire's cheeks. The last thing she wanted was for Matthew to know that she'd freaked out. She wanted to lie to him, to tell him she'd taken a wrong turn on the way to the bathroom.

Claire shrugged. "It was just a little claustrophobic in there. I needed some air."

Matthew stepped into the room and set down the drinks on the nightstand. He stood close enough to her that Claire swallowed hard.

"So, are you feeling any better?"

"Not really," she admitted. Damn, why was it so hard to lie to him?

"Then let's get out of here," Matthew whispered.

Claire's pulse sped up, and a little glow of anticipation sparked in her middle.

"Really?" she asked.

He leaned in. "Of course. What I really want is to spend time with you. Just you. And since we don't have a lot of opportunities to do that, maybe we should take advantage of what we've got, you know?"

Claire nodded. Half of her was jumping up and down with excitement, but the other half was worried. "Won't it look weird if we leave?"

"Nah," he murmured. "Most of them are three drinks in already. They won't notice if the couch is on fire."

He was right—Claire hadn't really thought about that.

"So, how come you're not drinking?" The question popped out before she stopped to think about how it sounded. She bit the tip of her tongue and winced.

Matthew shrugged. "Too risky. I get caught drinking, I'm off the soccer team. And that means no scholarships, no college team. I'd be stuck going to community college and living with my parents. And that is definitely *not* part of my plan."

He smiled at her.

"Come on," he said, grabbing her free hand. "Let's get out of here."

They headed down the hall and through the living room. Claire was so tense that the back of her neck was practically an armored plate. She could feel everyone sizing her up, judging her. Matthew edged them toward the front door without being obvious about it.

Once the front hall was empty, the two of them slipped out the front door into the almost-dark, and Claire was pretty sure no one had seen them.

The night was quiet after the shouting and music of the party. They were alone. Really alone.

"Thanks for the rescue. So, um, where are we going?" she asked as they walked toward Matthew's car.

"Wherever you want," Matthew answered, pulling her in close.

"What about that coffee shop over on Fourth Street? The one next to the bookstore? Emily and I hang out there a lot." As soon as she said it, Claire remembered that the last time she'd been there, she'd run into Victoria. Crap. What if she was there again?

Matthew smiled at her. "That sounds great."

There were very few cars out—people really were staying home after dark these days. When they got to Fourth Street, Claire could see that the little row of businesses were all dark, the coffee shop included. Matthew slowed down as they passed it. A bright-pink piece of paper had been taped to the inside of the shop's glass door.

"'Temporary New Hours,'" Claire read, "'ten a.m. to six p.m.'"

"You can see that from here?" Matthew's voice was incredulous. "I must need my eyes checked."

*Oops. Damn.*

"It's closer to my side of the car," Claire offered. "I didn't think about them being closed."

There was a flutter of movement at the far end of the row of businesses. Claire blinked at it as Matthew's car drew closer. It was a person.

Oh, God. It wasn't just a person. It was Lisbeth. She was walking down the sidewalk. Claire couldn't figure out why she would be here when everything was closed. Lisbeth turned to look at Matthew's approaching car.

Claire slid down in the seat so fast that her knees banged against the dashboard.

"Claire?" Matthew sounded shocked, and the almost-bitter smell of worry filled the car.

"It's Lisbeth!" Claire hissed. "Just—keep driving and tell me when you can't see her anymore, okay?"

"Oh, crap." Matthew sped up a little, and Claire stayed hunched down into the seat. Her legs had started to ache from being crunched into such a weird position. In her back pocket, Claire's cell phone started to ring. She managed to wriggle it out at the same time that Matthew turned a corner. Lisbeth's number was lit up on the caller ID.

"Nooooo," Claire moaned.

"Don't answer it," Matthew suggested.

"She'll be *furious*," Claire said. But if she answered in the quiet car, Lisbeth would know that she wasn't at the party. She was screwed.

"Wait fifteen minutes and then text her." Matthew suggested. "Tell her you couldn't hear the phone because it was so loud—that it's too loud to talk."

Claire licked her lips and nodded. Lisbeth would be mad, but she'd probably buy that. The phone in her hand beeped as the call went to voicemail, making her decision for her.

"You can scoot up now," Matthew said. "We're far enough away."

Claire slid back up in the seat. "Do you think she saw me?"

Matthew shook his head. "I think probably she saw *me* and got suspicious, you know?"

Claire leaned her head back against the seat. "I'm so sorry, Matthew. If my mom weren't being so stupid about all of this . . . ugh. I'm just sorry that I'm making you sneak around, I guess."

Matthew shrugged. "Look, I'd rather be honest about all of this, too, but my dad has screwed up enough stuff in my life that I totally understand. And who knows? Maybe she'll change her mind once this werewolf stuff calms down."

"I seriously doubt that. My mother doesn't change her mind."

"Well, either way." Matthew stopped at a red light. He

reached over and touched her face, his hand tracing the shape of her jaw. "It's worth it, either way."

They drove around for a while, marveling at the fact that everything really was closed at night. Matthew didn't seem to be nervous about being out after dark, which surprised Claire.

"Aren't you worried about the werewolf?" she asked.

"Well, we *are* in a car," he pointed out. "So we'd be faster than the werewolf. But mostly, I just think that the odds of being in exactly the wrong place at exactly the wrong time— they're pretty small. I wouldn't go for a hike right now, but driving around town? Nope. Not nervous about that. And anyway, you're here, which means you must not be terrified either, right?"

A little shock zinged through Claire. She hadn't really considered that he would turn the question back around on her. "Um, no, I'm not. For the same reasons you just said, really. Oh, crap!" She looked at the clock. "I'd better text Lisbeth."

Lisbeth *was* pissed, but she seemed to believe that Claire was still at Doug's. Claire felt bad about lying to her, but, she reasoned, she wouldn't be doing it if her mother would listen to reason. As it was, she didn't have any other choice.

Since nothing was open, they ended up driving aimlessly around town, talking about everything and nothing at the same time. When they ended up back on Doug's block, Claire looked at the clock. It was quarter till eleven. How had so much time gone by so fast? From the street, the music coming from inside was just a whisper of bass. Claire leaned back in the seat and sighed. She really, really didn't want to go in there and face everyone, even if Matthew was with her.

He leaned over and kissed her. Claire could feel him smiling.

"Come on," he said. "Let's go see who's still conscious in there."

"Okay," she whispered, still a little tingly from the feeling of his lips against hers.

If Matthew was with her, it wouldn't be that bad. And it was only fifteen minutes, right? The two of them walked across the front lawn and into the house. There were still small groups of people scattered though the family room, but their conversations were louder, and there were a couple of people passed out on the couches.

Claire stayed near the windows, watching for Lisbeth's car. The last thing she needed was Lisbeth coming up to the house—she'd be in twelve kinds of trouble for sure. When the car pulled up outside, Claire ran for the front hall.

"I'll call you later," she said, as Matthew quickly kissed her good-bye.

"Hey, Engle!" The slurred call came from somewhere in the living room. "Get your ass over here—we need a fourth for poker!"

Matthew laughed and headed back into the party while

Claire opened the door and darted across the dark lawn. She slid into Lisbeth's car.

"Now I believe you couldn't hear the phone—if the music's that loud out here, it must have been deafening in there!" Lisbeth shook her head. "So, did you have fun?"

Claire sighed. "I dunno. Sort of, I guess." It was true. The time she'd spent with Matthew had been amazing, but the rest of the party stuff had been pretty torturous.

"And what about Doug?" Lisbeth asked, her voice heavy with meaning.

Claire shrugged. She looked over at Lisbeth, wondering what she'd been doing on Fourth Street. "So, what did you do while I was gone? Anything fun?" she asked.

"Nah," said Lisbeth. "I went home and read for a while. That's about it."

"Oh." Claire turned to stare out the window. Everything was off tonight. Lisbeth was lying to her. Claire had lied to pretty much everybody. And Matthew—how could she date someone who was the center of attention when she was always trying to hide?

She slumped down in the seat and wondered if maybe her mother was right, even though her reasons were wrong. The thought made her stomach as heavy as a bowling ball, but maybe it really was impossible for her and Matthew to be together. What if she just ended up making him miserable?

Then again, maybe she should let him make his own

decisions about how he wanted to spend his time. He was the one who suggested they leave, just the two of them. It was possible that she was just being oversensitive. Overreacting.

Claire leaned against the glass and sighed. Things would be a lot simpler if she didn't like him so much. Or if she were just a normal human, like everyone else.

*But no,* I *get to be a werewolf. Just freaking great.*

# Chapter Twelve

THE NEXT FEW days dragged on forever. All Claire could think about was that every passing hour brought her closer to Tuesday night's full moon.

By the time the sun sank behind the trees on Monday, Claire was pacing her room, wondering why Matthew hadn't called back, worrying about what the next night would be like. She was so tense that her teeth ached. She had to get into the woods. Maybe if she could run for a while, could practice a little—maybe then she'd feel better about everything.

When everyone else had gone to bed, Claire crept out of the house. Sneaking out wasn't nearly as scary as it had been before. She knew where every creaky stair was, and just how far she could open the back door before it squeaked. In no time, Claire was in the little clearing she'd started to think of as hers—not nearly as big as where the pack met, but still. It was big enough to practice in. She wished she'd called Zahlia. It would have been nice to have someone to hang out with while she practiced. The scent of the pine needles tickled her nose when she bent to pull off her shoes. It smelled good. Comfortable.

When her socks were draped over a low branch, Claire stretched up and rolled her head from side to side. Her feet had changed so much that when she was in her wolf-form, her shoes didn't fit. Besides, she could run faster without them—it would be easier to get away if she heard something coming.

*And, anyway, we're the scariest things out here. That's one good thing about being a werewolf, I guess. You don't have to be afraid of so much stuff anymore.*

Claire thought about Matthew's dad. The stuff she was frightened of now was a hell of a lot more terrifying, actually. She shook her head to clear it and forced herself to focus.

The change came faster this time. Claire huddled on the ground for a minute, waiting for the adrenaline rush of trans-forming to pass. Even though she could transform faster, she still looked pretty much the same as she had that first night—mostly human. She swallowed hard, thinking about the next night's gathering. How much different would she look in twenty-four hours?

When her pulse had finally slowed after the stress of the change, Claire lifted her nose and sniffed. The forest smelled so much better when she was in her wolf-form. More complicated. The edginess she'd felt all afternoon still scratched in her chest, and Claire streaked off into the woods, determined to run it out.

After three sprints to the gathering clearing and back, her ribs were heaving. She lay on the ground underneath one of the pine trees and forced herself to take deep breaths. She felt great—exhausted, but great.

Claire closed her eyes and thought of Matthew.

"No, man, it's too late. I'll call her tomorrow. I don't want her to think I'm a totally inconsiderate ass."

The voice made her jump. Shaking herself, she realized she must have been listening to him, the same way she'd done with Lisbeth. Claire closed her eyes and concentrated on his voice.

"Yeah, see, there's just no way I'm telling you that."

There was a pause.

"Because I like her. A lot. I've never met anyone like her before, and I'm not going to screw things up by talking to *you* about *that*." Matthew sounded exasperated.

Claire rolled onto her feet and danced around in a little circle. He was talking about her. He had to be. But she couldn't hear him anymore. Crap. She'd dropped her concentration.

She sat back down and tried to hear him again, forcing herself to stay focused on his warm, rich voice. But it was no good. Either he'd quit talking or she needed more practice.

Claire sighed and forced herself back into her human form. She might as well quit while she was ahead, anyway. Matthew's words left a little warm spot in her belly that glowed all the way home.

When dark fell on Tuesday, Claire was surprised to find that she was more relieved than anything. Whatever was going to happen, at least she could quit feeling so anxious about it.

Lisbeth knocked on her door.

"Yeah?"

Her blond head poked around the door. She was dressed for yoga, but Claire noticed she was wearing turquoise earrings, and the scent of lavender body lotion wafted into the room.

"I'm going to class. I'll be back by ten, okay?"

Claire looked surprised. "They're having yoga at night?"

"It's just for tonight. A special thing, kind of."

"Oh, well, have fun, then."

Lisbeth closed the door behind her. The scent of some emotion lingered in the room, but there was still so much lavender body lotion smell that Claire couldn't tell what Lisbeth had been feeling.

She looked at the empty room and sighed. Her mother had shut herself in the darkroom after dinner, and there was nothing to do but wait. Reality shows and commercials blared from the television behind her, but Claire stared at the shadows on the lawn, willing them to lengthen. She could feel the fur itching underneath her skin.

A couple of hours after Lisbeth bounced up the stairs to announce that she was home and going to bed, Claire heard her mother's soft knock. They crept down the stairs and out the back door in silence. When they were safely hidden in the deep woods, Claire's mother turned to her.

"Claire, this is your second moon. You know that the change will be more complete for you this time, yes?"

She nodded. "How much different will it be?" she whispered.

Her mother shrugged. "It is unique for each of us. At your next moon you will change fully, but this time—there is no way to know for sure." She stared into the woods, listening. "Are you ready?"

Claire nodded nervously and followed her mother farther into the trees. Eventually, the firelight flickered in the distance—they were close. Claire could see Beatrice, Victoria, Judith, and Katherine already in the clearing.

When she and her mother broke through the circle of trees, Victoria looked up at them, her face painted with fear. She threw her arms around Claire's mother.

"Marie, I greet you." Victoria's voice shook. She hugged Claire and greeted her.

"It was good to see you at the coffee shop—you handled yourself perfectly, you know."

"Oh—um, thanks. It was good to see you, too."

Judith and Katherine skimmed their eyes over Claire the same way they had last time. It was like she was half-transparent to them. She fought an urge to roll her eyes.

Claire scanned the trees for any sign of Zahlia. The shadows were empty and still.

She turned to Beatrice. Anxiety tightened the wrinkles around the old woman's eyes.

Once they had greeted each other, Victoria sniffed at the air. "Where is Zahlia? She can't be late—not tonight of all nights!"

Beatrice eased herself off the log where she had been sitting and stood by the fire.

"We'll have to start without her, I'm afraid."

Claire arranged herself around the edge of the fire with the others. The idea of transforming in front of everyone sent needles of panic shooting through Claire's limbs, even though she'd done it once before. She wished Zahlia were there— she'd feel a lot more comfortable. Her concern immediately turned to guilt. It didn't seem right to be worrying about how she looked. Victoria could lose her baby any second.

Beatrice raised her wrinkled hands and took a breath.

Before she could begin the chant, an enormous black wolf streaked into the forest, her lips flecked with white foam and her pelt marred with twigs and burrs. Zahlia had arrived.

Claire watched as Zahlia forced herself back into her human skin. She stayed on all fours on the forest floor, her ribs heaving and her black hair dripping sweat. Without bothering to greet any of them formally, she lifted her head and looked at Beatrice. "We are not alone in the forest. There is a *seule*—I smelled her on my way here, and when I approached, she ran. She headed east, toward town." Zahlia rose to her feet, still panting, her eyes wild.

Claire felt her mother shift into a tense posture. Victoria looked torn, her lip caught between her teeth and her hands curled into fists at her sides. Only Beatrice remained calm.

"What does it mean, that she's here?" Claire asked tentatively.

"A wolf without a pack is rare but not unheard of." Her mother's voice was flat. "Often they are frightened, or dangerous. Sometimes both."

"Of course," Zahlia said, her voice still breathless. "But this time, it may be more than that. She could be the one who is killing humans in town. We must catch her—question her. We cannot let this one go silently."

"And we would hunt her to what end?" asked Judith, her hands on her hips. "Force her to join us? Demand she leave? Kill her?"

"I don't think Zahlia was going to suggest tearing off into the woods without a plan." Katherine pursed her lips. "But this doesn't seem like the best time for strategizing."

Beatrice stared into the fire for a moment, her hands raised, then shut her milky eyes.

"This ceremony cannot be delayed. We determine the fate of Victoria's child, and then we will track the stranger."

The scent of disappointment—bitter, almost charred—wafted off Zahlia as she slunk into place.

"Heya, Claire," she muttered. "Everything okay?"

Claire nodded and her mother shot Zahlia a poison-dart look. Beatrice began to chant. Across the circle, Victoria sat with her arms wrapped around her midsection, staring hard into the fire. Her lips were pinched and tears sparkled in the corners of her eyes.

Without warning, Beatrice began a new chant. The others swayed slightly with the trancelike rhythm of the words, and the fire in the center of their circle began to change.

The flames no longer flickered at random. Instead, they began a slow, steady swirl, parting to reveal the logs underneath, and then drawing back together, each time rising higher and higher. As Beatrice's chanting reached a frantic peak the fire rose high enough to scorch the branches of the trees. Across the clearing, Claire saw her mother, shimmering as her form began to alter.

Claire hurried to undress, stumbling when she tried to yank

off her sweatpants too fast. *Please don't let anyone have noticed that.* She should have been practicing the clothes part, too. Her embarrassment washed away when she began to change.

The transformation took Claire's breath away. She felt her too-tight skin melt away faster and more completely than it ever had. Fur erupted all over her body, and her hands and feet took on a cramped, misshapen look. Her arms and legs were caught somewhere between human and animal, and with a start, Claire realized that the sudden heaviness at her lower back was a thick tail.

No one paid any attention to the fact that she was incomplete—they were all staring at Victoria. The hazel wolf sat in front of the fire with her eyes closed.

No one breathed.

No one moved.

*Oh!* Victoria sucked in a sharp breath and bared her teeth. Sorrow swooped down on the group like a black-winged bird.

*Oh, no—it's not—I mean, I'm okay! There's no pain! Oh, it's a girl.* Victoria let out a gasp. Her tongue lolled out of her mouth and she began to pant. *Oh, thank you, thank you, thank you, thank you.* She rocked back and forth again and again in relief.

Beatrice threw back her gray-muzzled head and *yipped* in delight. Claire's mother and Zahlia immediately followed suit, with Judith and Katherine coming in a half second later. The five wolves surrounded Victoria, butting up against her and nudging her flank with their snouts. Silky fur covered every inch of their skin and their sharp teeth fit neatly into their jaws. None of their paws were tipped with pink-painted human fingernails. But Claire's were.

She hung back, embarrassed by her own half-changed appearance and the sympathetic tears that trickled down her cheeks.

*Oh, Goddess, I look hideous.* She felt the thick rope of muscle in her tail twitch as it curved underneath her body in shame. Claire hung her head, keening a strange, canine whine. A whiff of frustration, tangy and sharp, made her lift her eyes back to the group.

Claire's mother looked at her and dropped her ears the tiniest bit.

*Do not be rude,* chérie. *Come and congratulate Victoria.*

*Oh, lay off her, Marie.* Zahlia huffed and shook her head. *Like any of us had to deal with this much on our second moon. Give her a minute.*

*You have no right to tell me what to expect of my daughter!* Claire's mother's ears were laid flat back against her skull.

*Cut it out, you two—this is no time to argue.* Victoria looked over at Claire. *Come celebrate! Good Goddess, you look wonderful. You should have seen me at my second moon—my fur was so patchy, it looked like I had mange! Your fur's all the way in—that's so lucky! I'm so lucky.* She rolled over onto her back and wriggled against the dusty ground. She looked maniacally happy. *Can you believe it? I'm having a baby!*

Claire slunk over to Victoria on her awkward limbs as the others moved back to their places around the fire, still barking and keening in celebration. Her tail dragged on the ground, catching stray twigs as she walked. With her half-changed head, Claire butted Victoria's shoulder as gently as she could.

*Just think,* Victoria nipped at Claire's furred ear, *in nine months, there will be eight of us!*

Victoria's words sent a shiver of unease through the group, distracting Claire. She turned to her mother, curious, but before she could form the question, her mother shook her sleek-furred head at Claire, ever so slightly.

Beatrice snapped her jaw shut and sat neatly in front of the fire. *Victoria, go home and get some sleep. The rest of us will track the seule.*

*Why? I feel wonderful. I'll go help with the tracking.* Victoria stood, her tail wagging happily behind her.

*Absolutely not. If this seule is dangerous enough to kill humans, then she will not hesitate to attack one of us if we try to stop her. We would be putting the life of your baby in unnecessary danger. I know you can track. But tonight you will not. I want you to ensure Claire gets home safely, and then I want you to go rest.* The authority that rang in Beatrice's command was unmistakable, and Victoria bowed her head, her tail curving underneath her body. Beatrice turned her milky eyes to Claire.

*Do you know your way out of the forest?*

The tilt of the old wolf's head told Claire that this was not so much a question as a command. Claire's half-changed nose scented the path she and her mother had taken through the woods earlier. She looked over at her mother and her stomach lurched at the idea of going home without her. What if something happened to her mother while they were hunting the *seule*? What if it attacked her mother? Or Zahlia? The idea of one of them getting hurt—or worse—made her sick.

"Can't I go, too?" Her half-human voice sounded strange in the clearing. Behind her, Katherine let out an irritated snort.

Beatrice's ear twitched. *At the next moon, you would have been able to go with us. But half-changed you would hinder us far more than you would help us. I'm sorry, Claire.*

Claire opened her mouth to protest, but Marie's voice filled her head, stopping her. *Our pack has survived without you for sixteen years, Claire. Tonight will be no different. Go home and wait for me.*

"Okay," Claire whispered.

Zahlia tilted her head to one side in a can't-win-'em-all gesture. Then the five wolves turned and disappeared into the trees like smoke, their noses twitching in anticipation. Claire looked at Victoria. Victoria pressed her ears back until they were flat against her head. Fear flickered across her face as she scanned the trees. Just by looking at her, by smelling her tangy, damp scent on the breeze, Claire knew that Victoria was suddenly terrified to go through the woods—that her pregnancy made her feel vulnerable.

"I'll be okay on my own if you'd rather just go home," Claire said.

Victoria licked her lips. *No—Beatrice told me to take you home. We have to listen to her, Claire. She's our Alpha—her word is law. I'll be okay. Having a violent* seule *around just makes me nervous. I hadn't really thought about it that way, before my mother forbid me to go, but she's right. I have to protect this baby.*

"If you're sure . . ." Claire hesitated. She knew Beatrice was supposed to be obeyed, but she hated to make Victoria stay in the woods any longer than she had to.

*It'll be fine. Really, as long as we're not hunting her, she won't want to bother us. We'll be safe, I promise. Let's go.*

Before she could second-guess herself again, Claire grabbed her clothes in her half-changed mouth, turned, and scampered into the trees. Every time a twig cracked in the distance, Victoria's head jerked up, away from the scent Claire and her mother had left along their path, and her ears swiveled back and forth, listening for any sign of the *seule*.

Victoria was so nervous that Claire started to get jumpy, too. What she needed was a distraction.

"So, it's really great about the baby, huh?"

Victoria whined. *It is. As long as I can keep her safe, it will be wonderful.*

Claire grimaced. She'd been hoping for more of an I-can't-wait-to-buy-baby-clothes reaction.

*Sorry. I know I'm being twitchy.*

"It's okay. Hey—thanks for saying that I did okay at the coffee shop. I think Mom secretly believed that I actually jumped up and down and shouted about how glad I was to see another werewolf."

Victoria let out an amused *whuffling* sort of noise. *I'm sure Marie doesn't mean to be so hard on you. She just doesn't want to see you go through the pain of making mistakes, you know?*

"Yeah. Maybe." Or maybe not.

*One day, you'll understand. The beginning is hard for everyone.*

Victoria picked up the pace, and Claire struggled to keep up with her. By the time Claire made it back to the edge of the forest, she was panting with exertion. It took her two tries to force herself back into her human skin.

Claire looked back at Victoria. "Be careful going home."

Victoria cocked her head and flicked her ears, but since Claire was in her human form, she couldn't understand what the golden-brown wolf was saying. With a wave, Claire slipped through the opening in the wall and pressed herself against the ivy-covered brick. Relief flooded through her—she'd made it home, at least. All that was left to do was slip back into the house and wait for her mother to join her.


Claire sat in the dark kitchen, watched the microwave clock count away the night, and wondered what the hell was going on in the woods. An hour passed, then two. Exhausted, Claire put her head down on the table and stared at the glowing green numbers with heavy eyes.

A warm hand shook her shoulder and Claire started awake, confused. "Wha—"

"Ssshh," her mother warned her. "Don't wake Lisbeth. We must get you into bed, *chérie*. It is nearly dawn."

Claire glanced out the window at the graying sky. "Did you find her?" she whispered.

Marie shook her head, her lips pressed into a thin line. "No, the trail was unclear, and we split up to track her, but we came too close to town to search any further. We won't know what happened until the town wakes." She rubbed a hand across her eyes. "Go to sleep, Claire." Her voice filled with weariness. "These things will still be here to deal with in the morning, and we will meet with the pack a few nights from now to discuss what should be done."

# Chapter Thirteen

THE MOONLIGHT GLEAMED against her pale skin as she ran naked though the woods, celebrating. She'd confused all of them—led them on a wild goose chase until one by one they dropped away. Stupid packs with their stupid rules and stupid loyalties. None of them knew what it really meant to be a wolf. None of them knew how to treat humans like the playthings they really were.

She hadn't intended to kill anyone tonight, but she was still so high from the chase. And that moron had been so eager to see what the noise was outside. Holding that gun like it would help him. She barked gleefully, the sound bouncing off the trees around her. His finger hadn't even twitched on the trigger.

*Now that she knew they were all fooled, it was time to make the next move—time to lure the one she'd grown to hate most into the trap that she had set so perfectly. To make it work, she just needed that greedy little man, Dr. Engle, to get angry enough to take matters into his own hands. And when he'd caught her enemy, put the blame of so many deaths on her head . . . well. She'd never have to worry about that particular wolf again.*

Claire lay in bed, watching the pink dawn creep across the sky. There was no way she could go back to sleep—not after everything that had happened. When Claire heard Lisbeth banging around in the kitchen, she slid out of bed.

Lisbeth stood in front of the stove, scrambling a pan of tofu and peppers. At the kitchen table, Marie sat in front of a plate of limp bacon, her hand wrapped around an enormous mug of coffee. She stared at the television set with bleary eyes.

"Morning, Claire!" Lisbeth chirped. "You're up early. Want some juice? I put some ginger in it today—it gives it a little extra zip, I think." Lisbeth held out a pitcher of revolting-looking green sludge. The smell of wheatgrass and spinach hit Claire like a slap. *Man, she's really perky this morning. . . .*

Claire shook her head and stumbled over to the coffeepot. She poured herself a huge mug full and dumped two heaping spoonfuls of sugar into it. Once the first sip had burned its way down her throat, the voice of the news anchor penetrated Claire's exhaustion.

"... police said that the latest murder, happening so far to the north, indicates that the werewolf may have relocated to the denser woods north of Highway 34. The male victim was found outdoors, with a firearm nearby. Citizens are reminded not to leave their homes after dark for any reason. Suspicious activity should be reported to the police, or the Protective Action Council, headed by Dr. Charles Engle. They can be reached by calling 555-0194. Now, let's turn to Angie for a check of the weather—Angie?"

Claire turned to look at her mother. The coffee sloshed against the side of her mug. The *seule*. She really was the one killing people, and she was still in the woods. The pack hadn't caught her, and she'd killed that poor man. *Maybe if they'd had more help—if I'd been there—maybe they would have been able to find her.* She set down her coffee mug too hard on the counter.

"I don't mind if you want to drink that poison, Claire, but for God's sake, don't spill it everywhere, 'kay?" Lisbeth dug a fork into her tofu.

Marie met Claire's eyes and mouthed, "Later."

\* \* \*

"Hello?"

"Hey, Claire." Matthew's voice was quieter than usual.

"What's wrong?" Her mind flashed to the party. They hadn't really talked much in the days since then—maybe she'd been right. Maybe he'd been disappointed that she wasn't exactly the social butterfly type.

He sighed. "It's my dad."

*At least it's not me. Damn, what made me think that, anyway? I must be the most narcissistic person on the planet.*

"What about him?"

"He's freaking out. And I mean *freaking.* That guy who got killed last night—it just pushed him over the edge. He's been ranting all morning about how the FHPA and the Protective Action Council were both supposed to be out patrolling, and it still happened. All of a sudden, he's all action-hero about the situation. He keeps saying he's the last line of defense, and he's called in all of these other people for some big strategy meeting tomorrow. He's making me crazy with his whole saving-the-world thing. It's just about him getting into the stupid Lycanthropy Researchers International so that he can prove he's worthy of his FHPA spot, anyway."

Claire squeezed her eyes shut. If Matthew's dad had decided to do something drastic, that put the whole pack in danger. She forced her shoulders to relax, focused on sounding normal.

"That's really crappy. Do you want to go somewhere this

afternoon? Get away from the insanity for a while?" Her mom and Lisbeth would be home. It would be hard to sneak out without them catching on, but she'd figure out a way.

Matthew laughed bitterly. "I'd like that more than anything in the world. But apparently, I'm picking up some tracking expert at the airport this afternoon. Dad's orders."

"Oh, Matthew, I'm so sorry."

"Yeah, me too. I guess we're both at our parents' mercy these days, huh?"

"Yep. But I'm glad it's just your dad you're frustrated with." The words tumbled out of Claire's mouth before she could stop them.

"What do you mean? Who else would I be frustrated with?"

"Um—I just thought . . . We haven't talked much since Friday, and . . ." She sighed. "I'm not exactly as popular as you are. I don't really go to that many big parties—I thought maybe you were wishing that I was more like the rest of your friends. That I liked that sort of stuff more."

*Not that you even know how different I really am from them, but still. God, I wish I could tell him everything.*

The silence on the other end of the phone made her squirm in her chair, and she struggled to keep her mouth shut.

"Claire."

Matthew's voice was very, very quiet, and she could feel the first tingle of tears behind her eyelids.

"I cannot believe you even thought that for a single second."

"Well—" Her throat closed up before she could say anything else.

"Spending time with you is so much better than getting blind drunk with a bunch of people who only care about how many goals I can score, or what my clothes look like—I can't even tell you how much better it is. You're more interesting than anyone at that party by a long shot."

"I just don't want to be taking you away from your friends or anything."

"You're not. Believe me, you're really not. No more worrying about this kind of stuff, okay?" His voice was gentle.

"Okay." Claire struggled to keep her voice even. His voice was so sincere—there was no doubt he meant every word. She struggled not to sniff into the phone. "Good luck this afternoon."

"Thanks, I'll need it. I'll talk to you soon, okay?"

"Yeah, okay."

Claire hung up and flopped down onto the carpet. She'd gotten so used to the truth being the absolute wrong thing to say. But somehow with Matthew, it always seemed to be absolutely right.

*I'd better not get too comfortable with that idea.* She sighed and stood up. Sometimes it seemed like she'd never get all of this figured out.

As Claire and her mother made their way into the woods a few nights later, her mother laid a warning hand on Claire's arm.

"You are allowed to come to the gathering this evening, but you must understand something. Until your transformation is complete, you will have no say in our proceedings. Beatrice always has the ultimate say in what course we take, but the rest of our pack are allowed to voice opinions. Except for you. As far as you are concerned, this is strictly a learning experience." Anxiety tightened her mother's voice like a guitar string.

"Yeah, okay." Claire shifted from one foot to the other. *It's not like I have anything to add, anyway. Why is she freaking about this?*

"Good."

Claire could smell her mother's relief, sharp and clean.

"What you do in our pack—it reflects on me as well. Your mistakes can affect my status. I do not wish to give my position in the pack to Zahlia. Am I making myself clear?"

Claire nodded and tried to ignore the headache that blossomed behind her eyes. *So if I screw up, I hurt both of us. Yeah, no pressure there at all.*

The shadows around them seemed darker than usual.

"Um, Mom?"

Her mother turned to look at her, her lack of patience pinching her lips.

"I was just wondering—Victoria said the other night that

the *seule* wouldn't be dangerous if we weren't hunting her. Is that true?"

"I wouldn't say that she's not dangerous. But I think her desire to stay hidden, to be left alone, would prevent her from attacking a wolf who wasn't tracking her. You don't need to be concerned."

Her mother stopped speaking as the clearing appeared before them. Beatrice squatted near the fire, watching as Victoria adjusted the logs.

"Claire, I greet you." Beatrice's eyes were bright with anticipation.

"Beatrice, I greet you," Claire answered smoothly. She turned to Victoria, whose wide grin was infectious. "Victoria, I greet you," she said, with genuine happiness. Claire's mother put a hand on her shoulder and squeezed it appreciatively.

So far, so good.

Zahlia, Judith, and Katherine arrived almost simultaneously, and greetings were offered. Zahlia turned to Beatrice and showed the older woman the side of her pale neck. Claire sensed the submission in her posture. Zahlia opened her mouth to speak, but Claire's mom beat her to it.

"We should transform before we discuss the issue. It'll be easier, and there's less chance we'll be overheard that way." Claire's mother scanned the woods around them with her sharp photographer's eyes.

Zahlia looked up from her spot by the fire. "That's not fair to Claire. You know she can't fully transform. Besides, if we're discovered in the woods, we'll have bigger problems than having been overheard."

"Claire is not permitted to participate in our discussion tonight—and she will still be able to hear us, even partially transformed." Claire's mother sounded irritated.

"Marie is right," Judith said. "Since Claire won't be any help, we need to do what's best for everyone else."

Claire crossed her arms. She was glad to have Zahlia sticking up for her, but having everyone talk about her like she wasn't even there made her feel like a five-year-old who'd been caught coloring on the walls.

Everyone looked at Beatrice.

"Claire," she said slowly. "I am sorry, but your mother is right. We need to remain as concealed as possible, and it is easier to do that in our wolf-forms. We will transform."

Claire's mother looked pleased that Beatrice had sided with her. Zahlia stiffened and walked over to sit next to Claire.

"I just wanted to say that I'm sorry they're going to keep you muzzled tonight."

At the edge of the firelight, Claire's mother stalked back and forth impatiently.

Without waiting for Claire to respond, Zahlia got up and went to kneel in front of Beatrice. With her finger, she sketched a rough map in the dirt of the paths where she'd tracked the *seule*.

Claire's mother shot an exasperated look at the back of Zahlia's head.

"Perhaps," she suggested, her voice tart as a lemon, "we could discuss your findings as a group, Zahlia?"

Anger skittered across Zahlia's face as she turned to face Claire's mom. "That's not your command to give, Marie. Watch your place."

"I am merely asking why we are waiting, Zahlia."

Her mother's cool restraint made Zahlia's outburst seem childish. Claire's mom had used the same move on her plenty of times, and it sucked.

"I was just trying to get a map drawn before we started. To cut down on the confusion."

"She's not wrong, Marie," Katherine said. "We need to know where we're looking."

"Enough!" Beatrice's voice was firm. "Zahlia is right—the map is important, and we have not wasted our time by having her draw it."

Claire's mother took a deep breath and sank down near the fire. "Certainly, Beatrice."

Claire scooted back until she was in line with the other women, and her mother shot her a quick look that clearly said *watch yourself.*

*She really doesn't trust me at all.* Claire gnawed on a ragged cuticle and focused on keeping her bitter feelings from trailing across her face.

"Well," Zahlia huffed, "I didn't mean to cause a delay." She arranged herself on Beatrice's right side, completing the circle. "I'll be happy to discuss our strategies whenever you're ready."

She turned to Beatrice and bent her head so low that Claire could see the sharp part in her dark hair.

Beatrice got to her feet and raised both hands. She began to chant, and a hush fell over the women as they transformed.

When Claire looked around the firelit circle at the six wolves, a wave of hot jealousy rolled through her. It caught her off guard. She'd gotten used to the idea that she was not like everyone else—that she would change—but she'd never found herself *wanting* to be a wolf like this. Claire crossed her arms in front of her chest, her fur-covered fists clenched beneath her armpits. It didn't make the longing that ached in her ribs any less intense, but at least she didn't feel like she was about to fly apart.

Zahlia glanced in her direction, and Claire read the sympathy in the quick flick of her dark-furred ears. Claire hunched over in front of the fire, trying to hide her thoughts. She knew the others could read her body language like a news ticker on the bottom of a television screen, and she hated it.

Beatrice gave one rough bark, and the other wolves turned to face her, ready to begin.

In spite of Zahlia's bragging, she really didn't have much information about the *seule*. No one knew where the lone wolf had come from or where she was hiding. Claire was surprised when Victoria complained that the *seule* hadn't presented herself to their pack.

*I mean, I know that* seule*s aren't exactly all about following the rules, but come on. If she's not going to move on, she should at least have the courtesy to let us know how long she's planning to stay here—and why.* The sandy-brown wolf shook her head once, like she was trying to clear it.

*If she is hunting humans, I assume she believes that we would not receive her with great warmth.* Claire's mother sat very still, confidence pouring from her steady gaze. *We must either force her out, or find and confront her. She will do nothing—it is up to us to resolve the situation. I believe that with all of us searching, we can find her tonight and end things before they get even more out of hand.*

*I already suggested that, Marie!* Zahlia gave an agitated whine. *That's why I was out pacing the woods long after the rest of you had gone home the night of the full moon. You can't act as though no one else has thought of that idea! I'm the best tracker here—there's no reason for the rest of you to be out confusing the trail.*

The black wolf began to pant, and Claire wondered if she was imagining the faint smell of panic—thin and biting—that seemed to waft from Zahlia's fur.

*Send me,* Zahlia begged, bending her head low to the grizzled wolf next to her. *I will find her for you, I swear it. I don't need the pack's help for this. It will be better if I go alone.*

*No. We act as a group—you know that.* Claire's mother laid her ears back. *We should all search.*

*Agreed.* Judith's eyes were bright in the firelight. *You cannot cover the whole area alone, Zahlia. And since Katherine and I live in the opposite direction, there is no reason for us not to search that portion of the woods. You are not the only decent tracker among us.*

Victoria lay down in the dirt, hiding her nose between her paws. Obviously, she wasn't going to be hunting a crazed *seule*—not while she was pregnant.

Beatrice stood up, the claws on her four feet digging into the earth.

*I will not force anyone to participate in this—especially considering that two of our number are unable to do so.* She glanced at Claire. *Nor will I prevent anyone from working alongside Zahlia, if they so wish.*

A soft grumble rolled in the black wolf's throat.

*I will go with you tonight, Zahlia. Together, we can cover more ground.* Claire's mother got to her feet, ignoring Zahlia's irritation.

*As will we.* Katherine pressed against Judith, who flicked her ears in agreement.

*Good. I think I would only serve to slow you down, and I can see that Victoria would not be very helpful, either.* The disappointment in Beatrice's posture was faint, but it was there.

The sandy wolf dipped her head. *We will make sure Claire arrives home safely, and then we will return to our house.*

Claire's mouth dropped open. They were really going to split up and search the woods for some sort of freaked-out lone wolf serial killer.

*Oh my God.*

"Wait—" Claire's human voice sounded strange even to her as it echoed off the trees surrounding the clearing.

The wolves all turned to face her, surprised that she had spoken. The knife-sharp gaze Marie trained on Claire stopped the rest of the sentence from leaving Claire's mouth. Panic fluttered in Claire's chest like a sparrow. Her mother had told her to keep quiet, and she couldn't even get that right. Crap.

"Never mind, sorry," Claire mumbled, staring down at the ground. She couldn't meet her mother's disappointed eyes. *Of course. I would screw it up right at the very end.*

*Are you ready to go?* Beatrice's voice was gentle but firm.

Claire nodded.

*Then you may lead the way, and we will follow you.*

Claire nodded again, her skin crawling with embarrassment. Her eyes filled and before she started to cry, Claire wheeled around and ran through the woods, her feet pounding down the now-familiar path back to her house. She could hear Victoria and Beatrice behind her, following, but not intruding.

When Claire reached the wall at the edge of her yard, she heard Victoria give a quiet *yip* before the two wolves turned and left her alone.

Claire stopped and leaned against the cool, uneven bricks. The salty tears stung her cheeks and she welcomed the discomfort. She wanted to punish herself for being so stupid, for doing something that could damage her mother.

*And I did just exactly what she told me not to. All I had to do was keep my freaking mouth shut, and I couldn't even get that right. How could I be such an idiot?*

When her sobbing had slowed enough that the she could see again, Claire crept through the hole and went home to wait for her mother. She slipped into the house, halfheartedly washing the tear streaks from her face. Even though she was sure she wouldn't be able to sleep, Claire climbed into bed. She lay there and stared at the ceiling. Eventually, her exhaustion won out, and she dozed off.

When she woke, sunlight streamed through her window, and her neck was stiff from being in one position for too long. In the hall, Claire could hear her mother and Lisbeth talking, but she couldn't make out what they were saying.

There was a soft knock on her door before her mother peered in. Tight lines ringed her mouth and dark circles curved underneath her eyes. Marie glanced back at Lisbeth's room before she began to speak.

"When you're up, would you come down to my darkroom, *chérie*? I'd like to get your opinion on something."

Her voice changed the setting on Claire's heartbeat to *panic*.

Claire slid out of bed. "Just let me brush my hair, and I'll be right down."

# Chapter Fourteen

CLAIRE HAD HER hair halfway into a ponytail when the phone rang. It was Emily.

*I so* do not have time for this right now.

Even though she was desperate to hear what her mother had to say, Claire couldn't ignore the guilt that poured through her, thick and sticky as honey. She picked up the phone.

"Hello?"

"Oh my God, Claire I am seriously having the worst week *ever*," Emily groaned. The connection fizzed with static.

"Lean more toward the window," Claire instructed. "You're breaking up."

"Sorry. But you'll never guess what Dan did."

"Dan?" Claire adjusted her ponytail in the mirror.

"The guy? Mr. Wholesome? Come on, Claire." Emily sounded hurt.

"Right, sorry, what happened?"

"He tried to give me his freaking class ring last night. Can you believe it?"

Claire scowled at her reflection in the mirror, confused and antsy. She sort of wanted to care about Emily's guy problems, but she just . . . didn't. "That's sort of 1986 of him, huh?"

"It's worse than that! We've only been hanging out for a couple of weeks—I mean, we've barely even, you know, fooled around, and he's trying to—like, *claim* me or something. It totally freaked me out, and then when I wouldn't take it, he actually teared up. God. That was the one good thing about being stuck in this hellhole and now it's all screwed up."

"That sucks, Em." Claire glanced at her watch.

"What am I going to do now?" Emily moaned.

"Don't freak out. We'll think of something. Listen, I totally hate to do this to you, but my mom's waiting to talk to me. Can I call you back in a couple of hours and we'll figure it out then?"

Emily made a disgusted noise. "Fine, leave me all alone in my misery. Maybe I'll go ask the stupid chickens what they think I should do."

"Emily—," Claire protested.

"No, it's okay," Emily relented. "I'm just pissy. Go talk to your mom and call me when you're done. I'm going to go eat some chocolate or something."

As soon as she'd hung up, Claire tossed down the phone and sprinted for the door. *If the worst thing that had happened to me all summer was some nice farm boy trying to give me jewelry, I'd be freaking ecstatic.*

Claire ignored the jealousy that wound its way around her neck like a snake and swung open the darkroom door.

Things were bad. Claire knew it before her mom said a single word. The table in front of her mother held four cameras, neatly arranged. There was no film on the table. There were no prints. Behind her, the computer monitor cycled through its screen saver—no digital shot filled its wide frame. Her mother was just *sitting* there, her dark-circled eyes staring into space. She never did that.

"Mom? You, uh, wanted to see me?"

"Yes. Claire, I don't want to scare you unnecessarily, especially at such a . . . vulnerable time in your transformation. But I really don't see how I can keep this from you."

Claire sank onto one of the high stools that surrounded the table, her heart jumping up and down in her chest.

"I have little proof—only suspicions, but I went back out alone after you were in bed last night, and what I found . . . Claire, we are in much more danger than any of us had thought. Until I know for sure that I am right, I won't say anything else. It would be unfair. But you must be incredibly careful, Claire. I am no longer sure who—or what—to trust. Please, you must promise not to go out at night without me until I say." Her mother took Claire's chin between her long fingers. "Promise me."

Claire nodded. "All right. But, Mom, what—" A faint ping interrupted Claire midsentence.

Her mother glanced down at the phone on her hip and frowned. "We'll discuss it later, *chérie*. I need to answer this. I'm going out later to look for more proof, and Lisbeth will be running some errands for me. If she comes home before I do, call me immediately." Marie spun toward her computer and lifted the phone to her ear. "This is Marie."

Claire slid out of the darkroom while her mother made plans for a shoot in Turkey. Her mother hadn't really told her anything at all. *Well, at least things are back to normal in one way. And why the hell does she care if Lisbeth gets home before she does, anyway?* Without a backward glance, Claire bolted away from the darkroom and went straight upstairs.

In her room, the phone stared at her accusingly. Matthew was the only person Claire really felt like talking to, but she had promised Emily she'd call back.

Claire sighed and dialed Emily's number.

"Hey, thanks for calling back." Emily sounded genuinely relieved.

"No problem." *It turns out that I'm in mortal danger,*

*apparently, but sure, let's solve a boy problem. Huh. Can I still be in* mortal *danger if I'm not really human?* Claire shook her head.

"So? What am I going to do about Dan?" Emily asked.

Claire wanted to tell Emily that she was being ridiculous, that she should be grateful that this was the worst thing that had happened—but that wasn't fair. None of this was Emily's fault. *I'm the abnormal one here.* Claire struggled to imagine what she would have told Emily if this had happened last summer.

"I don't think you should do anything. I mean, either he'll get over it or he won't, you know? It's not worth stressing over. If he has any brain cells at all, he'll realize he's being an idiot and come crawling back to you. If not—well, your parents can't leave you out there forever, right?"

Emily sighed. "It already feels like I've been here for ages, but I guess you're right. I'm just pissed. I mean, so much for a silver lining, you know?"

Claire heard the crack of a soda can being opened. Emily was the worst Diet Coke addict Claire knew, and that one little sound made Claire miss her more than ever.

"I wish you were home," Claire said. "Everything's more fun when you're here."

"Like what? What have you been doing without me? God, Claire, I miss you so much! Seriously—I want to hear what's been going on with you."

"Not that much, really. And, um, I sort of need to make another call."

Claire was dying to talk to Matthew. It was a whole lot easier than talking to Emily. It made Claire squirm to realize that, but it was true.

"Matthew?" Emily squealed.

"Yes, and I really do not want to talk about it right now."

"Okay, but I am so serious, Claire, if I do not get some details *soon* I am going to freak out on you."

"I know, I know. We'll talk later, okay?"

"I'll say hi to the cows for you."

Claire could hear Emily giggling as she hung up. *At least she's in a better mood.* She shook her head while she dialed Matthew.

"Hello?" The rasp in his voice caught Claire by surprise.

"Matthew, hey—are you okay?" she squeaked. *Oh, very sophisticated, Claire.*

"Yeah, I know I sound like crap. Ever since Dad planned his meeting for today, the phone's been ringing nonstop." He sounded exhausted.

"So, how come you're stuck answering it?"

Matthew sighed. "They're all upstairs in Dad's stupid 'War Room,' trying to figure out where they need to set the traps."

Claire's heart stuttered against her ribs. "T-traps?"

"Yeah, for the werewolf? It's his new plan. They're gonna try to get them put up before dark—they think the werewolf may be following the press coverage, so they're keeping it supersecret." He paused. "Oops. Uh, don't say anything about that, okay?"

"No problem." The lie came easy. Too easy. Her mother's voice echoed in her head. *In this world—we are driven to lie a great deal, Claire. More than most.* "So, are you playing secretary all day?" she asked.

"Nah. I'll be finished pretty soon. Can you hang out?"

"Yeah—" The memory of Dr. Engle's piercing eyes made Claire's wolf-brain twitch. "Mom and Lisbeth will be gone later this afternoon, and it's gonna be wicked hot again. Maybe you could come over and we could hang by the pool?"

"Sounds great to me."

Claire snapped her phone shut. Having Matthew over was probably a bigger risk than she should take. But between the memory of Matthew's warm, crooked smile and her mom refusing to actually talk to her, *again* . . . maybe it wasn't such a bad idea after all. And her mother had said that she didn't want her alone any more than necessary, right?

A few hours later Claire sat in the kitchen with Lisbeth while she made up an enormous grocery list.

Her mother appeared in the hall, beckoning Claire with a long finger.

"Claire, may I speak with you for a moment?" The sharp lines etched in her mother's forehead were a bad sign. Claire slid out of her chair.

"I'll be right back," she mumbled to Lisbeth. Claire followed her mother into the hall. "What's up?"

Her mother frowned. "I'm going out. I think I have an idea wh"—she stopped, her eyes trained on the kitchen where Lisbeth was banging the cabinet doors closed a little too obviously—"in regards to our earlier conversation."

Claire's mouth went dry. She couldn't let her mother go traipsing around the woods with Matthew's dad and his whackos out setting traps, especially not if she was in her wolf-form. And she probably would be, since it was the best way to hide her identity.

"Mom, I need to talk to you first, okay? Let's, umm, can we go talk in my room or something?"

Marie shook her head. "I don't have time, *chérie*. We'll talk when I return. I may be out a bit later than usual. And no matter what happens, you are not to leave this house until I tell you that you may."

The closed-off look that Claire knew all too well slid across her mother's eyes. Before she could say anything, her mother turned and strode down the hall with unnatural speed. *Werewolf speed.*

"Mom!"

Marie turned, her face a mask of irritation. "Not now, Claire!" Her voice was a growl, the command in it clear. "Later" wasn't a request—it was an order from a higher-ranked pack member.

"Just—be careful," Claire sputtered, her gaze darting to the kitchen door. "There's . . . dangerous stuff out there." As warnings went, it was pretty crappy, but between her mother's insistence and Lisbeth hovering in the kitchen, it was the best Claire could manage. If her mother really was planning to transform and search the woods, then she was taking a huge risk.

Lisbeth left a few minutes later, looking distracted and irritated.

Claire sat in the empty house and waited for Matthew, wondering if it were possible for time to pass any slower.

"Hey."

Matthew's smile hit her like a blast of tropical air. So did the actual air—the heat wave showed no signs of letting up any time soon.

"Wow, it's awful out there." Claire waved him into the house. "Ready to hit the pool?"

Matthew waved the rolled-up towel in his hand. "Absolutely."

"Great. I just need to change into my suit." Claire left Matthew in the kitchen and threw on her bathing suit as fast as she could.

Ten minutes later, they were floating in the pool chairs with the sun beating down on them. Claire kept glancing at the kitchen windows, half-hoping to see her mother staring back at her—even if it meant getting caught with Matthew. She was worried enough not to care.

"This is heaven," Matthew announced.

Claire looked at the drops of water sparkling on his chest. *I'll say.*

"You okay?" Matthew asked. "You seem sort of distracted."

"Sorry, I guess I am, a little. My mom and I had some . . . weirdness this morning, and I can't shake it." That was putting it mildly. But she couldn't exactly tell him that she was worrying about what might happen if her mother ran into his dad in the woods. *Maybe she's not even there. She didn't say exactly where she was going. . . .*

Claire sighed and bit her lip.

Matthew slid off his pool chair into the water and swam over to her. "Sounds like it's been a bad parent day all around." He took her hands and gently pulled her off her floating chair. "Is there anything I can do?"

Claire leaned into his chest. "Distract me?" she suggested.

He smiled. "That could be arranged." He leaned in and kissed her, tightening his arms around her. Claire felt the two parts of herself rise up and begin to battle. The human in her relished the touch of his soft mouth, welcomed the pressure of his hands against her shoulders. The rest of Claire—the werewolf—wanted to go off by herself, to think about what she could do for her mother. She didn't know which side to listen to—didn't know which voice was the angel on her shoulder, and which was the devil.

*I tried to warn her . . . There's nothing I can do about it right now, anyway.*

In spite of her anxiety, Claire gave into the familiarity of being human, and wrapped her arms around Matthew's warm back.

Long before the sun threatened to sink, Matthew suggested that they'd pushed their luck far enough for one day. After his car had disappeared down the drive, Claire slipped out onto the front steps and sat down. She wrapped her arms around her legs and stared out at the trees in the distance, shivering in spite of the heat. *Please let her be okay. Please.*

Darkness fell, and Claire's mother still hadn't come home. She couldn't stand the waiting anymore. Something had gone wrong. Claire could feel it. She had to talk to Beatrice.

The phone felt hot in her sweaty hand. After a quick Internet search to find the number, she dialed, and then stared at the digits glowing on the tiny screen. All she had to do was hit SEND. Claire closed her eyes and pressed the button.

It rang only once before Victoria answered. "Hello?"

"Victoria? It's Claire. Listen, I really need to talk to Beatrice."

"On the *phone?*"

The dismay in Victoria's voice sent doubt slithering through Claire's stomach like an eel.

"Um, yeah. It's kind of urgent. Is she there?"

"No, she's not. What on earth is going on?"

Claire's voice wobbled when she answered. "Mom took off, Victoria. I think she went to look for something in the woods—the *seule*, I guess—but Dr. Engle put traps out there, and if she's been caught—" Claire couldn't finish the sentence. The words were too horrible to say. "We have to look for her. She might need help."

"Claire, there's no reason to think anything's wrong. Your mom probably just wants to catch the *seule* before Zahlia does. I'm sure she's fine. Marie is a very capable woman—and she's an even more capable wolf."

Claire's jaw tightened in disbelief. "You think this is just about her wanting to beat Zahlia?"

"Probably. I know you're too new to know all of this, but your mom and Zahlia aren't exactly best friends." Victoria hesitated.

"Okay, so they don't love each other. Victoria, I really think my mom might be in trouble—"

"Claire," Victoria said, interrupting her. "Your mother is fine. Trust me. Go watch a movie or something, and try to relax. I'll talk to you later."

"Fine." Claire hung up. If they were going to treat her like that—like she was just some stupid newbie—then maybe she'd go ask someone who thought she was capable of doing something.

She called Zahlia, but it went straight to voicemail.

"Hey, it's me, Claire. Could you call me as soon as you get this, please? Thanks."

Claire hung up the phone and stared out at the dark lawn, desperately wishing that there was an easy answer to just one of the questions that spun through her mind.

# Chapter Fifteen

LISBETH GOT HOME a few minutes after the first stars glimmered to life.

"Claire?" Lisbeth poked her head into the living room.

"Yeah?"

"I'm gonna put some steaks on the grill. Is your mom home?"

"Um, no, she's not here." Claire wriggled her toes, willing herself to hurry up and invent some plausible reason her mother wasn't back.

"Okay." Lisbeth's voice was slow and thick with suspicion. "Well, where is she?"

"She, uh, she called and said she had to fly to Denver right away. Something about a big, last-minute shoot."

Lisbeth crossed her arms. "Since when does your mother have a client in Denver? She's never mentioned it."

Sweat prickled on Claire's forehead. *Be calm, be calm, be calm.* She shrugged. "I dunno. You know she doesn't tell me anything. So, um, since she's gone, I guess we can go ahead and eat whenever." Claire tried to brush past Lisbeth.

Lisbeth's grip on her upper arm startled Claire. "Not so fast. I want to know what's going on. What's *really* going on. You've been prowling around here for *weeks*, sleeping all hours of the day—you never tell me anything anymore. And your mother's no better. When I mentioned that I was worried about you, she just brushed me off. I know we're not actually related, but I love you, and I'm worried. Please, Claire, talk to me."

Claire stared at Lisbeth, remembering all the hours Lisbeth had spent with her—helping with homework, teaching her to knit, listening when she griped about boys and school and her mother. She trusted Lisbeth and she wanted desperately to tell her what was happening. Maybe the two of them could figure out what to do, how to find her mother. The words tickled the tip of her tongue, but she could never actually say them.

"Claire, please." Lisbeth shook her arm, not bothering to hide her desperation. "You can trust me. I mean, what, do you think I'm the werewolf or something?"

She meant it as a joke, Claire could tell, but the secret shriveled and dried in Claire's mouth like an autumn leaf. Maybe Lisbeth wasn't a werewolf, but she was definitely keeping something from Claire. And that meant Lisbeth didn't *totally* trust her. So why should Claire confide in her? When she looked back at the woman who had taken care of her for so many years, the lies came pouring out of her as easily as if she'd turned a tap.

"Lisbeth, nothing is going on. Really. Mom took off for a random work thing—just like she always has. It's not like she's ever given us a ton of notice, so I don't see what the big deal is this time. And I talk to you plenty. Just because I don't tell you every little thing about my social life doesn't mean I don't like you or anything. It's not like you tell me everything about your life."

Lisbeth blushed and dropped Claire's arm. *Bingo. She knows I'm right about that.*

"Okay, I'm sorry. Let's—let's just go eat."

"Sounds good, I'm starved." Claire watched Lisbeth's shoulders slump in defeat. A shower of guilt that felt all too familiar pattered down on her. "Maybe after dinner we could watch some TV or something," she added.

"That would be great!" Lisbeth perked up at the suggestion. "I better go get the meat on the grill."

When she'd left the room, Claire called her mother. It didn't make sense that her mom wanted to know when

Lisbeth was home, but still . . . The call went to voicemail and Claire's heart sank. Her bad feeling about all this had just become really terrible.

After dinner Claire sat curled up on the couch with Lisbeth. She bit her cuticles and tried to look like she was paying attention to the sitcoms that blared on the screen. *If something had happened—if she'd been caught—the news would interrupt this crap.* The thought only half-comforted her. If her mother had run into the *seule*, the news wouldn't know about that, now, would they?

Hours later, Lisbeth stood and stretched. "Ugh, that's as much mass-market media as I can take tonight. I'm going to bed, Claire-bear. You sure you're okay?"

"Yeah, I'm fine. And don't call me that."

Lisbeth sniggered and headed for the shower. Claire walked over to the window and stared out at the dark lawn, willing her mother to come loping across the grass. The desire to sneak into the dark forest was so strong it made Claire's bones ache. She couldn't stop imagining her mother, caught in some sort of hideous trap or mangled by the *seule*. But no matter how badly she wanted to go, Claire couldn't just ignore an order from a senior pack member. Some primitive compulsion to obey emanated from deep inside her wolf-brain, keeping her trapped in the too-empty house. When she heard Lisbeth close her door, Claire wandered upstairs and watched the woods from her bedroom window.

For three nights, Claire kept her vigil. She gave Lisbeth fake messages from Marie, and hoped desperately that Beatrice would decide to do something.

By the time the sun crept over the horizon after the third night, Claire had collapsed onto her window seat, frightened and exhausted. When the first bright rays touched Claire's face, a fierce determination swelled inside her. Why should she be the good little listener she was supposed to be? It wasn't getting her anywhere and it wasn't helping her mother.

*Screw the pack order. Screw my mother's command. If she's dead*—Claire forced herself to think the word—*it won't make any difference, anyway.*

Claire flipped on her computer and looked up Victoria's address. It was halfway across town, but there was no way she could ask Lisbeth to drive her there. She'd have to bike it. Claire drummed her fingers against the edge of the keyboard. It was like teetering on the edge of the high dive. She knew she could jump—she knew she *should* jump—but the animal part of her brain screamed at her not to do it, not to endanger herself so foolishly.

Claire's muscles twitched with indecision. *Go. Stay. Go. Stay. Okay, I'm definitely going. But if Mom's okay, she'll be freaking furious with me. Crap.*

Outside, the forest waited, wearing an early-morning haze like a nightgown. Matthew's dad might already be out there, checking his traps again. The idea shook Claire to the core. She had to go—if he wouldn't waste any time, Claire couldn't, either.

After she scribbled a bogus note to Lisbeth about where she was going and blew the dust off her bike helmet, Claire took off down the sloping driveway.

*This is so stupid. If I'd gotten a car for my birthday like every other sixteen-year-old, I could still be in the air-conditioning.*

By the time she pulled into Victoria's driveway, her shirt was soaked with perspiration, and the smell of fear and exhaustion wafted up from the damp fabric.

Claire rang the doorbell, and then looked at her watch. *Holy crap. How did I get here in twenty minutes? It should have taken an hour to ride here!* She'd have to be more careful. When she was scared it was too easy to do things faster than a normal human could.

Victoria opened the door.

"Oh, Claire, I should have guessed you'd come." She pulled Claire inside with her free hand. In the corner of the room, Beatrice looked up from her knitting.

"I'm sorry," Claire panted. "It's just—my mother still hasn't come home. I know you said it's no big deal, but I think she was looking for the *seule*. If she's hurt, if something's happened to her—we have to find her."

Beatrice glanced in the direction of the TV. The BREAKING NEWS banner scrolled across the screen. "Have—you haven't seen the news," she said, her eyes trained on the pastel square of yarn in her lap. "Claire—your mother has been caught. I am so sorry."

"Caught?" The word twined around Claire's throat as she said it, choking her.

"Yes. I'm afraid it's only a matter of time before they force her to reveal her identity, and then Dr. Engle will administer his 'cure.'"

Beatrice's hands trembled when she spoke, and that was the last thing Claire noticed before the floor swirled up to meet her and everything went dark.

"Claire. Claire! Wake up."

The fingers that pinched her cheek were gentle, but Claire slapped the hand away from her face without thinking. Beatrice's eyes glowed with concern.

"Sorry," said Claire, instinctively ducking her head low. The old woman sniffed and turned away. Claire had been forgiven, this time. "So, what are we going to do?"

"You must go home, and you must wait." Beatrice lowered herself back into her chair and picked up her knitting needles. "Once we have a better idea of what Dr. Engle plans to do, the pack will meet to discuss our next move."

Claire scrambled to her feet. Her still-weak knees wobbled, and she grabbed the back of the couch for support. It was only the hot anger, shooting up her spine like a lightning bolt that kept her vertical. "They—they have my mother." Claire's voice faltered. She forced herself to look at the face of the familiar, beautiful wolf on the TV screen. Her mother paced in the tiny cage where they held her, her ears laid flat against her head.

Claire looked at Beatrice in disbelief. "They have my mother! Everyone already knows what they're planning to do to her—they'll give her their freaking 'cure' at the full moon! The longer we wait, the less chance we have of getting her out. Waiting will kill her."

Beatrice didn't look up. "Time spent planning is not wasted. And also, we are not certain what effect Dr. Engle's experiments have upon a true werewolf. Even if we are unable to rescue her—which is likely, given the sort of security Dr. Engle is using—it's still possible your mother may survive his treatment. We must take the time to explore all of our options." She took a deep breath and met Claire's gaze. Tears glittered in the corners of her eyes. "Please know that this is not a decision I have made lightly, Young One. The safety of our pack comes before everything else. If it means the sacrifice of one, then we must accept it even though it hurts. I will not risk everyone's future for your mother's sake," she said, stroking the blanket she was making. "And your mother would do the same thing, would make the same decision, if she were in my shoes."

Claire looked over at Victoria, hoping she would speak up, would change Beatrice's mind. Victoria leaned against the wall. Her shoulders were hunched, every muscle in her body leaning toward her middle, protecting the tiny baby that grew there.

*They're scared. They're scared for the baby and so they're going to let Dr. Engle destroy my mother.*

"It's not the pack you care about at all, is it?" she spat. "You're scared for yourselves and you're just going to let them have my mother because of it." Claire stared hard at Victoria. "What would you do if it was Beatrice—your own mother—that they'd captured?"

"I know how hard this is for you, Claire. Marie is like a sister to me." Victoria's voice broke. "But just because your mother did something she knew wasn't safe, that doesn't mean she'd want the rest of us to endanger ourselves. I'm sure of that."

A growl caught in Claire's throat at Victoria's words. How dare she hint that Marie had acted irresponsibly? "My mother was trying to save us, all of us, and she risked her own life to do it. If you're too *weak*"—she spat the word—"to help me, I'll go find help somewhere else. I'm sure Zahlia will do it."

Beatrice's left eye twitched when Claire mentioned the dark wolf, and Claire knew she'd hit a nerve.

"Zahlia may be brave, but she is also loyal to the pack," Beatrice said gently. "Even if you will not obey me, I would think twice before asking her for help."

*Manipulative bitch.* Claire spun and headed for the front

door. "I'm not interested in taking lessons in loyalty from someone who obviously knows nothing about it."

Claire slammed the door hard enough to make the hinges ring and slung herself onto her bike. The helmet she left lying in the grass like an upended turtle. She was protected by the speed and strength that had pumped through her on her way through town, and the heightened senses that meant she could hear cars coming long before she could see them, could smell the people on the sidewalk before they ambled out in front of her. Helmets were for humans. Claire was *loup-garou*.

# Chapter Sixteen

THE LOOK LISBETH gave Claire when she stormed into the kitchen was pure worry. "Where on earth have you been? Have you lost your mind, riding around in this weather? There's a heat advisory out, for God's sake. And you're *purple*. Did you even think to take any water with you?" Lisbeth didn't wait for her to answer. She thrust an enormous glass at Claire. "You sit down right this minute and drink this. What if you'd gotten heat stroke? Your mother would never forgive me, Claire!"

The words came automatically. "Sorry. I—"

"You can apologize later. Drink that, and then go get in

a cool shower." Lisbeth yanked a mug of tea off the counter, sloshing pepperminty water on the floor. While she was wiping it up and muttering something about *job security* under her breath, Claire took her water and slunk upstairs.

She locked her bedroom door, and then went into her bathroom and turned on the shower, letting the water run cold over her shoulders. Claire stood under the icy spray, feeling the anger in her gut pull into a tighter and tighter knot until it was a little ball of blue-white rage.

She tried to call Zahlia, but her voicemail picked up. Fine—all she had to do was find her address and go over there.

It was not as easy to figure out where Zahlia lived as it had been to locate Beatrice and Victoria. By the time Claire had an address—an apartment in a sketchy part of town—her hair had dried. It was too far to bike. She'd have to take the bus. Claire dumped a handful of quarters into her pocket. *Always be prepared, right?* As casually as she could, Claire went downstairs and rummaged in the kitchen for some lunch.

Lisbeth stood in the doorway, glowering. "I hope you didn't have any plans today, missy, because you are not leaving this house until your mother gets back from her trip."

Her words brought a rush of bile into Claire's mouth. How was she supposed to get her mother home if she couldn't leave the house?

"I said 'sorry,'" Claire started.

"Not good enough this time. Besides the fact that you scared me half to death, I had something I really needed to take care of this morning, but I was too busy waiting for you to go anywhere. You're sixteen years old now. Old enough to start taking other people into consideration once in a while."

Claire ducked her head. "I didn't know you had plans. You didn't have to wait for me. I'm old enough to let myself in the house when I get home, you know."

Lisbeth sighed. "That's not the issue here. Now, I'm going to go see if there's any news on that *monster* they caught last night, but I will be checking on you, Claire. And you had better be where I expect you to be, every second, do you understand?"

Lisbeth was usually so Zen about things, meditating on problems and coming up with what she liked to call "gentle solutions." Claire opened her mouth, ready to apologize again, and stopped short. The smell that filled her nostrils was unmistakable. Underneath Lisbeth's anger, she smelled of fear.

Claire's mouth snapped shut when she took in the way Lisbeth was standing—arms crossed over her chest, fists clenched. *She really was freaked out about me being gone. Crap.*

"I know I screwed up big time." Claire automatically twisted her head to one side, baring her neck a little. Lisbeth might not know the signs of submission the way another wolf would, but it couldn't hurt. "I really am sorry, Lisbeth. If it's okay with you, I'll just go upstairs and eat in my room."

"Fine." Lisbeth uncrossed her arms. "But don't get crumbs on the carpet. I just cleaned, and I'm not revacuuming that pigsty you call a room." Claire could see her anger fading.

"I'll be careful."

*All I have to do is wait. Just a day or two. Then I'll go find Zahlia.*

True to her word, Lisbeth checked on Claire every couple of hours, even setting her alarm clock so she could do a few middle-of-the-night bed checks. Claire tossed under her covers, feeling the frustration of being trapped, jailed.

Two worry-filled days later, Claire and Lisbeth ate a silent dinner together in the kitchen. Lisbeth sat glued to the news, which was nothing more than footage of Marie pacing in her cage, mixed in with statements by Dr. Engle about what "great progress" they were making and an occasional weather report, just so that they could mention the drought again. Claire couldn't wait anymore. She had to go find Zahlia. The only good news was that with Dr. Engle announcing that the werewolf had been caught, there should be plenty of people out after dark, so no one would notice her on her bike.

When she finally heard snores coming from Lisbeth's bedroom, Claire snuck in and turned off Lisbeth's alarm, and then slipped out of the house the same way she had almost every other night for the past several weeks. A loneliness that Claire wasn't used to feeling sliced through her. She could feel a howl building inside her, the urge to voice her feelings almost too strong to push away.

Beatrice and Victoria—her own pack—had refused to help her find her mother. The thought filled Claire's mouth with the bitter taste of bile. She stashed her bike behind some bushes a few blocks from the nearest bus stop and waited, struggling not to cry. When the bus finally arrived, Claire got in and sat on the edge of one of the hard plastic seats, watching the stops tick by, getting more furious by the block. By the time she reached Zahlia's, she was glowing with rage.

Rusted wires hung out of the buzzer outside Zahlia's apartment building. Claire tugged on the greasy handle of the lobby door. It swung open easily. Inside, the fluorescent lights buzzed and flickered overhead. She shivered. Beatrice and Victoria's house hadn't exactly been glamorous, but this was one step above condemned. She'd had no idea Zahlia lived somewhere like this.

Claire took the rickety stairs three at a time until she arrived at the fifth floor. She knocked on the door of Apartment 503 and waited. Down the hall, two people shouted at each other in a language Claire didn't understand. When she heard the sound of glass breaking, she knocked again. The current of danger, the coppery smells of fear and malice and desperation—it was too much to bear with her heightened senses. The next full moon was just over two weeks away, and with each night that passed, Claire could feel her transformation becoming more complete. Everything around her pressed in harder, filling her brain with so much information that it made her head ache.

Where was Zahlia? The hair on the back of Claire's neck stood up. What if something had happened to her, too? She reached out and tried to open the door. Locked. But there was no deadbolt—it was only the flimsy push button lock keeping her out. Claire hesitated for only a second before she kicked hard at the door. It swung open with a satisfying pop, and Claire said a silent prayer of thanks.

The contrast from the dark, urine-scented hall made Claire do a double take. Inside, the apartment was immaculate. There was almost no furniture: one stiff-looking loveseat, a glass coffee table, and a small television. The walls were bare, and the only thing on the kitchen counter was an expensive-looking coffeepot. It looked unnatural, somehow. Like someone had put together the things they assumed people had in their houses, but with the details all wrong.

"Hello?" Claire called softly. "Zahlia? Is anyone here?"

There was no answer. Claire walked a little farther into the apartment. A small hallway opened off the kitchen/living room combo. Two doors stood open, the rooms behind them dark, but at the end of the hall was one closed door. A strip of light shined out from underneath it. Claire's heart stammered in her chest and she instinctively moved down into a half crouch. She slunk down the hall.

The first door she passed was a tiny bathroom. The shower curtain hung perfectly straight, towels neatly folded over the bar. In the next room were a small desk and a wooden chair. The only nongeneric stuff she'd seen in the entire apartment was in this room, but it was a strange mishmash of things. A wilted sunflower had been pinned to one wall, and a little garden gnome sat on the desk, his paint flaking and peeling like he'd been outside for years.

On the floor was a man's briefcase with the initials DRM monogrammed on the edge. Three round stones sat on top of it in a neat row.

Claire walked down the hall and stood in front of the last door, working up the courage to open it. *Please let her be sleeping in there.*

"Zahlia?" she whispered, cracking open the door. When no answer came, Claire pushed it open all the way. The overhead light shined down on a small bed with a faded quilt pulled up tight over the pillow. There was no headboard—in its place hung an enormous photograph. It was grainy from being blown up too big. The woman in the picture looked shockingly like Zahlia, except that her hair was gray and her cheeks were rounder.

*Her mother.* The thought popped into Claire's head automatically. Before she could process it, her nose twitched.

In the middle of the bed, a small white dog lay curled up, its eyes closed tight.

The dog was dead. Claire could smell it.

Without a backward glance, Claire bolted out of the apartment and tore down the stairs. Whatever was going on with Zahlia, it wasn't good. Outside the building, she leaned against the grimy bricks and gulped deep breaths of the garbage-scented air, trying to calm herself. Across the street, a couple of guys dressed in dark clothes, their hats pulled low over their faces, watched her.

When the bus pulled up to the corner, Claire dumped in her change with even shakier hands than the strung out woman who climbed on behind her. When the bus made it back to the stop closest to Claire's house, she practically crawled off. It was nearly one a.m. and she was exhausted.

No matter how badly she wanted to rescue her mother, there was nothing Claire could do until morning. The town may have relaxed with her mother's capture, but Claire hadn't. Somewhere, the *seule* was still out there, and Claire had no desire to run into her alone. Claire couldn't shake the image of Zahlia's apartment from her mind—she hoped the black wolf hadn't gone looking for the strange wolf by herself.

Claire crept back into the house. Upstairs, Lisbeth's snores echoed like a buzz saw. Claire's shoulders slumped in relief. *At least I'm not in any more trouble*. With any luck, Lisbeth would think she'd just forgotten to turn her alarm on. Claire collapsed on her bed and fell asleep, wrapped in guilt because she lay in her comfortable bed while her mother was trapped in a cage somewhere. All night long, she dreamt of dead dogs, suspicious-looking men, and cages. Lots and lots of cages.

In spite of her exhaustion, the sun woke Claire shortly after dawn. She felt more rested than she'd expected to. Her mother never needed much sleep, always working late in her dark-room, and then getting up early to prep for a shoot or go to a meeting. Maybe it was part of the whole werewolf thing. *If I get her out*—Claire stopped herself. *No, when I get her out, I'll ask her.*

She slid out of bed, grabbed her phone, and wandered downstairs. Even now, walking into her mother's darkroom uninvited made Claire's palms sweat. The cool, dim air smelled of Marie. Claire slid onto one of the stools in front of the worktable and put her head in her hands.

Her cell rang and Claire jumped.

"Hello?"

"Hey." Matthew's voice was gravelly, but the excitement in it was clear. "I hope I'm not calling too early."

Hearing his voice lightened the blackness in her chest, just a little bit.

"No, I'm up," she said, trying to keep her voice normal. Part of her wanted to just go ahead and break down—tell him everything. But his dad actually *had* her mom. If Matthew panicked, he might go to his dad. And Claire couldn't risk that.

"Cool. So, listen, since things are, you know, safe again, I was wondering if you wanted to go out tonight."

Just the idea of seeing him made Claire feel calmer, made it easier to think. And if Matthew knew anything about where her mother was, then she needed to do everything possible to get that information.

"That'd be great. What do you want to do?"

"I was thinking we could go over to Greenway Park—maybe have a picnic?"

"That sounds fun. Can you pick me up?"

"Um, sure—is that okay with everyone there?"

Claire struggled to keep her voice level. "My mom's not here today. It'll be fine."

And who cared, anyway? Her mom wasn't around to punish her if she found out. And Lisbeth would probably let her go if she said that she was going out with Doug Kingman after all.

They sorted out times, and Claire got off the phone before her mask of I'm-just-a-normal-sixteen-year-old cracked.

*"Since things are safe,"* he'd said. *That's what he thinks. Things aren't ever going to be safe for me, not with a monster like his father on the loose.*

Claire took one last look around the darkroom before she went upstairs to see if Lisbeth was awake. Her gaze flicked over her mother's computer desk and she stopped dead.

If Marie Benoit was anal about one thing, it was her

photography equipment. Everything had a place in the darkroom, and if it wasn't in her hand, it was in its assigned spot. In anyone else's house, the two cameras sitting on the desk next to the computer would look innocent enough, but the sight made Claire shudder. One of the cameras was turned on its side, still plugged into the computer. Claire picked it up and flipped it on. The memory card was empty—whatever photos had been there, her mother had already uploaded and then deleted them from the camera.

Unable to believe what she was doing, Claire slid onto the chair in front of the monitor and jiggled the mouse.

On the screen, a gray box popped up. THESE FILES ARE PASSWORD PROTECTED. PLEASE ENTER PASSWORD. Claire bit her lip. Okay. She could figure this out. She started with the obvious words, like "password," "pictures." None of them worked. Claire had worked her way through her mother's favorite artists, foods, and hotels before she sucked in her breath and tried the one thing that kept darting through the back of her mind—the one password no one would be likely to guess. With shaking hands, she typed it in: *loup-garou*.

INVALID PASSWORD, the computer announced.

*Well, crap.* If that hadn't worked, Claire couldn't think what else it could possibly be. With a heavy sigh, she snapped off the monitor and headed upstairs to sweet-talk Lisbeth into cooking her some breakfast.

Claire ate as slowly as she could, forcing herself not to

check the time. When she'd meticulously rinsed her dish and put it in the dishwasher, making sure it faced the right direction, she finally glanced over at the clock. Her heart sank when she saw the numbers. How could it only be ten forty-five? Matthew wasn't due to pick her up until eight! If she couldn't find something to distract herself from the tension that knotted her shoulder blades together like wings, she'd be crazy long before he got to the door. She headed for the living room, hoping she could find something mind-numbing on television.

After forcing herself to sit through two bad movies and one infomercial, Claire trudged upstairs to her room and looked around. She picked up her phone and called Emily. Maybe there'd been more drama with the country boy that they could dissect, or mouse encounters Emily could tell her about. Any distraction would be a good distraction.

"I was just about to call you!" Emily started talking without even saying hello.

"Oh, yeah?" Claire shoved aside a pile of clothes and flopped into her armchair.

"I mean, can you believe it? It's totally amazing news, right? I haven't been able to get a hold of Mom and Dad yet, but I'm demanding they come get me as soon as humanly possible."

Claire's mouth opened, but no words came out. Of course

Emily would get to come home, now that everyone thought the werewolf situation was over. With everything else that was going on, Claire hadn't really thought about it.

"That's—that's great, Em."

"Well, don't break a nail celebrating, or anything," Emily huffed.

Claire closed her eyes. "Sorry, Em—it's fantastic news, really!" She forced herself to sound enthusiastic. *It is fantastic news. Or at least, it should be. So why am I not excited?* If she was being completely honest, Claire sort of wished that Emily would stay at her aunt and uncle's—at least until Claire had things with her mother sorted out.

*How can I feel that way about my best friend?*

"So, are you packing yet?" she asked.

"Everything but my toothbrush," Emily announced proudly. "And I gave Dan the 'thanks for the memories' speech already too."

"Wow. How'd he take it?"

"Ugh. Let's just say there were lots of tears involved, and none of them were mine. Anyway, I'm going to call Mom again and see if she's out of her meeting yet. I'll let you know as soon as anything's definite, okay?"

"Can't wait," said Claire, willing Emily to believe her. "Good luck with your mom."

"Won't need it," Emily reassured her, "but thanks anyway. Talk to you soon!"

Claire hung up and stared down at the phone in her hand. Having Emily around would only make things more complicated than they already were. She was starting to see what her mom meant when she said it was too hard to be friends with a human.

Disgusted with herself, Claire crawled into the shower, hoping it would make her feel less slimy.

The hot water ran out before she could calm down completely. Claire dried off, tossed on a shirt, and ran a comb through her hair. She sighed, wishing that this was just a regular date. If she were normal, she'd be wondering if she should wear a prettier bra, or if her jeans were too tight around the thighs. Instead, all she could think about was finding out how to get to her mother. Claire threw her hairbrush down onto the vanity. It was so unfair. *He's a really great guy, and I'm planning to use him in the worst way possible. Fabulous. I'm sure ordinary human girls are always trying to get secret information from their boyfriends. Yeah, I bet that happens all the freaking time.*

Claire scraped her opinion of herself off the floor and slicked on some lip gloss. She stuck some silver hoops in her ears. The irony brought a tiny smile to her lips. Whichever werewolf had convinced the humans that silver would kill them, all those centuries ago, had created an awesome cover.

Claire looked over at the clock glowing on her nightstand. Six o'clock on the dot. Claire stared at herself in the mirror, trying to conjure up the excited, crush-stricken girl she had been two and a half months ago. The eyes that stared back were too anxious, too calculating. *I'm only doing what I have to do to save my mother. It's not like I'm going to hurt him. Come on, Claire, try harder.* She forced her lips into a smile, but no matter how hard she tried, her eyes gave her away. They were too much wolf, and not enough human.

# Chapter Seventeen

CLAIRE STOOD IN the foyer, one hand on the door, hoping Lisbeth wouldn't look too closely at the boy behind the wheel of the car.

"Okay, here's the deal. I want you to have a great time, but do not make me regret the fact that I'm allowing you out of the house. And if you're not home by ten . . . well . . . Just be home by ten." Lisbeth put her hands on her hips, trying to look stern.

Claire resisted the urge to roll her eyes. *She can't even think of something to threaten me with.*

"Don't worry, Lisbeth, I'll be back in plenty of time."

Claire rushed out the door, practically slamming it shut behind her. She looked over at Matthew as she climbed into the car next to him. The sun caught in his hair, and when he turned and smiled at her, it stirred up the same fluttery feeling in her belly that it always had. Claire could smell the excitement and nervousness pouring out of his skin. Underneath it was the scent of his desire, sweet as a peach.

*Focus, Claire. You need to know what he knows.*

Every second that ticked by brought her mother closer to the tip of Dr. Engle's needle. Claire hated all this secrecy, all the double agent crap. She wanted to just ask him about it, to tell him that she needed to know. He trusted her, right?

But then he'd want to know why she was asking. And she'd just have to start lying all over again. And he might get suspicious and clam up. Or worse, tell his dad.

"Are you okay?" he asked. "You seem sort of distracted tonight."

"Sorry," said Claire. "I guess it's just, uh, weird to see all these other cars and people with the sun going down."

Matthew nodded. "Yeah. Everyone's back to enjoying the long, hot summer, thanks to my dad's 'service to the community.'" A harsh little laugh tore out of him. "Whatever."

Claire's ears pricked up. *"Whatever?" What did he mean by that?*

Matthew pulled into a parking space at the edge of the park and turned off the car.

"What do you mean?" Claire asked gently.

Matthew let out a long breath that filled the car with the scent of his confusion and anger. "It's just—you know how I told you that I wasn't sure about what my dad was doing? That I wasn't sure he was right?"

Claire sat frozen, as motionless as an animal who knows it's being hunted. She forced herself to give a stiff nod. Claire tried to collect herself enough to keep her voice from shaking. "I don't really know that much about werewolves. No offense, but I don't know why I should take your dad's word for it that they're the most awful things ever, you know?"

*One lie, two lie; red lie, blue lie.*

Matthew stared at her, a happy glow seeping into his eyes and sweetening his scent. "Not offended," he whispered.

"So." Claire swung open her door and climbed out of the car like they were having the most normal conversation in the world. "What's actually going on? Making you question your dad again?"

Matthew grabbed an enormous cooler out of the back of the car and set it on the ground. "If I tell you—Claire you couldn't tell anyone. I mean, if my father found out, I'd be dead."

Claire met his gaze with steady eyes. "I'm really, really good at keeping secrets."

*And that's more truthful than you'll ever know.*

He sighed and ran a hand through his messy hair. The sky

behind him shimmered with the last of the day's light. "Okay. Let's eat while we talk—I think better on a full stomach."

"Sure. Here, I'll help you with that." Claire grabbed the cooler's handle and lifted with him.

Matthew's eyebrows shot up in surprise. "Wow. You're really strong." He and Claire blushed at the same time.

"I've been doing a lot of swimming—"

"Yeah, I didn't mean that you looked weak, or anything."

They grinned at each other. "Forget it," said Claire. They set the cooler down near the center of the field. "I'm starving," she said, anxious to change the subject.

"That's good—I packed enough food for an army." He opened the lid and tossed her a blanket.

Claire spread it on the ground while Matthew unpacked the cooler. When they were each on their second chicken leg, Claire couldn't stand it anymore. "So?" she asked, stripping the meat off the bones with her teeth. "What's the deal with your dad?"

Matthew poked his fork into a container of potato salad. The first stars glimmered overhead and the growing darkness hid his expression. "Well, you know how they're keeping the werewolf at the lab until they can give it the cure?"

Claire suppressed a shudder. "Yeah?"

"Okay, really, he'll kill me if he finds out about this." He twisted a paper napkin in his hands.

"Matthew. I won't tell anyone. I promise."

He looked up at her. "I know. I trust you. Okay." He took a deep breath. "I sort of snuck into the lab one night. I was curious, you know? And it's not like I would have gotten hurt—that thing's cage is stronger than Fort Knox. Anyway, when I got in there, the wolf—it was crying. Like, really, really crying."

A ripping sensation tore through Claire's chest. She struggled to breathe.

Matthew barreled on, like he couldn't quit telling the story now that he'd finally started. Claire could hear in his voice how much he'd been aching to tell someone. "So, I felt bad for it all of a sudden, and—the look in its eyes, I just didn't think that it could have killed someone. I know it was stupid, but I wasn't thinking about getting hurt, and I just sort of stuck my hand through the bars and petted it. And it was the weirdest thing, Claire." He stared up at her from beneath his shaggy bangs.

"It butted its head into my hand and whimpered and—it was awful. I could just *feel* how lonely and scared and, I don't know—how *gentle* it was. I mean, not like a human, or anything, but not any more dangerous than any other animal, you know? I know it sounds crazy, and I wouldn't blame you if you didn't believe me, but I could just tell that it hadn't killed anyone. Or, if it had, it hadn't really meant to." He leaned over and lit the lantern that held down the corner of the blanket.

Claire hurriedly wiped the tears out of the corners of her

eyes. Matthew stared at her. He looked shocked. "I—I just feel sorry for it, that's all," she stuttered. *Truth number two.*

"Yeah. I just wish my dad would . . . I don't know. He's so freaking desperate to get everyone to take him seriously, to prove he belongs on the FHPA. But I wish he would investigate more before he gives it his cure. The way this werewolf is—I'm just more convinced than ever that he's wrong. I know they've done plenty of terrible things—my dad has a billion books about it, right? But, I mean, maybe they're not all like that. Maybe this one isn't like that. And his cure leaves them half-alive at best. I just don't think this werewolf deserves that. I don't think it's the one who's done all these horrible things."

"So, who do you think has?" The question popped out before Claire could stop it. The idea had been nagging at her all day. She couldn't help wondering whose crimes her mother was paying for.

Matthew leaned a little closer. "Maybe there are more werewolves out there than people think there are."

The adrenaline flooded Claire's veins so fast that the hairs on her arms stood on end. He was too close to the truth. Much too close. "What makes you think that?" she whispered.

"I saw something once—my dad left some classified reports on the computer desk. Government stuff. I was curious, I mean, anything that has TOP SECRET stamped across it . . ."

Claire nodded.

"So, the reports said that twice, after they caught a werewolf and my dad 'cured' it, the killings didn't stop. The government covered it up to keep the public from panicking—I mean, if people thought there were packs of werewolves roaming around, they'd freak."

"Wow, that's—that's really surprising." Claire said, breathily. *Really surprising that your dad knows he's not right, but he's still torturing us anyway.*

"Yeah, I was shocked as hell. That's when I really started to wonder about the stuff my dad does. He always works pretty closely with the government of whatever country he's 'helping'—he did that even before he got appointed to the FHPA. Maybe it's more about PR than anything, you know? I mean, what if there have been more werewolves like this one, really gentle ones, and they're taking the blame for some other killer? Just so that all us humans can feel all safe and self-righteous."

He stared off into the woods. "Maybe there's another werewolf who's been killing people here. That's what I think, anyway."

"But if you think that, how come you're not scared to be out here at night?"

Matthew ran his fingertips across the back of her hand. "Everyone else is out, too, right? 'Cause my dad says it's safe. I'm not gonna hide in the house forever. I can't. I guess I just don't think my number's up yet."

Claire wasn't sure what to say.

"Do you think I'm crazy?" he asked finally.

She shook her head. "No," she whispered. "I think you're the only sane one out there." The tears welled up in her eyes, and Claire didn't think she could stop from sobbing if Matthew kept looking at her in that relieved way. "I, uh—need to grab something out of my purse. I'll be right back, okay?" Without waiting for an answer, Claire scrambled off the blanket and headed toward the car, more surefooted than any human could ever have been in the newly dark night. She struggled to control the tears that coursed down her cheeks.

This wasn't at all the sort of "information" she'd been expecting to get from Matthew. Claire had known her mother must be terrified, lonely—but to have it confirmed like that just about broke her.

She yanked open the car door and made a show of rummaging through her purse while she tried to make sense of the thoughts spinning in her head. Maybe she could get more than just information from Matthew. Maybe he could actually help her—even if he could just get her into the lab where they were keeping her mother, it would save Claire an enormous amount of time and energy. Excitement hummed under her skin; the adrenaline overtook her sadness and she dried her eyes. She could do this. Even without Beatrice and Victoria, she could save her mother. It was just a question of how.

Claire snapped her purse shut and tossed it on the floorboard. She slammed the car door and turned to head back to

Matthew—and at that exact second, she heard the first low growl behind her.

Claire's eyes were still blind from the interior light of the car. All she could make out was a dark figure weaving through the trees at the edge of the forest. Another snarl rang out. The threat had been issued in a very familiar voice, and the flash of recognition that shot through Claire burned like an electric shock.

It was Zahlia. Behind her, Matthew knelt in the center of the blanket, focused on getting the food back into the cooler. The car stood between him and the wolf on the other side of the road, so even if he looked up, he might not see anything.

Claire edged around to the far side of the car and hunched down behind it, confused and scared. Whatever would make Zahlia show up in front of Matthew, it had to be serious.

At the edge of the forest Zahlia hesitated. Claire couldn't figure out what Zahlia wanted, and she didn't have much time before Matthew came looking for her. Claire threw off her clothes and transformed. Her true nature shattered her human disguise, and Claire stood in the shadow of Matthew's car, surprised by how much more complete her change was. She'd expected the transformation to be the same as it had been at the last full moon, but she looked every inch a werewolf. Still, she could feel something missing, could tell that her strength and her senses hadn't yet reached their full potential.

*Zahlia, what's going on? Matthew will see us!* It was the

first time Claire had needed to communicate the way the rest of the wolves did, since her lupine mouth made speech impossible. It felt as natural as talking, and Claire's confidence grew.

*Watch yourself, Young One.* Zahlia's warning echoed off the trees. Claire laid her ears flat against her head. She hoped Matthew hadn't heard that. He would notice that she was missing any second—she had to get back into her human body. Zahlia took a step forward, stalking her.

*What are you talking about? I'm trying to save my mother. If Matthew sees you, it'll screw up everything! Why didn't you just call me back? Can't we talk later?* Claire could smell her own fear and frustration. Her confusion. It made her smell weak.

Zahlia, upwind, caught the scent, too. She gave a little leap, bounding farther into the clearing. At the same moment, Matthew called out.

"Claire? You okay over there?"

Zahlia took advantage of Claire's distraction and launched herself at Claire.

*You. Stay. Out of this.* Zahlia growled, and pressed closer, knocking Claire into the car. *Your mother has made more than her share of mistakes, and you are following in her footsteps. If you don't back off, I will be more than willing to let that* boy *pay for your errors.*

Claire crouched low, her shoulder aching where it had slammed into the wheel well. A guttural rumble tore against her throat, and in spite of her confusion she tensed to spring, ready to defend herself.

*Zahlia, what is going on with you? I'm trying to ask for your help. Why are you pissed? I don't understand!*

Zahlia squared off against Claire. She panted in anticipation, her hot breath washing over Claire's face. It reeked of the hot-pepper scent of fury. *I'm helping you by not crushing you here and now. Consider yourself warned.* Zahlia turned and streaked off into the woods.

Crouched behind the metal bulk of the car, Claire squeezed herself back into her human form and yanked on her clothes. She kept one shocked eye trained on the woods as she stood. Her hands trembled.

*What the hell just happened?*

The wolf who'd just threatened her was nothing like the person—the friend—that Claire had trusted so much. She'd been sure Zahlia would understand, that she would want to help.

*And she threatened Matthew, too. Crap.*

"Matthew?" she called, hurrying back to the blanket where he lay on his back in the pale glow from the lantern.

"Yeah, you okay? You were gone awhile. I was starting to worry."

"Sorry. I couldn't find what I was looking for."

Claire stared at the trees, thinking she saw Zahlia lurking in every shadow.

She leaned in and kissed him.

"Claire," he whispered.

Claire cut him off with another kiss before he could say anything else.

"Let's get out of here," she murmured against his lips. She looked over his shoulder at the woods, wondering where Zahlia was. Had she gone? Claire scanned the trees. No eyes flashed in the lantern light, but the black wolf was a master at hiding from her prey.

"Sure, no problem."

Together they wadded up the blanket and headed for the car. The drive home was quiet, with Matthew focused on the dark roads and Claire scanning the ground on each side, looking for wolves. It was too soon to press him anymore about getting in to see the lab. She knew that. She could *smell* it. But all the same, the words "please take me to see my mother" were ready to leap out of her mouth, and she struggled to keep them contained.

"Now you're the one who seems quiet," said Matthew.

Claire shrugged. *Yeah, if you only knew how hard I was working to stay quiet.* "A little, I guess. Hey, um, are you busy tomorrow night?"

"Yeah—I have soccer practice until late. I'm not free again until Saturday."

Claire swallowed her disappointment. Saturday seemed like a year away. "Okay," she said finally. "Saturday sounds great."

Matthew lit up like a struck match. "Great! I have soccer practice until five, but after that, I'm all yours. Was there something special you wanted to do?" He squeezed her hand.

"I don't know. Let's just see how it goes." Claire squeezed back.

*That's the understatement of the year.*

The feel of his palm, warm against hers, sent a little ribbon of excitement sliding between her shoulder blades.

When he kissed her good night, guilt and desire and the sinking feeling that she was in too deep with Matthew spun together inside her. It would all be so much easier if she didn't actually care about him, if he hadn't just admitted that he thought his father was wrong.

# Chapter Eighteen

CLAIRE SLIPPED INTO the house and found Lisbeth on the couch, curled up around an enormous bowl of ice cream. "I'm home and I'm not late, and I'm going to go take a shower now, okay?"

Lisbeth squinted at her. "You haven't been smoking, have you?"

"Huh?"

"Well, you're rushing to take a shower . . . ," Lisbeth said pointedly.

For one second, Claire felt like every other sixteen-year-old on earth. "Lisbeeeth, that's crazy. It's hot outside. I got sweaty. I want to take a shower. I don't smoke! God." . . . . *dess*, she added silently.

"Well, good. You'd better not. I mean, the toxins they put into those death-sticks . . ." She wrinkled her nose.

Claire rolled her eyes and stalked upstairs to her bathroom. She pulled off her shirt, examining the bruise on her ribs where Zahlia had crashed into her. Why would Zahlia have threatened to attack Matthew? It could have been her idea of revenge—Dr. Engle's son in exchange for Marie. "An eye for an eye" sort of thing. But then, why would she have charged at Claire like that? And her creepy apartment . . . Claire couldn't make sense of it all, but whatever was going on with Zahlia, she needed to be stopped before she got captured too. *Or before she kills a human.*

Her phone rang and Claire flipped open the phone without even looking at the screen.

"Hello?"

"Claaaaaaaire!!! Guess what? I'm coming HOME!"

It was Emily. A very excited Emily.

"I—really? Already?"

"I know I said I'd call, but when I talked to my mom, she said she'd come right out to get me, and then my battery died—anyway, long story short, I'm coming back! And in time for Drama Club tryouts, too! I'm absolutely dying to see you, Claire. I'll be home Friday. When can we get together? What about Saturday?"

Claire felt a half smile twitch across her mouth. She could imagine it—Emily lounging on Claire's bed, painting her toe-nails, digging through Claire's closet to try on anything new she found there.

*Except that I can't let her in my closet—not with the stuff I've got hidden there.* The bloodstains from her hunts had refused to come out of two shirts and one pair of pants. They were wadded up in the back corner of her closet, but Emily would find them.

*And I can't exactly try to find Mom and give myself a pedicure at the same time. Dammit.*

There was no way she could hang out with Emily. In a flash, Claire understood why her mother had never had any real friends. Their lives were too different, and it hurt too much to have it constantly thrown in your face like that.

"I wish I could, but I have plans with Matthew." At least it wasn't a lie.

"Hey, that's fantastic! You guys are getting pretty serious, huh?"

"Yeah, we are, actually."

"Fine, then I'll let you off the hook for Saturday on *one* condition: I. Want. Details. And I mean, like, boxers-or-briefs details." There was a wicked edge to Emily's voice. "When can I see you?"

"Um, actually, my phone's about to die and I'm totally exhausted, but I'll call you, okay?"

"Oh, uh, sure." Emily sounded let down and Claire felt responsible.

Claire hung up and flopped back on her bed. The truth of who she was, *what* she was, hung over her like a lead umbrella. Her mother had told her over and over that it would get easier, that Claire would become like an oyster. *"The truth,* chérie, *the secret—it is like a grain of sand. You must hold it inside the way an oyster does, smoothing it over and over until it becomes a jewel that makes you stronger, more valuable, even though no one can see it inside you. It will only hurt at first."*

*But I'm not a damn oyster, Mother.* This truth was much bigger than a grain of sand, and it grew every day. Claire could feel herself straining at the edges, stretched to the point of explosion with the effort of keeping it contained. For what felt like the twelve millionth time, she went from feeling like being a werewolf made her superior to being certain that her condition was a curse.

She curled up on her comforter. Outside the window, the moon rose, pale against the darkening sky. She was running out of time—in only a few weeks the moon would be full, and Dr. Engle would take her mother away from her forever.

Claire pressed a fist against her mouth to muffle her whimpers and let the tears roll down her cheeks. She was so alone that she ached with it.

Hours later, Claire rolled herself up in her covers and

closed her swollen eyes. She slept fitfully. Nightmares jolted her awake again and again.

Shortly after dawn finally broke, Claire stumbled downstairs and poured herself a cup of coffee. She wrapped her hands around the hot mug and wandered down the quiet hall.

Without exactly meaning to, she ended up in front of her mother's darkroom. Even with Marie sitting in a cage at Dr. Engle's lab, Claire couldn't bring herself to break the cardinal rule about food or drink in her mother's workspace. She set the coffee on the little table next to the door and went in. The computer screen stared across the room at her, like a giant eye. Claire sat down in front of it and pulled up the same file she'd tried to get into the day before.

She missed her mother. Terribly. *I wonder if she misses me as much.* Claire stared at the password box on the screen, just as an idea crept into her head. Was it possible?

Slowly, she typed the letters into the blank field and hit ENTER. The file opened immediately. All the words she'd tried before, and she'd never once thought that her mother would have used her own daughter's name. The password was *Claire*, after all.

Claire blinked back the tears that had gathered in the corners of her eyes and focused on the image of the forest at night that had appeared on the screen. It wasn't like her mother's usual work—the photo looked rushed, unprofessional. Claire let the slideshow run, squinting at the screen. It looked like her mother had been in the woods, taking pictures from behind the protective curtain of pines. There was something out past the tree line, but it was hard to make out. The pictures had been taken without a flash, but her mother had obviously been using a slow shutter speed so that whatever she was aiming at would show up on the photo.

But her subject had been moving.

Claire stared at the blur in front of her. A jolt of recognition shot through her and Claire whimpered. She'd seen pictures of that same house before. It was where the man had been killed and left right out on his lawn. *The man the* seule *had killed.* In front of the house was a half-light, half-dark blur. *Oh, Jesus. Mom saw it happen—she was photographing the whole thing!* The pictures darkened and sharpened as Marie tried to get a clearer shot of the struggle in front of the house. Claire could only make out the indistinct shape of a very dark wolf.

As the slideshow flicked forward, the man's body suddenly stood out as clearly as the bricks on his house. He lay perfectly still, his mangled torso hideous against the cheerful daisies that bloomed behind him. Next to her victim, the wolf blurred as she moved away from the body.

The last two photos showed the wolf clearly. In the first she stared down at the mess in front of her, but her back was to the camera. The next photo showed her at the man's back

gate, her face mostly obscured by one of the sunflowers growing next to the fence. A dark lupine chin and a few gleaming
teeth were clearly visible beneath one of the blooms, but that
was it. Claire watched the two photos play over and over again,
her frustration building higher with each flash of the screen.
Something seemed so familiar about the pictures, the last one
especially.

Claire stared at the sunflower, blocking the *seule*'s face
with its too-big center and fringe of petals. She'd never really
liked that particular flower. They were corny, somehow. The
image of the sunflower in Zahlia's apartment jumped into
her mind.

*Zahlia never seemed like someone who would keep sunflowers*
*around.*

*Wait—why would she . . . ?*

*Oh. Shit.*

Maybe it was a coincidence. It could be a coincidence.
Claire sat frozen at the computer, remembering the other
things in Zahlia's weird little office. With her stomach churn-
ing, she clicked open the Internet and looked up the name of
the editor who'd been killed.

The search engine found it instantly. Dave McKinney.
The briefcase on Zahlia's office floor—the initials on it had
been DRM.

Claire pushed away from the desk, her hands clenched so
tightly that her fingernails cut into her palms.

The dog. The one on Zahlia's bed. One of the victim's dogs had gone missing when they'd been murdered.

It had been Zahlia. She'd killed every one of those poor people.

Claire turned and vomited all over the darkroom floor.

When she quit heaving, Claire snapped off the monitor and put her head down on the desk.

How could Zahlia have killed all those people? The same werewolf who had helped her when no one else would, practiced with her in the woods—how could she be so *savage*? Oh, God, and she'd threatened Matthew.

After Claire wiped up the mess on the floor, she picked up the phone and dialed Matthew's cell.

"Hello?" Sleep thickened his voice, but Claire was more focused on the fact that he was still breathing.

She glanced at the little clock on the computer. It wasn't even eight o'clock yet. "Oh, crap, I didn't realize it was so early, Matthew. I'm sorry—I'll call—I mean, why don't you just call me later?"

"No, Claire, it's fine. Really. The reporters start calling my dad at eight, anyway. I can't sleep with the house phone ringing off the hook like that. I'd much rather wake up to you than to the *Daily Herald*."

Claire blushed.

"Hey, do you still want to do something Saturday night?"

"Yeah, that'd be great."

*What I have in mind is probably not what you're planning, though.*

"Cool. Listen, I should get showered before the reporters start breaking down the front door. Is six o'clock okay?"

The idea of Matthew showering made it hard for Claire to focus on her answer.

"Sure. I'll have Lisbeth bring me over on her way to yoga."

Claire tried to focus on the thought of seeing Matthew, instead of dwelling on the fact that she'd be lying like hell the entire time.

On Saturday, Claire had Lisbeth drop her off two blocks away from the Engles', in front of Yolanda Adams's house. Fortunately, Lisbeth was running late enough that she didn't wait to see if Claire got into the house before she drove away. Once the car was out of sight, Claire walked over to the Engles'. As she paced up the front walk she noticed the front flowerbeds were dotted here and there with little statues.

Garden gnomes. Exactly like the one on Zahlia's desk. The rage that filled Claire stopped her, gluing her feet to the cracked concrete path. Zahlia hadn't just threatened Matthew. She'd been here. Watching. Planning. Claire struggled to control herself, to unclench her jaw. She was already late—if Matthew saw her like this, it could throw off the whole night. She'd deal with Zahlia later. And as long as she and Matthew were together, she'd make damn sure that no out-of-her-mind werewolf came within swiping distance of him.

Claire took a couple of deep breaths and walked up to the door, which had been left ajar. It was six fifteen on the nose when Claire walked into the Engles' kitchen. At the table, Matthew and his dad sat eating sandwiches and what smelled to Claire like canned soup. Dr. Engle smiled at her with too many teeth and waved to an empty chair.

"Claire, welcome. Please, sit and have a little bite with us." He was clearly trying to be hospitable, but he still creeped Claire out. "I made enough for three, but Mrs. Engle isn't feeling well."

The look on Matthew's face said that she had interrupted something—Dr. Engle's expression said he was glad that she had.

Claire slid into the chair. "I've already eaten, thanks." Under the table, she clenched her hands into tight fists. The urge to throttle the egotistical jerk until he admitted he'd been wrong about her mother was almost more than she could bear. The effort of holding herself in check made her bones hurt.

"We can go as soon as I'm done." Matthew's voice was acidic. He shoved a large corner of sandwich into his mouth and chewed like he wanted to hurt it.

Claire looked from Matthew to Dr. Engle.

"Ah, actually"—Dr. Engle stirred his soup, focusing on the letter-shaped noodles that floated to the surface—"Channel Six will be here in a few minutes. They'd like a family member to be in the story, and I think it's a good angle. I was hoping your mother would be able to participate, but that's obviously not a possibility. It won't take long—I'll just need a few minutes from you, and then you and Claire can go. I'm sure Claire won't mind waiting a bit, will you?" He turned the piranha-smile on her again, and Claire felt her lip curl in response.

*I know how to play you.*

She turned the curled lip into a simper and tilted her head to one side. "Oh, Dr. Engle, I couldn't possibly say. Whatever Matthew wants will be just fine with me." *Gag.*

He beamed and licked his lips. "See? What a help she is! So, it's settled. You'll do the interview."

Matthew tossed his sandwich crust back onto his plate and wiped his mouth with the back of his hand. "Sure, I'll do it." He shot Claire the tiniest look. "But you know what I'll be telling them."

"Wha—now. Matthew. I thought we were finished *discussing* the issue."

The look in Dr. Engle's eyes chilled Claire. The fury of the self-righteous nestled there like ice.

"You're right. I am done discussing it. You're wrong about the werewolf, Dad. You're not going to listen to me and I'm not going to listen to you. But I'm sure the thousands of people watching Channel Six tonight will be very interested to hear what I have to say. And I bet that someone from Lycanthropy Researchers will be watching too."

Dr. Engle stood up. "I will not tolerate you defending that soulless creature for one more second. It doesn't have the right to live among humans—it's a mistake, a mutation. It should never have existed at all!"

The snarl rose in Claire's throat before she could stop it. "You don't know what you're talking about." She stood and faced him, nostrils flared.

Matthew's mouth fell open.

Dr. Engle gave a short, hard laugh. "Of course not. I'm only one of the most innovative lycanthropy researchers in the nation. I'm part of the Federal Human Protection Agency. Why would I know what I'm talking about?" He looked up at the ceiling as though he could find patience in its smooth, white expanse.

Claire bit her lip. *Oh, crap. I really should have kept my mouth shut. What if he figures out that my mom is the wolf that he captured?* From underneath her lowered eyelids, she scanned his face. It held plenty of anger, but no suspicion.

"And you"—Dr. Engle turned to Matthew—"would do well to remember that it is never wise to bite the hand that feeds you." He threw his napkin down onto the table. "Now, if you'll excuse me, I need to go prepare for the news crew."

He stalked out of the room, and Claire heard a door slam in another part of the house.

Matthew pushed away his plate. "God, I'm sorry he's such an ass." He looked at Claire. "I can't believe you stood up to him like that. Everyone else just buys his crap without even thinking about it." Admiration shone in his eyes.

"Buyer beware, right?" Claire grinned. Tonight was going to be her night. Matthew was furious enough with his father that she was sure she could convince him to show her where the lab was. Once she knew how to get in, all she had to do was figure out how to sneak her mother out without being seen.

Maybe once she got her mother back they could start their own pack, just the two of them. Let Beatrice and Victoria clean up the mess Zahlia had made. Her mother shouldn't have to sneak around doing the work that their Alpha was too scared to do. That was the only reason she'd gotten caught, after all. If Beatrice had kept Zahlia in check, her mother never would have been captured.

"Ready to go?" Matthew asked.

Claire nodded. She blinked hard, clearing her head, and followed Matthew out to the car.

They drove around aimlessly while Matthew ranted about his father. Claire's senses strained as she tracked his scent, his expression, the way he held his body. Carefully, she fed his rage, using little comments and almost unnoticeable gestures. The last thing she wanted was for him to think that she was egging him on.

"It's just ridiculous!" Matthew pounded the steering wheel with the heel of his hand. "I mean, you should see this wolf,

Claire. It's the most gentle thing—I know it's an animal, but, dammit, there is nothing evil about it!"

Her surge of adrenaline was strong enough to be painful. This was the moment.

"I wish I *could* see it," she said softly. "If it's really as gentle as you say . . ." An image of her mother ripping at a newly dead deer flashed through her mind. *Well, she's gentle where people are concerned, at least.*

Matthew turned to her, his eyes ablaze. "You can!"

Success leapt through Claire. "Really?" She kept the excitement in her voice to the tiniest glimmer.

"Yes. Dad'll be busy with the freaking media for hours, and no one goes to the lab at night, anyway." His face turned serious. "You'd have to swear never to tell a soul that I took you."

"Of course," Claire said.

"Okay." Matthew's grip on the steering wheel turned purposeful. "It'll only take us about ten minutes to get there. My dad"—he snorted—"hates long commutes."

# Chapter Nineteen

THE BUILDING LOOKED exactly the same as the ones on either side of it: a long stretch of cinderblock, punctuated with corrugated metal doors. Far above, a lighted sign announced to the highway SELF STORAGE! FIRST MONTH FREE! Claire stared at Matthew. In the eerie light of the mercury lamps, his face looked drawn.

"Why are we here? Isn't your dad's lab at the university somewhere?" She kept her voice to a whisper.

Matthew shook his head. "He has two labs. That one's mostly for show. He kept the werewolf there long enough for the news crews to get their shots, but then he and his lab techs brought it here. This is where he does all of his actual experiments and stuff. No one knows about it, except for him and the techs. And Mom and me, obviously."

Claire trembled at the thought of what must be going on in this building if Dr. Engle needed to keep it so secret. The two of them pressed against the damp stone wall, waiting, watching. On one side of the facility, the highway wound past in a concrete ribbon, but the other side was bordered by a copse of trees at the edge of a farm. Finding her way back here later would be easier than Claire had hoped.

"No one's going to catch us sneaking in, right?"

Matthew shook his head. "It's Saturday. Everyone leaves at five on Saturdays, and they don't come back until eight o'clock Monday morning. My dad's always going on about how Sunday's a 'day of worship and rest.'"

*We'll have a whole day's head start after I get her out.* But all she could think to say was, "Oh, okay."

It was nearly impossible to be patient when her mother was so close. She had to do something to quiet the itching in her limbs. "So, which door is it?"

The corner of Matthew's mouth turned up. "All of them. He had the building converted. He rents this one, all the way down to the end. As long as he keeps sending the owners a fat check every month, I don't think they care what he does."

Claire's mouth fell open as she did a quick calculation. The lab was nearly a city block long.

"Okay, I think we're clear. We've gotta get down to the fifth door. The lock's broken on that one, but no one knows it. When I say go, we run."

"Got it." Claire's breath quickened and she bent her knees.

"Go," Matthew whispered and took off at a sprint. He was no match for a werewolf, but the hours of soccer training showed in the way he ran. For a human, he was fast.

He glanced back at Claire in surprise, one hand on the door handle. "You should go out for track," he said, wrenching open the metal with a twist. "You're wicked quick."

*You have no idea.*

Claire grinned to herself as they slipped into the lab and the scent of her mother washed over her.

In the darkness, the instruments glimmered like stars. No papers littered the counters, no school pictures stood next to the computer monitors—it was as bare and soulless as Zahlia's apartment had been. Claire grimaced at the memory of the dog lying on the black wolf's bed.

"I don't want to turn on the lights," Matthew whispered, "just in case. Can you make it through in the dark?"

Claire squelched an urge to snort. Her eyesight was good enough to read the brand names on the lab equipment. "Yeah, I'll be okay," she said. She could smell her mother at the far north end of the lab. *Make an effort to seem human, Claire.*

"So, um, where's the cage?"

Matthew took her hand, and Claire cursed the little electric tingles that shot up her arm. *This is not the time. I'm here to find my mother. I can ignore my hormones.* She repeated it like a mantra as he pulled her clumsily through the lab. He made it so hard to focus. Standing up to his father like that made it difficult for Claire to remember that he would run away screaming if he knew what she really was.

Claire's breathing grew ragged when she spotted the silver bars of the cage at the back of the lab.

Matthew peered over his shoulder at her. "Scared?" There was no taunting in his voice, just concern.

Claire shook her head. "Just, uh, trying not to trip."

The cage came into full view and Claire struggled to keep from whimpering.

Her mother lay curled up in the corner of the cage with her nose tucked underneath her tail. Misery shimmered around her like an aura.

Without thinking, Claire took a few quick steps toward the silver wolf.

A strong arm caught Claire across the chest. "Easy," Matthew whispered. "I don't want you to startle it."

Claire nodded and forced herself to move more slowly. In her human form, she couldn't communicate with her mother silently. Marie lifted her head and stared straight at Claire for a moment before she slunk to the front of the cage and pressed her flank against the bars. Ignoring Matthew's astonished gasp, Claire knelt down and pressed her forehead against the soft fur of her mother's neck. The wolf whimpered too softly for human ears to hear. Hot tears leaked out of Claire's eyes and dripped down onto her mother's pelt. Claire stroked her mother's haunches, feeling the bones underneath. On top of everything else, Dr. Engle wasn't feeding her enough.

"I'm so sorry," she whispered. Matthew was only a few feet away, so it was hard to talk quietly enough that he wouldn't hear, and there was so much Claire wanted to say. "I'm going to get you out before the full moon," she murmured, fighting off the dragging weight of her sadness.

Matthew's shoes squeaked on the linoleum when he finally walked up to the cage. "You really aren't scared of anything, are you?"

Claire looked up at him. "I'm not scared of this wolf," she said. "I can't believe anyone thinks it's okay to treat her like this."

Claire mistook the astonishment that flashed across Matthew's face when she turned to him. *He's surprised that I'm crying.*

"How—how did you know it was a female?" He knelt down next to her.

*Oh, crap.*

"I—I think I heard it on TV," Claire stammered. Her mother's ears pricked up, and Claire felt the muscles in the wolf's side ripple in concern.

"Really?" Matthew cautiously ran his fingertips along the wolf's shoulder. "Huh. Dad really wanted to keep that secret. He'll be megapissed if it's gotten out."

"Oh," Claire said. "Maybe I'm mixed up. I thought I'd heard that, but it must have just been a lucky guess." *Change the subject, change the subject!* "Um, how many times have you visited it?" Talking about her mother this way when she was close enough to touch made Claire nauseous.

"A few times," Matthew said. "It took me a while to get brave enough to pet it like this, though." While he stroked the wolf, Claire made the most of her night vision, looking for a way to get her mother out of the cage. The bars were solid—too solid to be harmed even by a werewolf in its prime. *Obviously, or Mom would already be free. They have to keep a key around here somewhere. . . .*

Claire's mother began to pant, and Claire could smell the hunger on her breath. "Is there any meat around here?" she asked Matthew.

"You—you want to *feed* it?"

"She looks hungry." Claire used the word "she" carefully. The sooner she could get Matthew to see that the animal in front of them wasn't a *thing*, but a feeling, thinking creature, the better.

Matthew pursed his lips. "There's food in the fridge, but my dad says if it's fed too much, it'll get bloodlust and they might not be able to control it."

"Do you think there's a chance he's wrong about that, too?" Claire stared at him intently. "Matthew, he's starving her." She got up and walked to the refrigerator. *Let him chew on that one for a minute.* Inside the immaculate fridge, test tubes and bottles covered the top rack, but the bottom two shelves were stuffed full of family-sized packages of hot dogs. *Cheap hot dogs,* Claire noted with disgust. She bent down and grabbed four packages of the food from the bottom shelf. After she pulled the other packages forward, it didn't even look like anything was missing.

Claire hurried back to the cage and knelt down in front of it. Matthew stared at her strangely while she ripped off the plastic wrappers and slid the meat through the bars. The smell of it hit her like a slap—it was no better than dog food. Her mother dragged the hot dogs to the back corner of her cage and gulped it down. The whine of relief that whistled through her nose as she ate sent desperation zipping through Claire. She couldn't leave her mother here for one more minute, not with what Dr. Engle was making her endure.

Claire looked at Matthew, her patience worn thin. "What?" There was more sting to the question that she'd meant to show.

He leaned back. "Sorry. It's just—I didn't expect anyone to understand why I didn't hate it—I mean, hate her. But you seem to feel even sorrier for her than I do. I'm just surprised, that's all."

Claire ran a hand across her forehead. She really had to

be more careful. "You told me she wasn't dangerous," she said. "And I trust you." Flustered, Claire turned to ball up the trash from the hot dogs. *It's the truth. I do trust him.*

Matthew's warm hand brushed her hair back from her face and he leaned toward her. Out of the corner of her eye, Claire saw her mother cock her head at them. Before he could kiss her, Claire ducked to the side and gave him a brief hug. *There's no way I'm kissing anyone in front of my mother.*

"It's late," she whispered. "We should get home before Lisbeth kills me."

"Oh, yeah, you're right."

Claire could feel his confusion through the shift of the muscles in his back.

"Thanks for bringing me," she whispered. Claire pulled away from him and they both looked at the caged wolf.

"We'll come back soon," Matthew said.

Claire couldn't tell if he was talking to her or to her mother. He started back to the door. Claire hesitated. She stared into her mother's gold-flecked eyes.

"Be ready," Claire mouthed. "I'm coming back for you."

The silver wolf blinked and twitched her tail once.

Before he could notice her dawdling, Claire followed Matthew back through the maze of equipment. If only she'd been able to find a key! *It doesn't matter. I'll find it next time, even if it means that I have to tear this entire place apart. Which might not be a bad idea, anyway.*

Outside, Claire took long breaths of the night air. The disinfectant smell of the lab lingered in her nose. She turned to Matthew. "I wish everyone could see that."

He suddenly looked uncomfortable. "Yeah, but we can't tell anyone, okay? I mean, I wish there was something we could do about it, but no one's going to believe us instead of my dad, you know?"

Claire opened her mouth, ready to disagree, when something moved at the far end of the building. She blinked and wondered if the tree shadows were playing tricks on her eyes. The security light showed nothing but a bare expanse of concrete and a chain link fence.

But then, whatever was out there twitched again and a pair of yellow eyes flashed in the darkness. Zahlia streaked toward the fence, her blackness separating from the shadows of the trees. She was coming for them.

Claire had always heard people say that certain things happened in slow motion—a car accident, a bad fall, the moment before a glass smashed against the floor. Each step Zahlia took registered in Claire's mind like a photo. She could almost hear the *snap* of the shutter. Matthew had his back to Zahlia. He didn't see her coming. Before Claire made her decision, she had time to register two separate thoughts: *If he sees me change, his father will kill me.* It was the second thought that was the strongest. *Not him, not now.* The moment those four words flowed though her mind, Claire threw off her clothes and burst into her true form. *Please,* she prayed, *let him not have seen me naked.*

Without looking at his face, Claire knocked Matthew into the alcove of the lab door and bounded past him. Zahlia cleared the fence with one leap and landed in the pool of bluish light. Her head lowered and she laid her ears back.

Claire mirrored Zahlia's posture while a low warning growl rumbled in her throat. She tried to tell Zahlia to stop, but Zahlia acted as though she hadn't understood. Her shoulders hunched under her dark fur.

*The cost of meddling is higher than you thought it would be, Young One. You will not stop me. You can't.* Zahlia growled, baring her teeth.

Claire shook her head and whined as the noise filled her ears. That moment of distraction was all Zahlia needed. Behind Claire, Matthew let out a gasp as Zahlia charged at her.

Claire crouched low and bucked hard just as Zahlia reached her. The black wolf flew over Claire's back and landed hard on the pavement, but not before she managed to grab the very tip of Claire's ear in her teeth. Claire spun around before Zahlia could attack again. Blood from her frayed ear dripped onto the ground below her.

Zahlia glanced at Matthew, crouched in the doorway. *You first,* she said, baring her teeth to Claire. *Then him.*

Claire slammed herself into Zahlia's flank, her teeth

snapping at Zahlia's dark neck. Zahlia twisted her head away at the last second, and Claire was left with a mouthful of fur. The pavement rushed up at Claire's snout as Zahlia spun out of her grip. Claire tucked her shoulder under and rolled hard. Zahlia's claws landed where Claire's eyes had been only a moment before. Leaping to her feet, Claire jumped hard and landed on top of Zahlia, knocking her to the ground. There was a huffing sound as the air rushed out of Zahlia's lungs. Winded, Zahlia rolled over onto her back. Before she could get her teeth around the soft underside of Claire's belly, Claire slashed at Zahlia's snout with her paw.

The dark wolf let out a howl. Blood poured down her nose and ran into her eyes. Claire looked at Zahlia, blinded and defenseless, her throat exposed. She faltered, unable to complete the kill. Without thinking, Claire snapped her jaws around Zahlia's front paw. She heard the bones crunch under her teeth. Zahlia screamed in pain.

Claire heard a metallic clang behind her and whirled around in time to see the lab door slam shut. Matthew had barricaded himself inside the lab. Good. When she spun back to face Zahlia, the black wolf was already halfway through the open gate. She hobbled along, three-legged and blood-covered.

Exhilaration flooded Claire. She'd stopped Zahlia, at least for a little while. Zahlia wouldn't attack anyone with a mangled paw—she couldn't. *Mom will know what to do.* The endorphins that surged through Claire started to fade. Her ear throbbed where Zahlia had bitten her, but it was nothing compared to the pain of realizing that Matthew had seen her transform.

*Now what do I do?*

# Chapter Twenty

CLAIRE'S FIRST INSTINCT was to hide. To go wait until Matthew left the lab and then find a way to free her mother. But if she could talk to him, reason with him, maybe he wouldn't tell his father what she was. Just maybe he wouldn't hate her.

Pain surged through her when she forced herself back into her human body. Claire winced when she yanked her shirt over her damaged ear. She kept one arm wrapped around her sore ribs and limped toward the lab door. It was locked.

"Matthew?" she called. "Please, let me in. I can explain!" Knocking on the metal door sent a stinging jolt down her arm. She'd been too focused to notice her injuries while she was fighting with Zahlia, but now they crowded around her, screaming for attention.

"Matthew?" she tried again. "Please, just let me in. Everything'll be okay, I promise. I—I won't hurt you. I *wouldn't* hurt you. Please, just let me in." Claire's voice broke and tears ran down her cheeks.

Inside, she could hear furniture being dragged across the floor.

"Just go away!" Matthew's voice sounded thin and panicky.

"Matthew, I'm not going anywhere until you listen to me. We can do it through the door if you want, but we have to talk." She was bawling in earnest now, hiccupping between words. Her ear ached, and the blood that coated the side of her neck had gone sticky. "Please. I only did it to save you, Matthew. I didn't know what else to do—she would have killed you!"

Claire heard him lean up against the door.

"How—how . . . all this time, you knew and you didn't tell me?" Matthew's voice sounded stronger, in spite of his stammering. "How could you?"

"Exactly," Claire wept. "How could I have told you? Matthew, your dad kills werewolves for a living. What did you expect me to do?"

"Cures them," Matthew muttered from inside the lab. "He . . . dammit."

Claire let out a keening sob. He didn't understand—she'd lost him. She'd only revealed herself to save him, and now she'd ruined everything. What if he told his father? Dr. Engle would kill her and her mother both.

She heard the sound of something heavy being moved on the other side of the door. The soft *click* of the lock being opened startled her and she jumped back. Slowly, Matthew opened the door the tiniest crack. "Oh my God, Claire, you're bleeding!" He threw open the door the rest of the way.

"Yeah," she said ruefully, "I know."

He reached out to touch her, but his hand started to shake.

"I'm sorry you had to see that," she whispered, "but I couldn't just let her kill you." Carefully, she took a step toward him and reached out her hand. "Let me—"

"No, wait!" Matthew interrupted, moving back into the lab. His foot tangled with the legs of a metal stool behind him and he fell.

"Matthew, I'm not going to hurt you!" Claire knelt down. "Let me help you up."

"Don't you touch me. You—you're one of them."

"If I wanted to hurt you, don't you think I would have done it already? You were right. There are more werewolves around than you think, but most of us are totally peaceful. Zahlia's crazy, Matthew, but I'm not like that. You have to believe me."

He scrambled to his feet, shaking his head. "Why would I believe you now when you've been lying to me all along? The only reason you didn't hurt me was so that you could find this place—see the other wolf."

Claire felt her cheeks burn.

"I'm right, aren't I?" The scents of fear and anger rolled off his skin in hot waves.

"Matthew, you don't understand." She looked up at him. He'd edged toward to the door. Claire could see his muscles bunched, tensed to run.

"What don't I understand?"

"The wolf your dad captured—she's my mother."

Matthew stopped dead.

"Please, Matthew. I'm telling you the truth. Think about it. Things started between us way before my mother was caught. I needed—I need—your help, that's true, but it's because you're the only one who sees how things really are. Didn't you just bring me here to see how gentle this supposed 'monster' really was?" Claire pointed at the cage in the far corner.

"We're werewolves. It's true. There's nothing I can do about that, or, believe me, I would have done it already. Do you think I want to be like this? To know that every month, I have to turn into something that everyone else on the planet wants dead? Do you think I *like* being the thing that gives people nightmares? I didn't ask for this Matthew, but I'm making the best of it that I can. So is my mother. She's never hurt anyone. She never *would* hurt anyone. Please. Even if you can't help us, please don't tell your father." Claire took a breath and played her last card. "I saved your life, and I would do it again. Don't make me regret that."

Matthew stared at her hard. He shook his head, once, twice, and then disappeared out the lab door into the night. Claire watched him go, her insides twisting with pain and fear. In the back corner of the lab, her mother whimpered, and determination settled over Claire like dew on the morning grass. Before she did anything else, she was going to get her mother out of that damn cage. On shaky legs, she walked back to the cage.

Claire was startled to see the body of a woman and not a wolf waiting for her. Her mother lay on the ground in her human form, bone-white and disturbingly thin.

*Why did she transform?*

"Where is the key?" Claire asked.

*"Dans le congélateur,"* her mother whispered.

She couldn't remember the English words. Claire suddenly knew how bad things really were.

"Mom, I—"

Marie heaved herself up onto the point of her emaciated elbow. "Freezer," she groaned.

Claire sprinted across the lab and wrenched open the freezer door. Inside was a bottle of imported vodka, three trays of ice cubes, and a tiny ceramic bowl with a silver key in it. The freezing metal bit at her fingertips when she snatched it from its dish. She yanked a long white lab coat from a hook next to the refrigerator and ran back over to the cage. It was only a moment before she had the key's teeth jammed into the lock, twisting it open so hard and fast that she nearly snapped it in half. The door swung open and Claire scrambled inside.

Gently, she covered her mother with the coat. Claire knelt and lifted her mother's head into her lap. She stroked her greasy, matted hair. "It's okay," she murmured. "We're going to get out of here."

Marie opened her eyes and looked at Claire. "You should have left me," she murmured.

"What?" Claire's hand stopped midstroke.

"It would have been safer, for you—for the pack. I would not be the first wolf in our history to sacrifice herself for the good of the rest." She closed her eyes and a pained expression washed across her face. When her gaze met Claire's again, there was no reproach in it. "But I am glad you did not leave me, *chérie*. You should have, but I am very glad that you did not."

Tears filled Claire's eyes and she struggled to hold them back. "I would never leave you," she whispered fiercely. "Never." Somewhere in the lab, a machine whirred, reminding Claire of where they were. "Can you walk? We really have to get out of here."

"That is why I transformed. You must help me, but, yes, I think I can walk."

Claire's mother rose gingerly, holding on to Claire for

support. Claire helped her button the lab coat. The fabric hung awkwardly from her mother's thin shoulders, but at least she was covered. With their arms wrapped tightly around each other, Claire and her mother slowly made their way out of the lab, stopping to put the key back in the freezer. They inched their way toward the safety of the woods. Every second that passed made Claire's blood hum with anxiety. She was sure that Dr. Engle and his antiwerewolf militia would appear at any moment, ready to kill them both.

When they reached the shelter of the trees, Claire lowered her mother onto the trunk of a fallen ash tree to rest. Marie sat with her hands on her knees, drawing in deep breaths of the clear night air. Claire sniffed at the breeze. There was no scent of Zahlia, but she couldn't keep her gaze away from the shifting shadows in the forest.

"What?" Marie eyed her suspiciously.

Claire picked at the bark beneath her. "I'm worried that Zahlia's out here."

"That bitch," she snarled. "I heard her assault you outside the lab tonight."

Claire hesitated. "I don't get why Zahlia did what she did. Why did she kill those people? Why come after Matthew and me?"

Her mother struggled to speak. "Zahlia has always wanted to be second-in-command of our pack. And she was poised to do so. But then Zahlia's mother—she thought that she had found evidence that showed our kind were to hunt humans once a year, as a tribute to the Goddess. Beatrice agreed with me when I said that Zahlia's mother was doing nothing more than searching for a loophole in our laws in order to fulfill her horrific appetites. Zahlia's mother left the pack before she could be disciplined. Because of her mother, Zahlia lost her chance at power. She has always felt that was my fault.

"I think that this was her idea of revenge. She thought if I were caught—blamed for murdering innocent humans— then she would be able to take my place." She grimaced. "It almost worked. But she didn't count on you getting in the way. I assume that's why she attacked you. After all, you ruined her plans."

Claire touched her mouth, remembering the feel of Zahlia's paw between her teeth. "When we fought, I—I hurt her pretty badly. I don't *think* she can sneak up on us tonight."

"I hope not," Marie moaned. "I do not think I am strong enough to fight her, and you have already been injured tonight."

"We just have to make it home," Claire said encouragingly. "We can pack some stuff and go straight to the airport, just leave and never come back. Let Beatrice deal with Zahlia." *Not that she will, but it's not my problem anymore.* Claire forced herself not to think about the fact that leaving Hanover Falls meant leaving Matthew and Emily, too.

The expression on her mother's face made her look like an old woman. "Claire, we cannot. It is our responsibility to help the pack. As soon as we make it home, I need to contact the others. Once we can arrange a gathering, then the pack can determine Zahlia's punishment. We must also deal with Matthew. He knows. And unless we can be sure that he will keep our secret . . . well. It must be taken care of one way or another before we could go. If he tells his father, then there will be no place where you and I could be safe."

"What do you mean, 'taken care of?'" Claire choked.

The thin slash of her mother's lips were all the answer Claire needed.

"You—you're talking about killing him?!" she gasped.

Her mother shrugged uncertainly. "Perhaps. But only as a last resort, only to protect our pack. It is permitted in our laws—and also in the laws of man. There may be one other way. In our traditions, there is something called a *gardien*, a secret-keeper."

"Yeah, I know about that, Zahlia told me." Claire flinched when she said Zahlia's name.

Her mother's lips thinned in disapproval. She sighed. "It is my hope that he will become one. The humans throughout our history who have known our identities without revealing them are offered the protection of our pack in exchange for their silence. You would be asking Matthew to carry a heavy burden, Claire." Her mother's eyes burned with fever and her gaze made Claire catch her breath. "It may be a very difficult choice for him to make. But it is the only way. I am sorry, *chérie*. Now. I suggest we go, before he makes a choice without even knowing that he has. Every moment we delay only increases the chance that he has already told his father what he has seen."

Claire knelt in the soft carpet of pine needles, her lungs burning with a scream she could not voice, while her mother stood and limped deeper into the forest.

In spite of the ache in her belly, Claire hurried after her mother. The deeper they went into the woods, the jumpier Claire got. Every twig that snapped in the distance, every rustle of a bird's feathers made her start, sure it was Zahlia. It took them longer to get home than Claire had thought it would. By the time they crept into the yard, Claire was shaking with the thought of what she had to tell Matthew.

She hurried ahead and peered in the window. One light burned in the kitchen, but there was no sign of Lisbeth. Claire got her mother into the house and they both crept upstairs. A note pinned to her door caught Claire's eye.

Claire-bear,
Sorry I wasn't here when you got home. Some last-minute plans came up, and I decided to jump on it. Hope that's okay! I'll be home around one—call my cell if you need <u>anything</u>. Hope you had fun!
—L

*She'll be back by one? Crap.*

It was already eleven. If she didn't leave soon, Lisbeth would be home before Claire could get back.

Claire got her mother into bed and then sprinted back to her room, ripping the note off the door as she went. She got cleaned up as fast as she could with her sore ribs. The shampoo she scrubbed through her hair burned when it ran into the wound on her ear. On the edge of the sink, her phone flashed at her—Emily had called four times. Claire reached out with a soapy hand and turned it off. She'd deal with Emily later. Tomorrow. Sometime soon. *Man, I am a really sucky friend.*

Claire snaked her arm back into the shower and scrubbed at the dirt under her ragged nails. When she was clean enough that she didn't look terrifying, Claire slipped into her mother's room.

The silk comforter was pulled up to her mom's chin—her frail body barely made a lump under the covers.

"Mom?"

"Yes, Claire?" Her mother struggled to keep her eyes open.

"Do you want anything? I have to go—to talk to . . . well. You know."

"Thank you, but I will be fine. Please tell Lisbeth, er . . ." her mother hesitated.

"I'll leave her a note saying that you flew home because you got sick. That's true enough. She'll probably come up here bugging you to drink some sort of miracle tea or soup or something, though."

"That will be fine. I know how to handle Lisbeth." A trace of humor tinged her mother's voice.

Claire grinned. "I'm sure you do."

"Be careful out there. And Claire?"

Claire cocked her head.

"Thank you. For everything. Not many creatures, human or wolf, would have done what you did tonight."

Claire waved away Marie's gratitude, but she couldn't keep herself from smiling. "You're my mother," she said. "Of course I did it."

Claire slipped out of the room and crept silently down the stairs. She left a note for Lisbeth on the table in her best imitation of her mom's handwriting. Then Claire walked out into the night, squaring her shoulders against the weight of what she was about to do.

All but one window of the Engles' house was dark. Matthew was still up. If his parents had been asleep when he got home, there was a chance that he hadn't talked to his dad—that Dr. Engle didn't know yet.

Claire picked up a handful of the smooth pebbles underneath a crabapple tree. Carefully, she lobbed them against the glass pane. As tense as she was, it would be all too easy to throw the pebbles hard enough to break the window. Matthew's face appeared in the window just as the fourth stone hit the glass. He leapt back out of sight and Claire cursed under her breath.

She waited until he peeked out again, and then waved frantically. Matthew slid the window up a few inches. "Claire? What are you doing here?"

"We have to talk. I'm sorry I lied to you before. I really, really am. But if you don't listen to me now, we're both going to regret it."

He crossed his arms over his chest. "Are you serious? Why should I believe you now? Can you give me a single reason to trust you?"

Claire's nostrils flared and she fought to control her temper. "Okay, I deserved that. I understand why you're pissed, Matthew, but this is serious. My mother sent me here." *He's right. I am a liar, but not this time.*

"I don't care if the pope sent you. I need some space. I have to think. And it's late. I'm going to bed, and you should go home."

"I'll go now, if you want. But let me talk to you before you—before you do anything about it, okay? Tomorrow, maybe, after you've had some time to think about stuff?" Claire hated the whine that crept into her voice, but she couldn't stop it.

Matthew sighed and rested his head against the window frame. "Fine. I'll meet you tomorrow night at Greenway Park, on the side where we had our picnic. I'm practicing with a couple of the goalies until eight thirty. I'll be there at nine."

Claire let out a long breath. Greenway Park would be really exposed, and who knew how healed Zahlia would be by tomorrow night? Still, she wasn't in a position to argue. "Awesome. That's perfect. Thank you, Matthew, you don't know how—"

He cut her off. "Go home, Claire. I'll meet you tomorrow." He closed the window, and Claire's gaze darted to the other darkened windows on the second floor. They stayed dark. Matthew hadn't woken his parents.

Claire slunk into the deeper shadows of the backyard and watched his window until he turned off his light. She checked her watch—12:18. If she hurried, she could still beat Lisbeth home.

When she made it back to her house, the lights were off. *I made it.* Claire hurried inside and checked on her sleeping mother. Exhaustion crept up on her like a spider and her injuries throbbed in time with her heart. She downed a couple of pain relievers and tumbled into bed. In spite of everything that had happened, Claire slept like the dead—still and dreamless.

Late the next afternoon, Claire slipped into her mother's room.

"Ah, Claire. How are you feeling?"

Her mother looked more like herself—still pale and sharply thin, but better.

Claire shrugged. "My ear hurts, and my ribs, but everything else is pretty much okay. As long as we don't run out of Advil, I think I'll be fine."

"I'm glad to hear it. I've just talked to Beatrice, and we're gathering early tonight, just before dark. It should give us time to make a plan and then take action before morning."

"Tonight?" Claire rubbed her eyes. "Crap."

"What?"

Claire sat down hard on the delicate-looking chair near her mother's bed. "Matthew was too mad to talk to me last night. But he said he'd meet me at the park tonight, and he promised not to do anything until after I'd told him . . . well, you know . . . what I have to tell him. He should be there just about nine o'clock."

"The timing will be bad." Her mother leaned back against the pile of pillows. "But talking to him is every bit as important as dealing with Zahlia. I will make sure you are able to meet him."

Claire licked her lips. "Does Beatrice know about the Matthew . . . thing?"

"She is the Alpha—I had to tell her. She is the only one who can truly grant permission to create a secret-keeper, and it is her duty to inform the rest of the pack."

Claire squirmed in her seat. "Is she angry?"

Marie turned, her dark eyes searching Claire's face. "She understands your actions. I know she believes you can convince

Matthew to accept this new role." She hesitated. "Are you sure you trust him? You are sure his father is not on his way here now?"

"I don't have any choice except to trust him. He could promise to be a *gardien*, and still tell. The only difference is that after tonight, he'll know what would happen to him if he does."

"True." Her mother sighed. "I hate being afraid, and I believe I will be for some time to come."

"I'm sorry. I know if I hadn't changed in front of him like that, we'd be safe." Claire hung her head.

"Yes. And he would be dead." Her mother put one finger under Claire's chin and lifted her face. "What you did puts us in terrible danger, *chérie*. But you did it for the right reason. To save a life is an honorable thing, always. I am not angry with you. Selfishly, I am frightened, but I am not mad."

"Thank you." Claire leaned forward until her head was pressed against her mother's shoulder. She'd come so close to losing her. Her mom wrapped her thin arms around Claire.

"I want you to be careful tonight, *chérie*. There will be more than one thing out there that would like to harm you."

Claire nodded against her mother's collarbone.

"Good. Now, go get ready. It will look less suspicious if we leave separately. I will meet you on the other side of the wall in two hours."

"Okay." Claire slipped out of her mother's embrace and stumbled into her room.

When it was almost time to leave, she brushed her teeth and threw on a sweatshirt, leaving her hair down to hide her injured ear from Lisbeth. She got out the door as fast as she could, claiming her headache was gone and she was going to bike over to Emily's for a brownie-gorging session.

Claire rode down the driveway, circling around to the far side of their property, where she stashed her bicycle in a stand of evergreen bushes. She sneaked back along the brick wall, watching the house for any sign of Lisbeth. When she reached the familiar hole, Claire practically dove through the ivy into the forest. She managed to catch herself just before she barreled full-force into her mother.

"I was beginning to wonder where you were," Marie said.

"Sorry. I had to hide my bicycle. Next time I'll come up with a story for Lisbeth that doesn't involve so many props."

Her mom laughed, but her face quickly settled back into its usual serious expression. The two of them set off through the already-dark woods.

They arrived at the clearing, where Beatrice and Victoria were already waiting. Judith and Katherine appeared before Claire had even settled herself on the ground.

"Well, we're just missing Zahlia," Beatrice said. "I don't expect her to come, but by failing to do so, she is disobeying a direct order from me." Her voice was tight. "We'll start without lighting the fire tonight—it's too early. And it's not a good night for sending unnecessary signals."

Claire glanced at the trees around them, wondering who else might be out there. She peeked at her watch. She had only half an hour before she was supposed to meet Matthew.

"So. What will we do?" Judith asked.

"Find her." Marie wrapped her arms around herself. "And then bring her back here."

Beatrice nodded. "Exactly. Once we have heard what she has to say for herself—what defense she offers for her actions—then I will decide whether she should be banished from the pack and sent to live outside the bounds of our territory, or whether her punishment must be . . . more severe." Beatrice stood up. "Are there any questions?"

The idea of seeing Zahlia again gave Claire the shivers.

"What about Claire?" Judith asked. "She's not fully changed yet. What role can she have?"

Claire stiffened, wondering if someone would mention Matthew.

"Her transformation is nearly complete, and from what Marie has told me, Claire has already proven herself to this pack. She will help us search tonight, which is even more important because Victoria won't be assisting us. I won't risk the unborn child."

Victoria stared miserably at the charred remains of their last fire.

Beatrice took a step forward. "Now. Let's try to finish this before the situation gets any uglier. You may transform whenever you wish. And please be careful. Very careful."

Claire's mother pulled her out of the circle before anyone began to change.

"I know you need to meet Matthew. I'll go with you as far as the park." Her mother bent to remove her shoes.

"How come no one said anything about him tonight?" The question popped out before Claire could stop it.

Marie pursed her lips. "Everyone already knows what happened. There is no need to discuss it until the situation is resolved. Hopefully he will agree to become a *gardien*, in which case there will be nothing to talk about."

Claire gulped. The words her mother hadn't said rang in her ears. That if he refused, there would be plenty to talk about.

*I just have to convince him. That's all. No matter what it takes, I have to find a way to make him agree.*

"So, when we get to the park—um . . ." Claire paused.

"I'll stay out of the way. I know my presence won't help. It will give me a chance to search that part of the woods." Marie straightened up. "And don't forget to carry your clothes with you."

*Right. Clothes.* Claire stood motionless, the weight of what she had to do pressing down on her too heavily to move.

"We're running out of time." Her mother shifted impatiently.

Claire shook herself. "Sorry. I'm ready when you are."

*At least, I guess I am.*

The two of them transformed and set off for the park.

By the time they arrived, a deep ache had settled into Claire's ribs and her injured ear throbbed. She dropped the clothes she'd brought and turned to her mother.

*I'll be as quick as I can.*

Marie's tail waved. *Take your time. This is every bit as important as finding Zahlia. I'm going to see what I can find in the woods.* She turned to go, leaving Claire alone.

Through the last fringe of trees, Claire could see Matthew. He stood leaning against his car, his hair still wet from his postpractice shower. Before her nerves could get the best of her, Claire changed into her human form and pulled on her clothes. Her shirt had a damp spot across the front from carrying it in her mouth and she hoped Matthew wouldn't notice it.

She shook the last of the pine needles off her shorts, smoothed her hair, and stepped out of the trees.

Matthew caught sight of her and headed across the clearing, closing the distance between them. Claire was relieved to see that there was no anger in his expression.

"Hey," she said.

"Hey, yourself." A smile twitched at the corner of his mouth—just a flash, but it was there.

When she looked at his mouth, the angle of his cheekbones, the realization of what might have been washed over Claire. They could have been together—gone to the prom and kissed in the hallways between classes. If she were human. Instead, they were meeting out here in the night to talk about keeping one of them alive. Tears stung Claire's eyes. "Matthew, I'm so, so sorry—," she blurted out.

He raised a hand to stop her. "I'm sorry too. I panicked."

Claire's mouth hung open. She hadn't expected an apology.

"You're right. I don't agree with my dad, but that doesn't mean it didn't freak me out to find out that someone I *know* is a werewolf. Sometimes stuff's just a little harder to process when it hits that close to home, you know?"

"Yeah, I have some experience with that." Claire snorted. The first night she transformed flowed through her memory—how unreal it had all seemed just a few months ago. Matthew turned and walked toward the trees. The thought of being in the woods where her mother might stumble across them made Claire nervous, but she fell into step beside him, anyway. They walked in silence across the field.

When they reached the edge of the forest, Claire's anxiety faded. It really would be easier to talk to him with the darkness of the forest shadows giving her a place to hide. And the only thing she could smell was a dead deer, deeper in the woods. Her mother must have circled around the other way. The fact that Matthew didn't hesitate to walk into the forest with her gave Claire the courage to open her mouth.

"Matthew." She sighed. "You cannot believe how much I do not want to say what I have to tell you now."

He cocked his head to one side. Claire crossed her arms tight in front of her chest and stared at the ground, not sure how to begin. Finally, she just told him exactly what her mother had told her. "The thing is, if you tell anyone who we are—my mother and I—then the rest of the pack will come after you. But if you don't say anything, hell, if you just pretend that none of this ever happened, then the pack will protect you. Forever. It's called being a *gardien*." She looked up at him. "I wouldn't ask you to keep this—us—secret just for my sake. I really wouldn't. But I couldn't stand it if anything happened to you. Please, Matthew, just forget you ever met me, and I promise, everything will go back to normal, okay?"

"But I don't want to forget about you." Matthew stuck his hands into the front pocket of his sweatshirt and looked at her hard, his eyes blazing in the faint light of the newly risen moon. "We can change things, Claire."

Claire swallowed hard. "I wish things were different too, believe me." She stared at the pine needles under her feet. "But—" Her mother's scent wafted through the clearing. Claire looked up and froze as her mother bounded into the clearing.

Marie's ribs were heaving and the fur on her hackles was raised. She stared hard at Claire, then looked away, the whites of her widened eyes flashing in the near-darkness. Next to Claire, Matthew backed up.

*At least he's not running away,* Claire thought.

Her mother was clearly upset, but without transforming, Claire couldn't tell what she was saying. Changing in front of Matthew seemed like too big a risk. He was already on edge, and that might just push him over. Before she could make a decision one way or the other, a ferocious growl rolled through the clearing and Zahlia ran in through the trees, favoring her injured front paw. Snarling, she leapt onto Marie's back, her front claws raking Marie's shoulder.

"Matthew, you have to hide!" Claire hissed.

Panicked and furious, she transformed so fast that she didn't have time to pull off her clothes. Shreds of fabric fluttered to the ground and somewhere behind her, Matthew gasped. Claire crouched low, her belly brushing the debris.

Still on Marie's back, Zahlia snapped at her face, her teeth just missing the other wolf's eye. Still weak from her time in Dr. Engle's lab, Claire's mother stumbled, her snout scraping the dirt as her front leg gave way. Zahlia slid forward, thrown by the change of position, and Claire sprang.

The force of Claire's impact knocked the black wolf off her mother, tossing her to the ground. Zahlia scrambled to get up but before she could regain her footing, Claire bit deep into the fur on the back of Zahlia's neck and rolled as hard as she could.

Claire twisted her head, using the momentum of their

bodies and the strength of her jaws to throw Zahlia away from Matthew and her mother. Zahlia hit a tree with a sickening *thud* before falling to the ground in a heap.

Claire staggered to her feet, ready for another assault, but Zahlia lay motionless on the forest floor. She was breathing— a high, whistling whine resonated in her throat—but she wasn't getting up.

Something in the woods beyond Zahlia caught Claire's eye. The scanty moonlight that trickled through the trees skittered across a grizzled pelt.

Beatrice was out there. Watching. Claire ducked her head, trying to see around the underbrush. Why wasn't Beatrice coming out here, into the clearing?

Claire barked once, asking the Alpha to come help them, to come deal with Zahlia.

In the forest, there was nothing but silence. A very answering sort of silence. In that second, Claire realized that Beatrice wasn't going to come to their rescue.

Claire stared at Zahlia. Part of her wanted to finish what she'd started—to kill the wolf who'd tried to kill her and her mother. To eliminate any threat to Matthew, or to the other humans she cared about. But she couldn't do it. Every time her muscles twitched forward, Zahlia's desperate whimpering stopped her.

Behind her, Claire heard Marie drag herself off the ground. Claire spun around to face her mother.

*Are you okay?*

Without answering, her mother stepped around Claire, edging closer to Zahlia. The black wolf's eyes rolled and she began frantically licking her muzzle.

Claire's mother stood over Zahlia's prone body, her ears and tail straining forward.

*Her neck has been broken.* She leaned closer, briefly snuffling at Zahlia's ear as she addressed the injured wolf. *This is a mercy, and one you do not deserve.*

Zahlia's keening cut off as Marie's strong jaws closed around her windpipe, choking her. In just a few moments, Zahlia's ribs stopped moving. She began to transform, but before she could completely regain her human form, her eyes grew still and glassy.

It was over. Zahlia was dead.

# Chapter Twenty-one

MARIE WOBBLED A few paces away from Zahlia's naked body and collapsed onto the carpet of dead leaves.

Claire crept over to her mother.

*Are you okay?* She sniffed at the blood trickling out of her mother's shoulder.

*I . . . will be . . . eventually . . .* her mother panted. *Go find Matthew.*

Claire whimpered. *Oh, shit. Matthew.*

She started to transform and realized a split second later that she'd ruined her clothes. Claire took a painful leap midchange and landed a few feet into the covering gloom of the forest.

"Matthew?" she called, trying to see into the clearing from her hiding place.

"Claire?" He stepped out from behind a massive oak tree. "Is it—is it dead? Are you okay?"

Claire felt her knees go watery. He wanted to know if she was okay. That had to be a good thing.

"Yes, she's dead. And I'm mostly okay. Are you?"

"Scared out of my goddamn mind, honestly. Why are you hiding?"

"It's . . . I don't have any clothes with me."

"Oh. Right." Matthew unzipped his massive sweatshirt and laid it on the ground. "I won't look," he promised, spinning away from her.

Naked, Claire darted across the clearing and threw on the sweatshirt. It hung almost to her knees. "Okay," she said.

Matthew turned around. "What about your mom? That is your mom, right?"

Claire nodded. "Zahlia hurt her pretty badly when she attacked us. She'll be okay, I think. Are you—do you hate me?"

"No. Why would I? That thing"—he pointed at Zahlia—"that *monster*, I hate. But you defended your mom. And me." His voice was shaking, but when he looked at Claire, confidence glowed in his eyes.

"Matthew—I'm no different than she was." Claire stuffed her hands into the sweatshirt's deep pockets. "I'm not a human girl, you know that. If you think she was a monster, then you must think I am too."

Matthew put a hand on her arm. "Of course not. You just proved everything I've suspected about werewolves. A monster wouldn't save a human. You could have pushed me out there as a distraction. You could have let your mother fend for herself and run away. Instead, you saved us both. You couldn't bring yourself to kill her, could you?" he asked seriously.

Claire shook her head. "No. I couldn't. Maybe it would have been kinder if I had. I don't know." Overwhelmed, Claire wavered on her feet. Matthew's arms slid around her, steadying her.

Claire slid out of his grip. "This is all my fault. You were only out here tonight because of me. If I weren't a werewolf, you wouldn't have had to see that—you wouldn't have been out here at all. I'm sorry I dragged you into all this. I'm so, so sorry. I should have stayed away from you."

"I know you're not human." He pulled her in again and wrapped his arms around her more tightly. "But that doesn't mean you're not a person. I was scared. I can admit that. But I'm not sorry I was here. I'm not sorry that I know who you really are. You shouldn't be, either."

Claire leaned into him, hoping that he couldn't feel her shake. "Will you keep the secret for us?" she whispered.

"I promise. And not to save my own skin—I'll do it for you. I'm no monster, either."

"Thank you. Really and truly, thank you." Claire eased herself out of his arms and looked at Zahlia, lying on the forest floor.

"What are we going to do about her, um, body?" Matthew asked. Claire could smell the sour, green smell of his nausea as he looked at Zahlia.

Claire ran a hand across her forehead. "I think I have an idea. Hang on."

She walked over to her mother, kneeling by the enormous wolf. "Can you get home on your own?"

Marie huffed and thumped her tail against the ground twice. Even while in her human form, Claire could tell that her mother was saying *yes*.

"Good. Don't worry, I'll take care of Zahlia." She turned to face Matthew. "Okay, so here's what I'm thinking . . ."

The picnic blanket was still wadded up in the trunk of Matthew's car. The cheerful red plaid looked inappropriately festive wrapped around Zahlia's body, but it was better than getting blood all over the car. While her mother limped her way home through the forest, Claire covered up the gore on the forest floor as well as she could and picked up the shreds of fabric from the clothes she'd been wearing. She wished her mother had been well enough to help them, but it was obvious that walking home was going to drain whatever strength Marie had left.

The memory of Beatrice, hiding in the woods like a coward, distracted Claire. As the Alpha, she was the one who should have killed Zahlia. She was the one who should have dealt with the evidence. Claire blinked away the anger that clouded her vision. There would be time to think about that later. She hitched up the too-big soccer shorts that Matthew had found for her in his car and took one last look around the clearing. It was good enough.

She and Matthew put the dead werewolf in the trunk and crawled into the car. They drove in silence. Matthew had snapped off the stereo when he started the car. It didn't seem right to listen to music with Zahlia dead in the trunk. When he turned onto the road that led to his father's lab, Matthew reached over and squeezed Claire's hand.

"This is the right thing to do."

"Yeah," said Claire, "but it's still hard, you know?"

"Yes. I do know." His voice was serious, and Claire was pretty sure he was talking about something more than just what they were about to do with Zahlia. Matthew parked the car in the shadows at the end of the facility and popped the trunk. He walked around to the back of the car. After a deep breath, Matthew reached in to grab the blanket, but Claire stopped him.

"I can carry her faster on my own," she said gently. "I'd let you help, but if we get caught . . ." She trailed off.

"It would be really bad," Matthew finished. "Okay. Go

ahead." He turned away, but not before Claire saw the relief that crossed his face when he realized he wouldn't have to touch Zahlia.

Claire wrapped her arms around the body and gagged as the smell of death filled her nostrils. She craned her head as far away from Zahlia as she could and lifted her out of the trunk.

"Go open the door," she panted.

When the faint squeak from the metal door echoed between the buildings, Claire ran as fast as she could. She darted into the darkened lab and nearly collided with Matthew.

Clearly, he hadn't expected her to be quite so fast. Inhumanly fast. The shocked expression on his face made Claire's chest ache. Adjusting the blanket-wrapped body in her arms, Claire eased past the lab equipment and headed for the cage. Matthew followed behind her. Claire could hear his almost-silent footsteps. In order to get Zahlia in the cage, Claire had to go in, too. Being inside the bars made the skin on her back crawl. As quickly as she could, Claire dumped Zahlia onto the floor and backed out of the cage. The sight of Zahlia's body lying on the concrete floor made Claire's mouth go dry.

*Don't start freaking out now. It has to be this way. Mom would be able to do this calmly. We're all a lot safer with Zahlia dead, and covering my mother's tracks with her body doesn't hurt her any.*

"Do you think your dad will call the police?" she asked.

Matthew shook his head. "He thinks cops are idiots. And he'd be totally humiliated if Lycanthropy Researchers International ever found out that his security sucked bad enough that someone could just break into his real lab. Not to mention the government. . . . Even if he realizes that another werewolf killed her, there's no way he can tell anyone without losing his credibility. I guess he might try to find the wolf that did it, but Dad won't call the police, and he's not going to be able to find any of you by himself."

Claire trusted him. She had to, especially considering how much faith he had in her.

"Okay." It was more of a breath than a word.

Matthew looked away from the body and let out a long breath. "Let's get out of here."

Claire hurried over to the freezer and grabbed the key from its dish. She locked Zahlia's body in the cage. After a silent moment, Claire wiped her fingerprints off the cage door and the key with the hem of the sweatshirt, put the key back into its dish in the freezer, and hurried out of the lab.

Matthew slid into the driver's seat and leaned his head against the steering wheel. Claire looked at the back of his neck, the set of his shoulders. She could see what they had just done in the way he held himself. And it was all her fault.

"I'm sorry," she whispered, and cursed herself for crying

*again.* "I wish I'd never—" With his head still resting against the steering wheel, Matthew turned to look at her.

"Don't," he said. "I'm not going to keep telling you that I don't regret this. I'll admit, when I first noticed you, first hoped you'd go out with me, this wasn't exactly how I envisioned things going. But I still wouldn't trade it." He leaned over and kissed her.

Claire backed away, leaning into the door behind her. "Matthew, being with me almost got you killed. Listen, I've wanted to date you ever since I first saw you, too." Admitting it made her blush. "But after all of the horrible things you've been dragged into because of me, because of what I am . . . I don't want to ruin your life. And that's exactly what I'm doing. So I think—I think maybe we shouldn't be together." The words burned like acid in her mouth.

Matthew pulled back and looked at her. "You are not ruining my life. I chose to be here tonight, didn't I? I know you're a werewolf, I know what it means, and I don't care. After everything that's happened, you can hardly say I don't know what I'm getting myself into. So, give me one good reason we can't be together."

Claire hesitated.

"Unless *you* don't want to?" He sounded surprised and a little hurt.

"It's not that! It's just—I don't know what's going to happen. I don't know how things will be now that I am . . .

what I am. I have to hide, all the time, and lie, to everyone, and—"

"But not to me. You don't have to hide from me and you don't have to lie to me because I *already know*. And I love you anyway." He took her chin in his hand and tipped her head up, holding her gaze with his. "I'm not asking you to marry me, Claire. Can't we just work things out as we go along? See what happens? Be a couple?"

The idea stretched out in front of Claire like a stream, shining with possibility. He was right—he already knew everything. There was no reason not to try. And just like that, all the feelings she'd kept wrapped up so tight burst out of their seams and filled her chest.

"I love you, too," she said. But what she really meant was *yes*.

The next morning, Claire crawled into her mother's bed. "Mom?"

"Mmm?" Her mother cracked open one eye. "Is it done?"

"Yes." Claire buried her face in the pillow, overwhelmed by the memory. She felt her mother sit up next to her.

"Tell me what happened."

Claire told her the whole story, including the part about seeing Beatrice in the woods. The only thing she didn't mention was the last conversation she and Matthew had. Her mother narrowed her eyes and looked at Claire.

"You are leaving something out, yes?"

Claire reburied her face in the pillow to hide the heat that rose in her cheeks. "I dunno," she mumbled.

"You want to see him," her mother guessed.

Claire felt her shoulders tense, and her mother sighed as she read Claire's body language.

"Well, it's not like it's dangerous anymore. It's not like he's going to guess what I am and tell his dad. Matthew chose, Mom, and he chose *us*. So why shouldn't I?" Claire turned her head just enough to peek at her mother.

"Oh, *chérie*." Her mother sighed and ran a hand over Claire's hair. "I just think love always ends badly, whether or not you are human. But maybe I am too cynical. And most everyone seems to survive heartbreak, at any rate. I am sure you will too, no matter what happens." She gathered Claire in her arms and hugged her tight. "You grow up too fast, you know that?"

"Mo-oom," Claire protested—but she didn't try to escape from her mother's embrace.

After a final squeeze, her mother let go and gave Claire a gentle shove in the direction of the door. "Now, go shower and ask Lisbeth to fix us something to eat. I could eat a horse."

Claire lifted her eyebrows into a question, teasing.

"Very droll, but how would you get it up the stairs? *Non,* for now, I think an omelette will do nicely. I am going to call Beatrice. She will not like it, but things have gotten out of hand, and something must be done about it."

"Okay." Claire walked out of the room. She leaned against the closed door for a moment, feeling something she hadn't felt in months—hope that things just might work out after all.

Buoyed by her optimism, Claire convinced Lisbeth to drive her to Emily's house. She wanted to see Emily, but preferably somewhere without any werewolf evidence stashed in the closets.

Claire bounded up the walk, knocked at Emily's front door, opened it, and stuck her head in.

"Helloooo," she called. "Anyone home?"

"Claire? Hang on a sec. Crap!" Emily's voice floated down the stairs, followed by a series of banging noises. "Oh my God, you're here!" She came flying down the stairs, the hems of her jeans dripping wet, and squeezed Claire into a tight hug.

"Is everything okay?" Claire asked, while Emily's jeans dripped on her toes.

"What? Oh, yeah. I spilled some watercolors. You surprised the hell out of me! God, I've been *dying* to see you." Emily's enthusiasm made Claire smile.

"So, do you have time to do something?"

"Um, of course! Do you mind waiting while I get the paint cleaned up? It shouldn't take long."

"Em, I'm even willing to help. Where's the carpet cleaner?"

Emily turned and headed for the kitchen. "Have I mentioned lately that you're the best friend ever?"

Claire followed her, still grinning. Things with Emily wouldn't ever be the same as before, but maybe she could make something new. A friendship that was good in its own way, even it if wasn't normal.

That afternoon, the local news interrupted the regular talk show. Claire had to turn it up—downstairs, Lisbeth had her music on loud enough that Claire could hear it in her room. The camera cut to a very pale Dr. Engle, his tie crooked and his hair a mess. Claire noticed that the building behind him wasn't the same lab where he'd imprisoned her mother.

"Ladies and Gentlemen, thank you for coming today. I am sorry to tell you that when my colleagues and I arrived this morning, we found the werewolf deceased. We are working to determine the cause of death, though we believe some sort of parasite—perhaps a nematode—may be involved. Of course, we are deeply saddened that we were unable to cure this, erm, creature. Its death marks a blow to our research and also to the small group of . . ."

Claire clicked off the television and walked over to her closet. Bitterness coated the back of her throat. She could taste it on her tongue like medicine. He hadn't even said that Zahlia had been killed. She'd guessed that he wouldn't. After all, if the public thought he couldn't keep his "research" safe, why would they trust him to keep the werewolves away?

\* \* \*

More than a week later, Claire pulled the last clean pair of shorts off her shelf and yanked them on. On top of everything else, she was going to have to do laundry. Great. The TV was on, and a flustered-looking Dr. Engle was being interviewed yet again about the mysterious death of "his" werewolf.

Her bedroom door swung open and Claire's mother peeked in.

"Don't you knock?" Claire asked, exasperated.

"Sorry. I did not think you would be up." She looked at the television. "Are you watching that?"

Claire nodded. "Yeah." Under her breath, she muttered, "What a total bastard."

Her mother smiled, her hearing good enough to catch what Claire had said. "The cowardly choice is often the easiest. At least there will be no investigation by the police—you should be grateful for that."

"I guess." Claire scooped up a heap of laundry and tossed it onto her bed.

"Tonight we gather," her mother said quietly, checking over her shoulder to make sure Lisbeth was still downstairs. "I am anxious to see everyone. We will leave at midnight and not a moment later. Please be ready."

Claire stopped sorting the laundry into piles and looked at her mother. "Yeah, I will. Be ready, I mean."

A smile darted across her mother's face so quickly that Claire wasn't sure she'd seen it at all.

"I think you will enjoy this gathering more than you anticipate. But you must trust me."

Claire looked down at the dirty T-shirt in her hands. "I do trust you. But I *don't* really trust Beatrice. Not after everything that happened." She looked up at her mother. "I know I'm probably not supposed to say stuff like that, since she's the Alpha and all, but it's true."

Her mother nodded slowly. "I understand that. But it is not Beatrice's fault, Claire. I blame myself—if I had been willing to teach you sooner, perhaps you would better understand our ways, perhaps you would not have been so surprised by Beatrice's decisions." She sighed. "But mostly, I blame Zahlia. Her stupid, selfish actions have seriously hurt the bonds of our pack. It will take some time to rebuild them." Her mother was quiet for a long moment. "Still, I believe something will happen tonight that you will like."

"If you say so."

Her mother smiled, slipped back into the hall, and pulled the door shut behind her.

Claire hated it when her mother got all mysterious like that. When she'd found out what her mother really was—that she'd been living a hidden life all those years—Claire had thought maybe that explained it. She thought that the cryptic little comments and secrets would stop. *Guess not.*

One of the piles of laundry in front of her started to ring, and Claire dug through the clothes until she found her cell phone.

"Hello?"

"Hey, Claire." Matthew's voice was unusually quiet.

"Are you okay?"

"Yeah, my dad's just on a megarampage, and I'm trying to stay out of the way."

"I saw him on TV. I thought he was at his lab. Where are you?"

"I'm with him. They finally moved the body today, and he needed help. He and his lab tech weren't strong enough to move her, and I figured if I helped, then it wouldn't look suspicious if they found my fingerprints there later, or something."

"Smart."

"Thanks. Anyway, he dragged me over to the other lab for his latest interview, and they're almost done asking questions, so I thought I'd call while I had a chance. Listen, if I can get out of here later, do you want to do something tonight?"

Claire sighed. "I wish I could, but I've got some, uh, girl stuff to do later. I think I'd better stick around here tonight."

"'Girl stuff'? Is that what we're calling it now?"

The teasing in his voice made Claire warm all the way down to her toes.

"You got a better idea?" she shot back.

"Nah. Oh—they're finishing up. Okay, not tonight, but tomorrow, then?"

"Yeah, tomorrow's good," she said.

"Good. I gotta go. I'll call you later."

When she'd flipped the phone shut, Claire sat between the mounds of laundry, turning the phone over and over in her hand, and smiled to herself.

Claire carried a basket of dirty clothes downstairs and found Lisbeth pulling a load of clothes out of the dryer.

"Hey." Claire tipped the basket of laundry into the empty washer and grabbed the detergent. Lisbeth smiled but didn't say anything. Something about her eyes looked funny too. "Are you okay?"

"Yeah, I'm fine." Lisbeth pulled a pair of jeans out of the pile and started folding.

Claire hesitated. *Something* was going on. "Are you sure?"

Lisbeth sighed. "Yeah. I guess it's time I told you. Do you remember Mark—the guy I met a while ago, the one from yoga?"

Claire nodded.

"Well, we've been seeing each other. A lot. And it's getting pretty serious. He wants me to move in with him."

Everything clicked into place and Claire felt her mouth drop open. The late-night phone calls, the weird outings after dark—Lisbeth had a secret boyfriend. Delight flooded through Claire. If Lisbeth moved in with him, everyone would be happy. She'd have more freedom. Lisbeth would finally have a life of her own. And maybe her mom would be forced to buy her a car after all. It was perfect.

"So, why do you look so worried? Don't you want to live with him?"

"Of course I do! I'm just—I've been anxious about you. I know you're not a kid anymore, but I feel like I'm abandoning you."

Claire rolled her eyes. "Come on. You wouldn't be abandoning me. I mean, I'm already doing my own laundry, right? And besides, we could still hang out."

Lisbeth looked relieved. "Of course. I mean, I'd still work here, if your mom'll let me. I just wouldn't *live* here."

Claire grabbed her empty basket. "You should do what you want—I'm going to be fine. Really." She stared hard at Lisbeth, trying to get her to see that she meant it. "You should go talk to Mom."

Lisbeth grinned. "Maybe I will."

At exactly midnight, Claire met her mother in the hall.

"Ah, thank you for being on time," her mother whispered. Her face looked drawn.

At first, Claire thought it was just because she was so thin from her time in the cage, but there was something else. She studied her mother out of the corner of her eye. *She's nervous.* The realization startled Claire. Why would her mother be nervous now? *Is she afraid I'll screw up, or something?*

"So, what's happening tonight?" Claire murmured.

"I'm not telling you. But it's nothing to be worried about, if that's what you're wondering."

"Then why are you tense?"

Her mother stopped and stared at Claire. "My goodness, *chérie*, you certainly have come into your own. I had no idea you'd become so observant."

The compliment glowed in Claire's chest, but she crossed her arms, waiting.

"Still not telling you." Her mother pulled open the back door and stepped out into the yard. "Surely you have twenty minutes' worth of patience in that young soul of yours?"

Claire tried to relax, but the idea of seeing Beatrice made her skin crawl. No matter what her mother said about the laws and traditions of werewolves, Claire still thought Beatrice had done the wrong thing. She hadn't even listened before she made her decision. She hadn't cared that Claire might have a better way, or more information. She'd just taken the easy, safe, mother-killing way out of the whole thing.

And now Claire was about to go submit to her. Again. She gritted her teeth and tried to focus on staying close to her mother as they made their way to the clearing.

They ran through the forest together, and the smell of the growing things, the scents of earth and night filled Claire's nose. The moon hung full overhead, its belly swelling with light. A tiny shock of excitement shivered under Claire's skin, pushing aside her bad feelings a bit. This time she would be able to completely change. She would be able to join the hunt. And she would be a full-on member of the pack, able to say what she wanted. The anticipation of it made her toes tingle.

Claire and her mother had loped all the way into the clearing before Claire realized that something was off. *There's no fire.* She looked at her mother, the question poised on her lips.

"Tonight, we arrive first." Her mother began dragging dead wood out of the forest and piling it in the center of the clearing with remarkable speed, even for a werewolf. She dropped a third limb on a pile she'd made near the kindling before she looked at Claire and put a hand on her hip. "You could help, you know," she said.

"Oh, yeah, sorry." Claire gathered an armful of smaller branches and placed them on top of the kindling, followed by the big logs her mother had piled up. Marie brushed a leaf out of her hair and surveyed the arrangement.

"*Oui. C'est parfait.* Stand back, Claire, and I will light it."

Claire stepped back to the edge of the clearing and watched as her mother knelt down in front of her, her back to Claire. She was still so thin that her shoulder blades poked out of the back of her shirt, like wings.

Her mother muttered a chant that was too quiet even for Claire to hear. As the first tendril of smoke rose from the wood, Claire's mother raised her hands over the logs and circled them three times. On the final circle, the first flame leapt out of the center of the fire, licking at the smaller branches nearby.

Claire rubbed the back of her neck. *Damn. I can't wait until I can do that.*

Her mother stood and brushed the dirt from her knees. She looked at the expression on Claire's face. "Perhaps, after things are finished here tonight, I could teach you how to create fire?"

Claire nodded, unable to stop the smile that crept across her face. "I'd like that. A lot."

"Good. Well, then, we are ready for the others."

# Chapter Twenty-two

JUDITH ARRIVED, FOLLOWED shortly by Katherine. Judith held Claire's gaze as she greeted her, and Katherine put a warm hand on her shoulder. Claire couldn't tell whether it was because she'd saved her mom, or just because she would be able to fully transform. Not that it really mattered—she didn't care what they thought.

By the time they heard Beatrice and Victoria coming through the woods, the fire lit the entire clearing with its warm glow. Claire noticed that Victoria's pants looked tight— her belly was already starting to grow. Claire didn't look at Beatrice's face. She couldn't bear to, not quite yet.

When the remaining pack members had greeted each other and were circled around the fire, Claire glanced into the woods. She could *feel* Zahlia missing. That the pack had not only lost a member but had been so completely betrayed—it made Claire sick. The faces of the others were serious in the light of the fire, and Claire knew she wasn't the only one thinking this way.

After a moment, Beatrice spoke. "When one of our own dies an honorable death, there are many ways we mourn her. Zahlia did not die in any way befitting a werewolf. In these circumstances, we will rejoin ourselves together, not speaking her name nor remembering her in any way for the rest of our time, so that when we are gone, so too will her imprint upon this world be erased."

The formality of her words and the flatness of her tone chilled Claire. She looked up, surprised by how different Beatrice sounded now, how confident and strong.

*She's so scared of the human world. She's totally confident when we're in the woods, when it's werewolf stuff. But anything involving humans freaks her out.*

It made sense. When Claire thought back, Beatrice had always seemed in control here, in front of the fire. But whenever something from outside the woods came up, she was no better than a cornered rabbit. Claire licked her lips. It was so obvious, now. But how could Beatrice run the pack like this? The human world was all around them, rubbing up against them. Frustration crawled through her.

Beatrice stepped closer to the fire and held out her hands. When they were all standing with their fingers clasped tight together, Beatrice bowed her head for a moment.

"This has been a trying time for us—our bonds have been battered, our ties frayed. We must work to rebuild. In the name of the Goddess I form this pack anew. Of one blood, one mind, and one being are we, bonded eternally. Forsaking all other allegiances, we pledge ourselves."

"By the Goddess," said the others, in unison.

Claire whispered it a half-beat behind. She really wasn't sure she wanted to say it at all.

Claire glanced over and saw her mother's face. A wrinkle had appeared between her eyebrows and she looked thoughtful, serious. Not as certain and celebratory as Victoria and Beatrice, who were both smiling. Not as relieved as Katherine, or Judith. Something about her mother's expression made Claire feel infinitely better. Her mother knew that things wouldn't be erased just by saying some stupid vow.

"Now," Beatrice began. "It has been the greatest honor of my life to lead this pack. But things have changed. Perhaps I have been a wolf for too many years now, but the minds of humans no longer make sense to me. I made an error when I failed to take into account the more"—she paused, looking hard at Claire—"unique aspects of Marie's abduction. The world is not what it once was, and I am not too proud nor too foolish to admit that neither am I. I have called down more moons than I care to count, and the time has come for me to stop. Marie, please step forward."

Claire's mother raised her head high. Slowly, she walked up to Beatrice and knelt in front of the older woman, her eyes shining. Claire's heart pulse thrummed in her ears, the emotions crackling through her like lightning.

Beatrice knew she'd been wrong.

And she was trying to fix it.

It seemed pretty obvious to Claire that her mother—the only member of the pack that she really trusted—was about to become their Alpha. And that would make Claire feel a whole hell of a lot better about the pledge she'd just made.

Beatrice reached down and clasped one of Marie's smooth palms between her roughened hands and pulled her to her feet.

For a long moment, the two women stood staring into one another's eyes. It was Beatrice who looked away first, turning her gaze to the ground. Slowly, she lowered herself until she was on her knees at Claire's mother's feet. She twisted her head to one side, showing her wrinkled neck, submitting herself to Marie. Claire's mother put one hand on top of Beatrice's head and they stayed that way. When Claire's mother removed her hand, Beatrice ducked her head low and took a silver chain from around her neck. Dangling from it was a crescent moon. Claire's mother took the necklace from Beatrice and clasped it around her own neck. Then she bent down to pull the old woman to her feet.

Victoria, Katherine, and Judith got down on their knees, and Claire followed their lead instinctively. Through her lowered eyelashes, Claire peeked up at her mother. The surprise had left her face. Power and pride in equal portions flowed out of her. It made her look so wild and beautiful that Claire's breath caught.

"You may stand." Her mother's strong, clear voice rang out across the clearing.

Everyone got to their feet, the others looking meek and a little bit nervous. A huge grin spread across Claire's face.

"Leading a pack is an honor and a burden, both. I look forward to the challenge, and I will rely heavily on Beatrice for guidance in these first few months. She is *La Sage Femme* now, our voice of experience, the keeper of our history. I expect reverence for her position from all the members of our pack."

The others lowered their heads, acknowledging Marie's first instructions as the Alpha. When they looked up, Claire's mother's smile had gentled.

"Now, before we transform in preparation for a celebratory hunt, there is one more thing I would like to do." She turned and gestured to the trees behind her.

Something rustled in the undergrowth and Matthew emerged from between two thin saplings. Claire gasped and then felt the heat rush into her cheeks when everyone turned to look at her. *How could I not have smelled that he was there?* She gave a tentative sniff and realized that she hadn't given her mother enough credit. Claire hadn't caught his scent because Matthew had been waiting upwind. Beatrice and Victoria were grinning at her like two kids at a surprise party. Judith and Katherine looked concerned.

Claire's mom put a hand on Matthew's broad shoulder, drawing him forward until he was part of the circle. "I'd like to introduce you to Matthew Engle, our new *gardien*. He has accepted this role and the difficulties that accompany it. He is under our protection now and you need not hide yourselves from him, though I would instruct everyone to use as much caution as possible."

"Um, thanks, Marie." Matthew shifted his weight. He seemed uncomfortable.

"Are you sure it's safe, having Dr. Engle's son as a secret-keeper?" The hesitation was thick in Judith's voice.

"We do not get to pick all of our roles in this life." Marie's words were sharp as a thorn. "You should certainly know that. What matters is the loyalty he has expressed for our pack. You will show at least as much regard for our laws as he already has. Is that clear?"

Judith nodded, dropping her gaze.

"Good. Now, I suggest that Claire walk Matthew back to the path. When he is safely on his way home, we will begin."

Matthew glanced over at Claire and grinned. Suddenly, he looked right at home.

Claire stared at him standing in the wavering glow of the

fire, in the middle of a pack of werewolves, and felt the pieces of her world slide together. It wasn't what most people would consider normal, but that was okay. She could be happy, and that was more than a lot of "normal" people got, anyway.

She jerked her head in the direction of the path and Matthew followed her, while everyone else gathered around her mother, congratulating her on her new status. When they were safely hidden by a thick wall of trees, Claire stopped walking. Matthew stopped too, peering at her curiously. Claire grinned, stretched up on her toes, and kissed him. "I can't believe you didn't tell me you were coming here!" she whispered.

"Your mother told me to keep it a secret—she wanted it to be a surprise."

Claire rolled her eyes. "You don't always have to listen to my mom, you know."

"Actually," Matthew said soberly, "I think I do." He squeezed her hand.

"Yeah, you're probably right about that." Claire sighed.

"Don't be upset—I'm not." He gazed back toward the hidden clearing. "You'd better get back, huh?"

"Yep. Can you find your way home from here?"

"Sure. I'll call you tomorrow, okay? We can figure out someplace to go eat or something. Oh, and I'll drive you on Monday, too."

"Drive me where?" Claire asked, confused.

"To school." Matthew looked astonished. "You do know that school starts Monday, right?"

"Oh my Goddess, no." She glanced up at him. "What? I've sort of had some other things going on, you know?"

Matthew shook his head. "Yeah, but still."

"Claire?" Her mother's impatient voice called softly.

"Coming!" Claire turned back to Matthew, who dropped a quick kiss on her lips.

"I'll talk to you tomorrow," he whispered, and turned to walk down the path, back toward civilization. Claire watched him go, smiling as he disappeared between the trees.

In the clearing, her mother stood, waiting.

"Sorry," Claire said automatically. "Where is everyone?"

"They are giving us a moment."

"Oh." Claire ducked her head. "Am I in trouble?"

"No, no. But I wanted to make sure you were okay before we begin the hunt. You looked . . . rather shocked, by everything."

"Well, you looked pretty surprised yourself." Claire tried to keep the accusation out of her voice, but failed miserably.

Marie waited silently.

"It was just weird, you know?" Claire kicked at the dirt. "I wasn't expecting Beatrice to—uh, retire? And then Matthew coming here . . . it was just a lot. That's all."

"I understand. And if I had known what Beatrice had planned, I would not have kept Matthew's presence a secret.

I meant it to be a happy surprise, you understand?"

Claire nodded. "I'm just—I guess I'm just tired of secrets, is all."

"I know. But for us, the time to hide things is finished. You are fully transformed. I can begin teaching you in earnest. From now on, things will make more sense to you. I am sure of it—but you must trust me."

Claire looked at her mother, at the certainty blazing in her eyes, and nodded. Listening to Zahlia had been the biggest mistake she'd ever made. Maybe it was time to listen to her mother, after all.

"Good. We will have more time to talk later, but now I am anxious to begin the hunt." She motioned Beatrice, Katherine, Judith, and Victoria back into the clearing.

When they had all taken their places around the fire, Marie raised her arms and began to chant. Though the words had always sounded strong when Beatrice said them, the power in Marie's younger voice gave them more energy, and Claire shivered as the sound washed over her. When her mother gave the signal, they all burst into their true forms.

It was the first time Claire's transformation had been complete. Every part of her felt *right*—her silky fur that caught the wind, the pads of her feet against the soft dirt—it was perfect. The feeling of release was so great that Claire couldn't hold back the cry that rose through her. She threw back her head and howled. Around her, she could hear the others join in, calling out to the moon above them, the ground below, and the forest that circled them tight.

*And now*—her mother's voice burst into Claire's thoughts—*we hunt!*

They raced off into the woods. Exhilaration flooded through Claire as she ran alongside the others, her nose full of the smell of the fire, the trees, and the endless, moonlit night.

Everything was just beginning—she could feel it. She could smell it. And she wanted to follow the trail all the way to the end, wherever that may be.

# Acknowledgments

WRITING IS A SOLITARY endeavor, but it is rarely accomplished alone. I am so grateful to the many people who helped me with this book.

Thank you to my amazing family, who have always encouraged me to follow my dreams—my husband and children, my mom and dad, and my brothers, Justin and Adam. Their support holds me up, keeps me going, and gives me light when things look dark.

My undying gratitude also goes to The Wordslingers—Trish, Heidi, Jean, Lisa, and Mandy—who help improve my writing every day. I rely on their invaluable advice, input, and support in all matters, literary and otherwise.

I have been lucky enough to work with some of the best professionals in the business. My intrepid agent, Caryn Wiseman, who believed in this project from the beginning and made sure it found the perfect home, all the while providing me with advice, hand-holding, and her own hard work. Of course, without the amazing editorial skills of Anica Rissi and her editorial assistant, Emilia Rhodes, this book would never have become what it is today. Their suggestions and insights opened whole worlds for me, and took Claire's story to a level I couldn't have imagined on my own. In addition to my thanks, I am pretty sure I owe them a whole box of mechanical pencils.

*Claire's story continues in*

# NOCTURNE

CLAIRE'S HUMAN FORM offered no protection from the chill in the moonlit clearing. She shivered as the early-October breeze licked at her arms and cheeks. Wrapping her arms around herself, she stared across the circle, wishing her mother would hurry up and start the ceremony.

A tangled pile of branches waited in the center of the pack. Marie kneeled down in front of it and leaned in, the mist of her breath kissing the outermost tips of the twigs.

Claire's mother closed her eyes, focusing. The graceful lines of her body tensed for an instant, and then it was over. The fire ignited with a roar, pulled into existence by the force of Marie's will.

The light and heat spread through the clearing, changing the texture of the air. The forest crackled with power—it was as though the fire had woven threads of lightning, tying the members of the pack together, linking them to something larger than themselves. As the flames grew, the feeling intensified, humming along Claire's skin, whispering to her about the things she could do.

Begging her to become a wolf.

The pack stood in a circle around the fire, all of them silent. Waiting. The flames leapt before them, the trees towered behind them, and the full moon shone down from above. Everything was ready for their transformation. Marie raised her arms, and with her voice full of the authority that came with being the pack's Alpha, she began to chant.

She called each of their names, and Claire shifted from foot to foot, aching for the warmth of her fur. As she edged closer to the fire, Claire noticed Judith staring at her. She quickly turned her attention back to her mother but kept Judith in her peripheral vision. From her spot next to Marie, Judith regarded Claire with narrowed, judging eyes.

Claire forced herself not to raise a what's-your-problem eyebrow and kept her attention trained on her mother. The chant was almost over, anyway. Anticipation tugged at Claire as Marie called her name. This was only her second full moon ceremony since she'd completed her transformation, but every second she spent in the woods—every time she looked at the moon hanging in the sky like an ever-changing jewel—she loved it more.

There were no secrets in the woods the way there were in her human life. There was just the pack. And the ceremonies.

And the hunt.

Marie lowered her arms.

"And now it is time. You may transform."

The words hung in the air, tantalizing as a ripe apple. Claire forgot about Judith. She forgot about everything but the unbelievable joy of slipping out of her human form and changing into her wolf self. Paws appeared where her hands and feet had been, and her skin gave way to thick gray fur. Claire's teeth grew sharp, and she felt the sudden, familiar heaviness of her tail.

The instant she changed, her senses sharpened. She could see the individual twigs high up in the trees. Could hear the rustling of something small—a mouse, maybe, or a chipmunk—in the undergrowth. And the smells . . . It was almost painful at first, how many things she could smell when she transformed. In her wolf form she could tell that there were four kinds of wood in the ceremonial fire tonight and she could smell the sweet, sighing scent of the autumn leaves dying on the trees above her.

And she could smell pain—the sharp, unbearable scent of pain. It startled Claire, and when she heard a worried whimper coming from Katherine, one of the other Beta wolves, she knew she wasn't the only one caught off guard by the odor. The scent was coming from Victoria, who sat on the forest floor, paws splayed awkwardly, panting hard. After Claire, she was the youngest wolf in the pack, but she was groaning like an old woman.

*Sorry*, she huffed, in the nonverbal language they shared in their true forms. *The more pregnant I get, the harder it is to change. I'll be okay in a second.*

She hadn't been pregnant that long, and Claire was horrified by how fast her belly had grown. Werewolf pregnancies didn't last as long as human ones, which made having a baby especially difficult, because it was so hard on the human part of the woman. Claire had seen it—the terrible way Victoria's skin had stretched, how the sudden change in her shape and weight had made her hips hurt so much that she could barely walk.

Beatrice, Victoria's mother, walked over and sat next to her, leaning against her flank like she was propping Victoria up.

*Marie, can you hunt without us?*

Victoria staggered to her feet, her belly swaying underneath her, dragging her spine into a bowl-shaped curve.

*No, no, no! I'm okay. I can go.* She licked at her muzzle anxiously.

*You reek of pain. You will stay here. And your mother will stay with you. The four of us can complete the hunt on our own.*

The weight of Marie's command made Victoria sink back down onto the ground. She looked relieved and disappointed in equal measures. Beatrice just looked relieved.

Marie turned to Judith, Katherine, and Claire. *Let's go.*

Without waiting for a response, Marie trotted off into the woods, her ears pricked forward and her nose high, searching for prey. The other three wolves followed. Claire kept to the back of the pack, since she was the newest wolf. She didn't mind—there was more to do at the back of the hunt than stuck in the middle, anyway. While Marie tracked in front, Claire kept her senses trained behind them, searching for an animal that might not have been able to find a good enough hiding place. Judith and Katherine loped along in between.

It was hard work, running along with the hunt. Marie set a punishing pace and expected the rest of them to keep up. Claire had taken to jogging in her human form, to make sure that she was in shape. She'd die of embarrassment if she was gasping for breath the way Katherine was. If Marie had taught her anything, it was that being a werewolf was a privilege, a life-and-death-risking double identity, and Claire had every intention of living up to that.

Behind her, there was a single, soft noise in the forest. The sound of a step.

*A misstep, more like.*

Claire whirled around, her head lowered and her shoulders hunched, sniffing the air frantically. The odor was not quite like deer—it smelled muskier. The animal part of her brain supplied the answer at once.

Moose.

Claire gave a soft yip. Her mother pulled up short and circled around, nearly colliding with Judith and Katherine, who scrambled to get out of the way.

Marie pressed close to Claire, her nose quivering.

Judith stared over Marie's shoulder at Claire, her lips drawn back ever so slightly, showing her sharp, pale teeth. It was a dominant move—almost an accusation. Everything in Judith's posture told Claire she should have stayed at the back of the line, kept her mouth shut, and let one of the senior wolves find the moose.

Before she could stop herself, Claire rolled her eyes. Judith took a warning step forward.

Marie's soft yip froze Claire and Judith in their tracks. Whether she hadn't noticed what was going on or she was just ignoring it, Claire couldn't tell. Either way, her mother's tail waved approvingly.

*Excellent. Well-spotted,* chérie.

The praise made Claire shiver. The anticipation of sacrificing a moose—even if it was a young one—zinged through her. The other two wolves shifted behind them, silent as the shadows themselves. Marie turned and acknowledged them with a look.

*Claire, you circle around with Judith, and Katherine and I will cut off the path.* The order was given noiselessly, all eye flicks and twists of her ears.

The wolves didn't waste any time. Judith and Claire ignored each other completely as they streaked through the trees toward the doomed animal.

In a matter of moments, the quiet of the forest was broken by the moose's panicked bellow. And then it was over.

They dragged the heavy, lifeless moose back to the clearing, in preparation for the feast.

Later, when the moose had been disposed of and their whiskers were clean again, the wolves ringed the fire once more. Claire hated this part—squeezing back into her human skin after the freedom of being a wolf. It was like slipping into a scratchy set of bedsheets. She got used to it quickly enough, but she dreaded the initial, prickly discomfort.

And Claire still wasn't used to going through the full moon ceremony without Zahlia. Zahlia had been dead for two months, and though they were not allowed to speak of her—even to say her name—the ragged hole she had left in the pack sent a shudder through Claire every time she passed too close to the memory.

After all, Zahlia had been her friend. Before Claire had found out that Zahlia was murdering humans. Before her "friend" had set up Claire's mother for capture. Attacked Claire's boyfriend. Turned on Claire.

Before Claire completely disappeared into the black hole of the Zahlia nightmare, Marie gave the signal and the wolves transformed. As much as she wanted to stay in her lupine form, her mother's command had to be obeyed. With a sigh, Claire slipped back into her human skin.

Victoria stood next to her, dressed, but with her distorted stomach uncovered. The hem of her shirt had twisted, and she struggled to yank it over her stretched belly. Embarrassed, Claire averted her eyes.

"Damn it!" The curse was quiet enough, but Claire could hear the tears in Victoria's voice.

"It's okay," Katherine soothed. "It'll be over soon enough. They say that the end is always the hardest part. Just think— probably only one more full moon to go, and then you'll be a mother. Oh, I'm so jealous. I always wanted a little baby to squeeze and hug."

Claire squirmed.

Marie cleared her throat, silencing them.

"As the Alpha of our pack, there are many decisions that fall to me, including when to hold the traditional celebration of our newly transformed wolves."

Claire forgot all about Victoria. She stared at her mother, her eyes wide with questions.

Marie looked over at her. "On the night of the new moon, two weeks from now, we will gather here especially for you. You will be expected to do a short demonstration of the basic skills—transforming, hunting . . ."

The tension drained out of Claire. She knew how to do those things. And she even had something extra: the ability to hear others talking even when they were miles away. Not all wolves had that sort of long-distance hearing. Sure, she had to focus pretty hard, but still, she could do it. It might even be sort of fun, to have the attention of the group like that. She started to nod at her mother, but Marie interrupted her.

"Of course, you will also be required to light the ceremonial fire."

Claire's head stopped moving mid-nod.

*The ceremonial fire. Shit.*

She couldn't do that.

She'd been trying for weeks, but in spite of all her efforts, the only way Claire could create a flame was if she had a match handy. Of course, she hadn't admitted that to her mother. She hadn't wanted to seem that inept. Not being able to light the fire was worse than embarrassing. She might as well be having trouble tying her shoelaces.

Without being able to light the fire, she wasn't a normal werewolf—she couldn't prove that she could connect herself to the foremothers and tap into their power.

*Oh, crap.*

Her mother smiled at her. "And to celebrate your success as a wolf, you will lead the hunt that night."

The idea lay in front of Claire, rich as chocolate cake. Just participating in the hunt was her favorite part of the gatherings. It was the only thing in either of her lives—human or wolf—that required her to use all her senses to their fullest. The wild intensity of the chase, the pride of completing the sacrifice to the Goddess, and the frenzied joy of the feast that followed were consuming. She couldn't imagine anything better than that.

Except actually getting to lead the hunt. She wouldn't let

anything get in the way of that. Not even her mental block against lighting the stupid fire.

Marie interrupted her galloping thoughts. "You are ready for this, yes?"

"Um, sure." Claire swallowed hard. She couldn't bring herself to admit that she actually wasn't ready. "I mean, it'll be fun, right?" The last word came out as a squeak.

"It's not just fun," Judith snapped.

Claire took in her mother's lifted eyebrows, and concern crawled over her, spider legged and sharp fanged.

Marie gave Judith a grudging nod. "True." She turned to Claire. "It does confirm that you are a complete wolf. There's no need to worry about it, though." She laughed. "Incomplete wolves are practically a myth, even the consequences for being one are almost medieval. It will be a wonderful celebration. I've been looking forward to it since you first changed—I can't wait to see you lead the hunt."

The words buzzed around Claire's head, and she struggled to stay calm.

Marie dismissed the rest of the pack and put out the fire. As the embers turned to ashes, Claire took deep breaths, letting the achingly cold air dull her panic.

When the only light in the clearing was the glow of the moon overhead, Claire and her mother headed for home. The sound of their feet crunching quietly through the last of the fall leaves was the only noise—there was nothing else to distract Claire from the worried pounding of her heart.

After a few wordless minutes, Claire couldn't stand it anymore. "Why didn't you tell me before? About the new moon gathering?"

Marie reached up and fiddled with the silver chain around her neck. "Because I didn't decide until tonight that it was time. After Victoria has the baby, she'll be excused from her pack duties for a few months. I didn't want her to miss the ceremony, but it was clear when I saw her tonight that she will certainly be pregnant for a while longer."

Claire started to say something but snapped her teeth shut before the words could come. Talking would just get her into trouble. And it wouldn't make any difference anyway. She knew her mother. There would be no begging for an extension. No bending of the rules.

She had two weeks to learn how to light a ceremonial fire or she was going to utterly humiliate herself. In front of the whole pack.

*Great.*

When they finally arrived home, Claire made a beeline upstairs. She was still fired up from the hunt and on edge from the announcement about the new moon gathering. It was already after two—if she didn't find a way to unwind, she'd never get any sleep before school the next day.

She looked longingly at her running shoes. Going for a

run, even in her human form, was the only thing that really calmed her down lately. But it was too late to go running. Anyone who saw her jogging at this hour was bound to think *something* suspicious was going on.

She kicked the shoes into her closet and grabbed her phone—there were two messages. The first was from Matthew, her boyfriend. He sounded exhausted. With only five days left until the state soccer finals on Saturday, the coach had them on a crazy practice schedule. Still, in spite of the fatigue in his voice, he told her that he hoped she'd had fun at the gathering and that he'd see her in the morning. And that he loved her.

The words sank into Claire like sunshine. Matthew always had that effect on her. No matter what, he made her feel like whatever was going on, she could handle it. It didn't hurt that he was the only human in Hanover Falls who knew about the werewolves. He was a secret-keeper for the pack, a *gardien*. He protected them, and they protected him. Being honest with him about who and what she was made it a lot easier for Claire to keep lying to everyone else.

Like her best friend, who had left the second message. Emily's words came out all in a rush. She demanded to know why Claire wasn't answering her phone at almost midnight, unless she was asleep, in which case Emily was very sorry for maybe waking her up, but she really, really needed the blue-black nail polish she'd left at Claire's the weekend before and could Claire bring it with her tomorrow, please?

Claire laughed, loving Emily's signature, caffeine-fueled intensity. She deleted the message and grabbed the little glass bottle off her dresser, stuffing it into her backpack. She looked longingly at her bed, but she was still too wired to sleep. Instead, she trudged into the bathroom and turned on the shower, hoping the hot water would help. With her mother's announcement tying knots of tension in her shoulders, though, there might not be enough hot water in the whole city to relax her.

School the next day was slow-motion torture. Her exhaustion from the gathering and the constant, nibbling worry about the upcoming new moon ceremony were a dizzying mix. Claire staggered through the halls toward her locker, having survived first-period history without falling asleep on her desk or chewing her nails down to the quick. Considering how she felt, that counted as a major success. She dropped her bag in front of her locker, sending a dust bunny flying.

"Oh, yay! Yayyayyayyay! You're here!" Emily bounced across the floor with a huge smile on her face. Her hair still startled Claire. After Emily had gotten back from her forced exile at her aunt and uncle's farm last summer, she'd chopped off her hair. It was short and sort of spiky in an irregular way that looked good on her, but Claire couldn't quite get used to it. She kept expecting to see the long, smooth ponytail Emily had worn since the fourth grade.

Emily started talking well before she actually got to Claire, her questions flying out of her mouth like a flock of sparrows. "Did you get my message? Did you bring the nail polish? Are you okay? I waited for you before class, but you never showed and I got worried. . . ."

Claire blinked, trying to digest all the words. She ticked off the answers on her fingers. "Got the message, brought the polish, fine-but-tired. I was up late and I overslept." She grinned at Emily. "Okay?"

Emily held out her hand. "Polish first. It's an emergency."

Claire dug it out of her bag.

Emily took it and then pointed the bottle back at Claire. "So, if you were up late, why didn't you answer my call?"

"My phone died. I didn't realize it until I went to bed, and by then it was way, way too late to call." The lie was as easy as blinking. She didn't even feel guilty anymore. Not really. Not when she knew what the consequences would be if anyone found out her identity. The thought made Claire's stomach sway inside her.

"You look like you're going to faint or throw up or something." Emily leaned forward. Claire could smell the fake-sweet scent of strawberry Pop-Tarts on Emily's breath, and it reminded her that she'd skipped breakfast.

"Your pupils are all funny. Are you *sure* you're okay?"

Claire blinked. Swallowed. Shook her head, then nodded.

*Oh great, Claire. Way to look totally together.*

"I'm fine. Just tired, really. And hungry. So, what's with the manicure urgency?"

Distraction was always a good tactic. And with Emily, it usually worked.

"So, that's the other reason I was calling." Emily glanced around the hallway and dropped her voice. "That guy Ryan, in art class? The one who does all the charcoal work?"

Claire nodded again. It was hard to keep track of Emily's endless string of potentially datable guys, but she vaguely remembered something about a blond guy who'd been making Emily's toes curl in the art room.

"So, yesterday, he came over while I was painting, and he told me that I held the brush like it was an extension of my hand. And the way he said it . . ." She shivered happily. "Anyway, if he's looking at my hands that closely, then I should probably redo my raggedy polish, you know? Because—"

Emily cut off midsentence as a pair of arms wrapped around Claire's waist from behind. For a wafer-thin moment she tensed, but then the familiar hint-of-cinnamon smell that meant only one thing—Matthew—wafted over her. She melted back against his solid chest.

"Hey, babe."

"Hey, yourself," she said.

Emily was staring at her expectantly. It was obvious that she wanted to say something more about Art Guy but that she didn't really want Matthew around while she rehashed the goings-on in her romantic world.

Matthew bent down and tucked his chin over Claire's

shoulder. "Can I talk to you for a minute?" There was a heavy, serious note in his voice that made Claire's skin prickle.

Emily's eyes widened.

"Hey, guys!"

From down the hall, Amy Harper's blond ringlets bounced as she waved frantically. She was loaded down with posters, and she had a roll of masking tape around her wrist. Even though she'd only been in town a couple of months, Amy had managed to get on practically every committee in the school. She had a dentist's-dream smile and boundless energy, and she was genuinely one of the nicest people you'd ever meet. She was also into pottery—seriously into it. Apparently, some gallery back in Pennsylvania sold her stuff.

She and Emily spent a lot of time together in the art room and had gotten close fast, which Claire had sort of appreciated, since it took some of the pressure off her. Amy was there for Emily when Claire couldn't be. Claire had to admit that it made her a little jealous—as much as she loved being a werewolf, all the power and freedom and feeling of specialness that came with the transformation had come with a price. And having to share her best friend with the petite, perky-sweet Amy was part of it.

"What's up?" Emily called back.

"Can one of you guys please help me tape up these posters? I have a quiz in precalc, and I don't want to be late!" Amy shifted the stack of paper from one arm to the other, blowing an errant curl out of her eyes.

The "you guys" surprised Claire. Amy wasn't friends with Claire or Matthew, but then again, she was so nice, she probably automatically included everyone. Like a kindergarten teacher trying to make sure everyone got a turn.

"Sure thing. Be right there." Emily looked pointedly at Claire, let her eyes skitter over to Matthew, and then twitched her lips. Which was Emily-speak for *I'm going now, but you will tell me what the hell he wants to talk to you about, and I don't mean next week.*

"We'll finish catching up at lunch," Claire promised, distracted by the catalog of things that might make Matthew sound so serious. Emily zipped off down the hall, arms already outstretched to catch the sliding pile of posters.

Claire turned to Matthew, her heart doing a sort of hiccuping stutter-step as she looked up at him. Claire had spent her entire sophomore year nursing a huge crush on Matthew—along with most of the girls in her class. Somehow, she'd been the one lucky enough to catch his attention. That he'd stayed with her after finding out she was a werewolf was nothing short of a miracle.

"You sound strange," she said. "What's up?"

Matthew nodded his head toward Emily and Amy. "It's about that, actually."

Claire looked at him expectantly. Her heart quivered against her ribs, nervous.

"The posters that Amy's taping up everywhere? They're for the Autumn Ball." He reached up and rubbed the back of his neck. "I—I really want to go. To take you. But I know that you're not exactly into dances, and I don't want to drag you if you'd be supermiserable."

Claire blinked, wondering briefly if she'd be less confused if she hadn't been so worried that he was going to tell her something terrible. "What makes you think I'm not into dances?" she finally asked.

Matthew cocked his head at her. "Well, I've never seen you at one before. Emily's usually taking over the dance floor, but I just thought . . ."

Heat rushed into Claire's cheeks. She cleared her throat, trying to get up the courage to admit the truth. Matthew was the one person she could always be honest with, so lying about something so small, so *human*—it seemed stupid. But that didn't make it any less embarrassing.

"I . . . um. Yeah. See, the thing is, no one's ever asked me before. And Emily always had a date, so I didn't want to tag along stag, and it was easier to just pretend that I didn't want to go in the first place."

There. She'd said it.

Matthew's mouth dropped open. If he laughed, she'd kill him.

"So, you're saying you'll go with me? You don't mind the dress and the corsage and the awkward photos and stuff?"

The girliest, most human part of Claire did a little dance of glee at the words "dress" and "corsage."

"Of course I'll go with you. I would love to!" She grinned, swatting his chest with her hand. "Geez, the way you looked before, it was like you were going to tell me that you were moving to Arkansas or something."

Matthew frowned. "Sorry. It's just—finals are on Saturday, and things have been—"

"Tense?" Claire interrupted. "Pressure filled? Insanely exhausting?"

"Yeah, those would work." He smiled the wide, genuine smile that made his eyes crinkle up the tiniest bit at the corners. "But after this weekend, it'll all be done, one way or another."

Down the hall, there was a series of high-pitched squeals as one of the show choirettes opened her locker and a flotilla of helium balloons drifted out. Claire wondered if she should stuff Matthew's locker before the state finals—usually it was something that guys did for girls and not the other way around, but she wanted to do *something*. Maybe she'd just make a sign to hold up at the game, the way the rest of the team's girlfriends did.

Claire stretched up and kissed him, just as the warning bell rang. "You're going to be fantastic. The match is going to be fantastic. And I'm going to be right there, screaming my head off. Now go, before you're late."

"Yeah, you're right. I hope you're right." He turned and hitched his bag up on his shoulder. "I love you."

"I love you, too." She threw herself into the scurrying mass of people who were scrambling for classrooms, and as she headed down the hall she caught sight of one of the leaf-framed posters. She was going to an actual dance. With an actual boyfriend.

Claire smiled to herself. Emily was going to die a thousand deaths of retail happiness when she heard.